Carol Townend was born in England and went to a convent school in the wilds of Yorkshire. Captivated by the medieval period, Carol read History at London University. She loves to travel, drawing inspiration for her novels from places as diverse as Winchester in England, Istanbul in Turkey and Troyes in France. A writer of both fiction and non-fiction, Carol lives in London with her husband and daughter. Visit her website at caroltownend.co.uk.

Also by Carol Townend

Knights of Champagne miniseries

Lady Isobel's Champion
Unveiling Lady Clare
Lord Gawain's Forbidden Mistress
Lady Rowena's Ruin
Mistaken for a Lady

Princesses of the Alhambra miniseries

The Knight's Forbidden Princess
The Princess's Secret Longing
The Warrior's Princess Prize

Discover more at millsandboon.co.uk.

THE WARRIOR'S
PRINCESS PRIZE

Carol Townend

MILLS & BOON

First published in Great Britain 2020
by Mills & Boon, an imprint of HarperCollins*Publishers*
1 London Bridge Street, London, SE1 9GF

Large Print edition 2020

© 2020 Carol Townend

ISBN: 978-0-263-08662-1

MIX
Paper from
responsible sources
FSC® C007454

This book is produced from independently certified FSC™ paper to ensure responsible forest management. For more information visit www.harpercollins.co.uk/green.

Printed and bound in Great Britain
by CPI Group (UK) Ltd, Croydon, CR0 4YY

To John, with love. Always.

Chapter One

*The Alhambra Palace
in the Emirate of Granada—1399*

Climbing to her bedchamber at the top of the tower, Princess Zorahaida dropped her veil on a ledge next to her elaborately carved bed and wished she did not see her sisters around every corner. Her sisters were long gone but she ached to see them.

She was feeding the songbirds in their gilded cage when light footsteps on the stair caught her attention. Closing the door of the cage, she turned, bracelets chinking.

Sama, her most trusted maidservant, stood on the threshold with her veil flung back. Her eyes were troubled.

Princess Zorahaida's heart constricted. What now?

The Princess's irascible father Sultan Tariq was

prone to the most bloodcurdling rages. Had he hurt someone? Zorahaida's greatest fear was that the day might dawn when she wouldn't be able to calm him. Thus far, she had managed reasonably well, though it was never easy. She felt as though for most of her life she'd been walking a tightrope.

She kept her voice calm. 'Something troubles you, Sama?'

Sama was the most sensible of her handmaidens. Rarely ruffled, her cool nature had been the reason she had risen so high in the Princess's favour. Zorahaida would trust her with her life. She trusted her other handmaid Maura too, of course. Maura had a heart of gold, though she was too nervous to be entirely reliable.

Sama stepped into the chamber and carefully shut the door.

'Princess, Imad has brought it to my attention that there are no more Spanish pigeons in the loft. Unless a delivery comes from Castile, the messages between you and your sisters will come to an end.'

Thankful it was nothing more serious, Zorahaida allowed herself to relax. A few years ago, her sisters had run away to marry Spanish noblemen in the neighbouring Kingdom of Castile.

Their father the Sultan had responded by banishing them from his Emirate on pain of death. She hadn't seen them since.

The three sisters were triplets, identical triplets. Perhaps that was why the bond between them was stronger than steel. Determined to stay in touch, they used carrier pigeons to communicate with each other.

Pigeons were astonishing birds. Faster than a horse and capable of flying hundreds of miles in a day, a homing pigeon was inconspicuous and reliable, perfect for taking messages between Al-Andalus and Castile. Best of all, there was no need for a human messenger to endanger life and limb by crossing the troubled border between the Kingdom of Spain and the Emirate.

There had been teething difficulties, but the system worked remarkably well. Zorahaida and her sisters, Leonor and Alba, regularly exchanged news. Mercifully, Sultan Tariq didn't have the slightest notion that his youngest daughter was in secret contact with her sisters.

'Don't worry, Sama,' Zorahaida said. 'All is in hand. More homing pigeons are on their way, they should arrive soon.'

Sama's expression cleared. 'That is a relief. I

know it's crucial that the three of you remain in touch.'

Sama left the chamber and Zorahaida gave a pensive sigh.

The links between her father's Emirate and the Kingdom of Castile, though tenuous, went back a long way. The Princesses' mother had been Spanish. Lady Juana of Baeza. Lady Juana had been captured by the Sultan's troops and when she'd been brought before Sultan Tariq, he had fallen in love with her on sight. He'd forced her to stay and had made her his Queen. She'd never been permitted to return to Baeza.

Sadly, the Queen had died so early in the Princesses' childhood that Zorahaida had virtually no memories of her. Her sisters Leonor and Alba had been her world. That was why losing them had been so devastating.

Zorahaida often wondered what life would have been like if she'd gone with her sisters. The Princesses' Spanish duenna Inés had painted Castile in the rosiest colours, she'd tempted them all with the thought of the freedom that might be found outside the enclosed world of the palace. Like Leonor and Alba, Zorahaida had dreamed about seeing her mother's homeland. Language wouldn't have been a problem. Thanks to Inés, the three Princesses grew up speaking Spanish fluently. None the less, they'd known adapting to life in Castile would be tricky after the confined world of their father's palace. They had known there would be obstacles.

As her sisters had been drawn to the men who were now their husbands, Zorahaida had initially been drawn to a third Spanish knight—Sir Enrique de Murcia. She shrugged. In the end, putting Sir Enrique out of her mind had been easy, he wasn't the hero she'd believed him to be. Parting with her sisters, on the other hand—to this day, Zorahaida felt as though she'd lost part of herself.

On the night of her sisters' escape with their Castilian noblemen, Zorahaida had been ignorant about Sir Enrique's true character. The idea of marrying a Spanish knight had been enticing, for surely no man would be as domineering and unforgiving as their father. Notwithstanding, Zorahaida had been torn.

What about their father? That rigid, complicated man who ruled his daughters with an iron hand, whilst at the same time showering them with gifts. She had actually felt sorry for him. Sultan Tariq had lost his beloved Queen and Zorahaida sensed he was terrified of losing his daughters too. The Sultan had no other children. How would he go on alone? He would have felt abandoned, and abandonment, she was sure, was what her father dreaded most.

Zorahaida's stomach clenched, as it usually did when she thought about the Sultan and she began to pace about the chamber. The various windows gave snatches of differing viewpoints. On one side lay the palace gardens with their fishponds, orderly orange groves and thyme-scented courtyards. On the other, she could see the wilderness beyond the palace walls and the deep crevasse, clear now of rocks. The scrubby trees on the other side of the dip climbed ever higher, drawing her gaze to the snow-capped peaks of the Sierra Nevada.

She stared at the snow-tipped mountain. She felt trapped in the palace. Suffocated. What would her life have been if she had run away with her sisters? These thoughts weren't new and, as she had done many times, she thrust them aside.

Regret was pointless. She had chosen to stay, and she had spent three years working to en-sure that loyal servants and guards escaped the worst of her father's wrath. It felt good to be useful even if the sense of being shut in was insufferable.

Sama reappeared. 'Excuse me, Princess, I forgot to ask. Will the homing pigeons be delivered to the market as usual?'

'I believe so.'

Sama bowed her head. 'With your permission then, I shall inform Imad.'

'Thank you. Sama?'

'Princess?'

'Would you also inform Imad that I am of a mind to accompany him when he goes to collect my sisters' birds.'

'Princess, are you certain? If Sultan Tariq, long may he reign, discovers you have gone into the city...' Sama's voice trailed off.

Zorahaida needed no reminder of the dangers. Every time she broke her father's rules, she risked disturbing the harmony she worked so hard to create. She also knew that most of the palace servants, yes, and the guards too, were grateful for her help. They wouldn't dream of questioning her, but that brought its own responsibilities. It meant that Zorahaida didn't often venture out and when she did, she was careful to be discreet. She didn't want anyone risking her father's wrath for her sake, yet seeing the citizens of Granada, ordinary folk, getting on with their lives was what kept her sane.

She drew herself up. 'I shall be careful, Sama, but if I don't get out for a short while, I swear I shall run mad.'

'As you will, of course.'

Sama opened the door and anxious voices floated up the stairs.

There was a swift pattering of feet, a light chattering sound and a small monkey hurtled across the patterned floor tiles. It was Hunter. Hunter had once belonged the middle Princess, Alba. Since Alba had gone, Zorahaida had adopted him.

Hunter skittered towards her and leaped on to her shoulder, quivering with tension. Zorahaida's heart sank, something awful had happened, she just knew it.

'Princess!' Maura, her other maidservant, was calling.

Pulled by the panic in Maura's tone, Zorahaida went to the head of the stairs. Maura stood a few steps below, panting for breath. Her veil was dark with sweat.

'Princess, come quickly! The lily pond. It's Yamina…' Maura's voice broke on a sob.

'She's fallen in?' Zorahaida went cold. Yamina was her cousin, the sweetest of children, she was not yet three. Mind filling with horror, Zorahaida snatched up her veil, tucked it into her belt and flew down the stairs. She passed Maura and raced along the flagged pathway that led to the pond.

This wasn't happening, Zorahaida told herself. Not Yamina…no, no, *no*.

At first glance, the pond looked undisturbed. Then Zorahaida saw a faint ripple. A small, starfish-shaped hand was flailing about near a water lily. Out of the corner of her eye, she noticed a dark shadow next to a pillared trellis. The shadow seemed out of place, but Zorahaida dismissed it. That tiny hand was all that mattered.

It was a small pond and it wasn't deep. She dropped to her knees. Yamina's hand was tangling in the lilies, sinking out of sight. Heart racing, Zorahaida caught the hand and pulled.

Yamina emerged. Her lips were blue, and her small body felt horribly heavy. Limp. She wasn't breathing. Zorahaida heard herself moan. She sat back, hauled the child over her knees and gave her a gentle shake.

'Yamina, sweetheart, wake up.'

Nothing. She gave a more vigorous shake.

Were the child's lungs full of water? Was she too late?

'Yamina, *please*.'

'God be merciful,' Maura muttered.

Yamina jerked and coughed and water left her lungs in a choking, sputtering rush. When she gulped in air and coughed again, Zorahaida turned her on to her side and watched the colour creep back into her lips.

Yamina opened her eyes. 'Princess?'

Zorahaida's throat closed. 'God is good.'

Pushing to her feet with Yamina cradled in her arms, Zorahaida turned to Maura. 'We must take my cousin to the harem. She needs her mother.'

Yamina started to cry.

Sama held out her arms. 'Allow me, Princess. She'll need dry things.'

Handing her cousin over, Zorahaida suppressed a shudder at the thought of what might have happened if she hadn't reached the pond in time. Her uncle, Prince Ghalib, doted on his little daughter. If she had drowned, he would have been out of his mind with grief.

A chill came over her. It hadn't been hard getting Yamina out of the pond. Maura could surely have dragged Yamina out herself, instead she had wasted time coming to fetch her…

'Maura, why didn't you get Yamina out yourself? Couldn't you reach?'

Maura's face was concealed beneath her veil, but she gulped and pointed towards the pillared trellis. 'I dare not, Princess. Didn't you see him?'

Vaguely recalling that dark shape by the trellis, Zorahaida swallowed down a feeling of nausea. All she could see was sunlight gilding the dancing leaves of a vine, the darkness had gone. 'Someone was there? Is that what you are saying?'

Another gulp. Maura's veil was trembling, she was terrified.

'Who was it? Did you see?'

Maura's head dipped. Her reply was inaudible.

'Maura?'

'He…he was standing in the shadows, Princess. It could have been anyone.'

Anyone? Zorahaida doubted it. She cast her mind back to the moment she'd arrived at the pond, trying to conjure the dark shape she'd seen. Stocky build. Bull-necked. A sense of solid strength.

'Abdul ibn Umar,' she said. Abdul ibn Umar was commander of Sultan Tariq's household knights, the head of his personal guard.

Maura let out a little moan. 'I didn't say it was Abdul ibn Umar.'

Zorahaida looked at her. 'I would take my oath it was the Commander under that arch.'

If her father's commander had been watching, why hadn't he intervened?

A cold stone lodged in Zorahaida's belly. Could he have pushed Yamina into the pond?

The rivalry between her father and his heir, Prince Ghalib, had become bitter of late. Had her father's hatred of his brother driven him to order the murder of an innocent child?

Indignation burned in Zorahaida's breast and she glowered in the direction of the Court of the Lions. At this time of day, her father would be meeting his counsellors in an adjacent chamber. To put it mildly, he would not take kindly to an interruption.

An icy calm descended on her. She didn't want to believe her father could order his niece's death. Yet she knew the tales. The history of the Nasrid dynasty was long and filled with bloody feuds. Brother fought brother in the ceaseless bid for power. Betrayals were commonplace. More damning than that though, Zorahaida had seen for herself how the Sultan had kept his brother incarcerated for many years in Castle Salobreña.

Yet feuding with his brother and heir was one thing.

Would he actually try to kill Prince Ghalib's tiny daughter?

It was possible. The Sultan had always been jealous of his brother's ability to father so many children when the Sultan himself had only sired three girls, Zorahaida and her sisters.

I cannot let this pass.

Bile in her throat, Zorahaida jerked her veil from her belt. It was damp with pond water and clung to her skin. None the less, she must wear it, at least until she was back in her apartments. If the Sultan found out she'd run out of the tower with her face bared to the world, he would have an apoplexy.

'I pray whoever was standing there didn't see me,' she muttered, though it seemed a forlorn hope. Turning towards the Court of the Lions, she beckoned for Maura. 'I need you to come with me.'

Maura hung back. 'Must I?'

'I would be grateful for your assistance. My father needs to know that it is unacceptable for one of his men to stand by when his brother's daughter is drowning.'

Maura made a squeaking sound and stood like a rock, slowly shaking her head.

Zorahaida sighed. 'Very well, I shall go on my own.' The tone of her voice was dry. 'If you could manage to find Prince Ghalib, I imagine he would like to know his daughter is safe.'

'Of course, Princess.'

Maura scuttled off and Zorahaida took in a sustaining breath. Now for her father.

The door to the council chamber adjoining the Court of the Lions was closed. The Commander of the Sultan's household knights was, as Zorahaida had foreseen, standing guard before it, huge arms folded, feet planted stolidly apart.

'May I help, Princess?'

Commander Abdul ibn Umar's voice was courteous, though his eyes were cold as stone. And Zorahaida didn't miss the insolent curl to his lip as he took in her damp veil and the water streaks staining her clothes.

Hiding her anger, she kept her voice calm. 'I need to speak to my father, Commander. Would you be so good as to ask him if he is free?'

Commander Abdul ibn Umar bowed. 'As you command, Princess.'

It wasn't long before the door of the council

chamber was opened and Zorahaida was announced.

Sultan Tariq, ruler of the Emirate of Granada, was seated on his wide, gilded throne. He was clad in white and a great ruby glinted in his turban. His crimson slippers rested on a large footstool. Slaves stood at the Sultan's either hand, palm fans in hand, valiantly attempting to create a breeze.

Despite the slaves' best efforts, the atmosphere was oppressive. The hanging braziers didn't help, smoke was wafting from them like grey snakes, filling the council chamber with the heavy scent of frankincense. The red and gold standard of the Nasrid dynasty hung limply in a corner, as though melting in the heat.

Hurrying in, Zorahaida fell at her father's feet and kissed his silken slippers.

Commander Abdul ibn Umar, she couldn't help but notice, took up a position behind her father, along with a handful of fellow officers, her father's most trusted knights.

'Father, a thousand blessings upon you.'

Gold rings glinted as a languid hand gestured for her to rise.

A smile began to form on her father's face. 'Daughter, you bring me joy, as ever.' The smile faded as the Sultan took in her dishevelment. 'But what is this? Your clothes are creased, and your veil—its dripping on the floor. What has happened?'

Heart in her mouth, Zorahaida decided bluntness was the only approach. Her father was a capricious and harsh master, she feared servants were beaten most days, but thus far she'd never known him to hurt a child. At the back of her mind remained a seed of doubt. Yamina was the daughter of her father's heir, Prince Ghalib. Even though the Sultan had all the power, rivalry between the brothers was nothing new.

'Father, something dreadful has happened in the gardens. I came straight here, confident you would want to be told.'

The Sultan's eyebrows formed a dark black line. 'Oh?'

'Yamina fell in the lily pond.'

The Sultan stroked his beard. 'Dear me, poor little thing.' His voice dripped with insincerity.

Zorahaida's anger flared and she fought to keep calm. Nothing would be achieved by alienating her father, yet this couldn't be ignored.

'Father, Yamina cannot swim.' She paused, her gaze flickering briefly to the Commander. 'Furthermore, while Yamina sank beneath the lilies, your commander stood idly by.'

Her father sucked in a breath. His face was an expressionless mask. 'My niece has drowned? May the angels protect her.'

'No, Father. You will be relieved to hear that Yamina is safe.'

Commander Abdul ibn Umar leaned forward and whispered in her father's ear.

Sultan Tariq's eyes flashed, dark and hard as obsidian. 'You saved her, Daughter. My commander saw you.'

'Yes, Father, I saved her.' Zorahaida cleared her throat, biting her lip beneath her veil.

She had heard that tone of voice before. Polite. Formal. Distant. Zorahaida knew her father and she shivered. Never had he used that tone with her. *I am his favourite,* she reminded herself. *Father loves me. He will be angry, but he will never hurt me.*

She clasped her hands together. 'Father—'

'Enough! Zorahaida, your insolence is disappointing. Worse than that though, is your disobedience.'

'I beg your pardon, Father, but I didn't disobey you. All I did was pull my cousin out of the water.'

Slowly and with such menace that her stomach turned over, the Sultan shook his head.

'You were running, tearing about the gardens like a wanton.'

Her mouth fell open. 'Father, I—'

'Where was your veil?' Several veins bulged in the Sultan's neck. 'Your face was seen. Seen. What has happened to you? You are a disgrace.'

Rising from his gilded couch, the Sultan stepped towards her. Zorahaida's chin lifted.

'What, no apology, Daughter? No show of contrition. Very well.'

He lifted his hand, rings flashing and struck her cheek. The thump of flesh meeting flesh stole Zorahaida's breath and she reeled sideways, seeing stars. Stunned.

'Daughter, you anger me. Get out of my sight.'

The next morning, Zorahaida lay on a cushion next to a window in the uppermost chamber of her tower, staring at the distant peaks of the Sierra Nevada. Even now, her face throbbed. She had a blinding headache.

'Princess, if you would turn your head a little,' Maura said, quietly. 'You need more balm on that cheek.'

Obediently, Zorahaida submitted to Maura's gentle hands. 'Thank you.'

'You will be bruised for a time, Princess,' Maura said.

'It is no matter.' Zorahaida spoke calmly, though her insides were churning. She'd never been hit before. Her father had hit her and that was bad enough, but what terrified her most was that he had taken his commander's side over hers. It made her think the unthinkable. *Father feels guilty.* Had he asked Commander Abdul ibn Umar to kill Yamina? Had he ordered her drowned? His own niece?

She reminded herself that, to her knowledge, Sultan Tariq had never brutalised a child. He was cruel. He dismissed servants on a whim. He beat them. He attacked anyone who threatened to defy him, including the three Castilian knights with whom her sisters had run away. The knights had been prisoners at the time, they'd been chained and unarmed. Helpless. That hadn't stopped him. Zorahaida would never forget how the Sultan had charged at the knights with his scimitar drawn. Fortunately, when Zorahaida and her sisters had intervened, he'd calmed down.

Zorahaida had always been confident of

calming him. Of making him see the error of his ways.

Not so yesterday. Violence ran through the Sultan's veins. She remembered the way his gold rings had flashed as he had struck her. Gold rings. Zorahaida had read several sacred writings and she understood that as a man, her father shouldn't be wearing gold rings. Much that he cared. Her father took heed of no one's opinion but his own.

Had he ordered Yamina's death? Hinted that something might happen to her? She no longer knew.

A soft rap on the door broke into her thoughts and Sama came in, carrying a gleaming casket.

'What's this?'

'Princess, Prince Ghalib sends you his warmest greetings and begs that you accept this humble gift as a token of his everlasting gratitude and esteem. It's a jewel box.'

The box was gilded metal, decorated with enamelled panels of great beauty. Zorahaida took it and ran her fingertips over the delicate enamelwork. Geometric patterns covered the lid—diamonds, lozenges and stars. The colours were extraordinary: vivid reds, the brightest of blues, greens gleaming like emeralds.

'How beautiful, it looks as though it came from France,' she murmured.

'Aye, your uncle said it is from Limoges.'

Turning the key, Zorahaida lifted the lid. On a bed of velvet, lay a pink rosebud with the dew still upon it. Tears stung the back of her eyes.

'Sama, please convey my thanks to Prince Ghalib. Tell him I will treasure his gift, it is beautiful.'

'At once, Princess.' Sama stood for a moment frowning at Zorahaida's face. 'Does it still hurt?'

'Not as much as it hurts inside,' Zorahaida said. The thoughts she couldn't say, not even to Sama, she kept to herself.

What hurt most was how helpless she felt. All hope had been crushed. She had believed that her father would eventually mellow. She had thought him capable of change as he grew older. She couldn't have been more wrong. In truth, he was getting more irascible and ungovernable by the day.

'Sama, did you speak to Imad about collecting my sisters' pigeons?'

'They will be collected on the morrow.'

'And you informed him that I should like to go with him?'

Sama's face fell. 'Oh, Princess, I thought…

after yesterday… I am very sorry, I told him you had changed your mind.'

'Sama, that was wrong of you, I intend to go.'

Maura gasped. 'Princess, you cannot!'

'I think you will find that I can.'

'No. Princess, please don't.' Sama hesitated. 'Last time you were almost caught. What if the Sultan, may he live for ever, finds out? After yesterday, he'll kill you. And if he doesn't kill you, he will certainly harm your guards.'

'Or us,' Maura put in, quietly.

Zorahaida looked at her handmaid. 'Maura, you need not fear. Our guards are loyal and intelligent. They know when Father's men are looking the other way. I shall take the greatest care and I will not be discovered.' She stood up, gently probing her bruised cheek. 'If I don't get out, just briefly, I swear I shall lose my wits. Please, Sama, convey my message to Imad.'

'As you command, Princess.'

Chapter Two

The heat from the furnace was intense and the armourer's face was dripping with sweat.

Jasim ibn Ismail, knight at arms, retreated a couple of paces and watched closely as the armourer gave the final taps to an armbrace damaged during his last practice session.

Being the best workshop in Granada, it was packed with rival knights. All were as eager as Jasim to see that their weapons and armour were ready for the coming tournament. The queue for last-minute repairs straggled into the street.

Prepared to wait, Jasim rested his shoulders against a wooden partition. There was no sense rushing the armourer, he wanted the job done well.

A knight standing behind Jasim cleared his throat. 'I assume you're here for the Sultan's tournament?' he asked.

'Aye.' Jasim smiled and waited. His red-gold

hair and beard often caused speculation. As he had anticipated, the knight was looking uneasily at Jasim's eyes, which most people said were the colour of amber.

'Where are you from?' the knight asked, cautiously.

Jasim pitched his voice to carry above the clang of hammer on steel.

'Madinat Runda. Jasim ibn Ismail at your service.'

The knight's eyebrows lifted. 'Your father was Ismail ibn Osman? The rebel? I'm surprised to see you in Granada after the stir your father made on his last visit.'

Jasim held in a sigh. If only people wouldn't rush to judgement. His father wasn't truly a rebel, though after his falling out with Sultan Tariq his reputation had suffered. 'I am not my father. And he, may he rest in peace, died some years' since.'

At least the knight hadn't made any comments about Jasim's mother. With his father having been so dark, remarks concerning his mother's ancestry often followed. And Jasim knew precious little about her. His father's second wife, Jasim's mother had died giving birth to him.

The knight held his gaze for a moment before nodding pleasantly. 'My apologies, that was badly done.' He gave a wry smile. 'I am sure you honour your father, though you must admit that his intervention with Sultan Tariq was disastrous.'

'Father wasn't a diplomat,' Jasim agreed coolly. 'Although in his favour, dealing with Sultan Tariq is rarely straightforward. I expect he did what he thought was best.'

'I'm sure. Well, I wish you good fortune in the lists.'

'My thanks. Good fortune to you too.'

'It's likely we'll need more than a little luck,' the knight said drily.

'Oh?' Jasim gave the knight a quizzical look.

The knight grinned. 'Clearly, you've never entered one of the Sultan's tournaments.'

Jasim lowered his voice. 'Are you saying the bouts are rigged in some way?'

The knight glanced uneasily over his shoulder. 'No, no, nothing like that. All I am saying is that you should take care. With your name, contestants may assume you are fighting to restore your father's honour. The Sultan's supporters could gang up against you, in a rush to prove where their loyalty lies.'

'That had occurred to me.' Jasim shrugged.

'I'm used to my father's reputation preceding me. However, I think it's more likely that the Sultan may refuse me entry.'

Jasim's entry had already been approved by the steward, though he was conscious that the Sultan himself—unpredictable and volatile as he was—might intervene and deny him the chance to fight. If that happened, Jasim would have to find another way of proving to his uncle, the Governor of Madinat Runda, that sometimes the best way to deal with a bully was to confront him. In Jasim's opinion, his uncle's policy of appeasement simply wasn't working.

The conversation turned and Jasim conversed easily with the knight until the armourer beckoned him over. 'Sir Jasim, your armbrace.'

Jasim approached the glowing furnace as another armourer was thrusting a sword into it. Sweat beaded the man's brow. How men worked in here was beyond him, it was hotter than the devil's pit.

He examined his armbrace. 'Good as new, I'd say.'

The armourer grinned. 'Thank you, sir.'

Jasim drew out his purse and made a point of grimacing as he weighed it in his hand.

The purse was almost empty, he'd deliberately

given half of his coin to his squire to carry, for he wanted word to get around that Jasim of Madinat Runda had entered the Sultan's tournament because he was eager for coin.

'How much?' he asked.

When the armourer named his price, Jasim winced and made a show of counting out the coins with grudging slowness. When he was done, he was almost certain that the armourer and anyone watching would assume that Sir Jasim and his squire would be on short rations for the next few days.

The Sultan had made a point of announcing that several caskets of gold dinars had been set aside for tournament prizes. Jasim wanted people to assume he was desperate to win a bout or two. In truth, Jasim had coin, however, he could always find a use for extra gold. His motives for entering the tournament were simple: he wanted his uncle to realise that he wasn't his father and to that end he intended to do well in the tournament.

God willing, Jasim wanted to find himself in a position where he could open negotiations between his uncle and the Sultan. The entire district around Madinat Runda had suffered because of his father's impetuosity. Jasim was determined to redress the balance.

He found his squire, Farid, outside.

'The horses are in the paddock?' Jasim asked.

'Yes, Master. And before you ask, they are well guarded.'

'Good.' Jasim was about to ask if Farid was hungry when he heard the tramp of marching feet.

It was a small procession of some kind. Half-a-dozen armed guards in grey surcoats were heading towards them. The guards' faces were hidden, swathed in white scarves. Out of habit, Jasim searched for an insignia. Catching a flash of red beneath the surcoats, he stilled.

Red. The insignia of the Sultan was red and gold. Who were they guarding? Jasim strained to see but his view was blocked by the guards, who were in very close formation.

As the party approached, the townsfolk drew back to allow them to pass. People nudged each other and some started to smile. Whoever was at the heart of this strange procession, they were well known and well liked, which must imply that this little entourage didn't have anything to do with the Sultan. Even in Granada, the Sultan was not universally loved.

Briefly the escort parted. A dark veil fluttered. It was a woman. Jasim stared, expecting to see a lady in vividly embroidered silks. A merchant's wife, perhaps. Many of them went about like princesses. But no, this woman's all-enveloping veil was unadorned, and as far as he could see, her clothing was as plain a grey as her escort's surcoats. If it weren't for her escort, he wouldn't have given her a second glance.

Whoever she was, she walked with a youthful, flowing step. After a moment, her guards—for there could be no doubt that despite the woman's humble attire, she was being protected—closed ranks about her. It was then that Jasim noticed that though she was simply dressed, she had servants. A man and a woman were carrying baskets and another woman had what looked like a lute case slung over her shoulder.

A lute case?

Curious, Jasim caught the eye of a fellow knight. 'Who is that woman, do you know?'

The knight shook his head. 'No idea. I'm not from these parts.'

The small procession wound on, turned into the next street and then Jasim had it. One of the hospitals was sited in that street.

'She must be a patron,' he murmured.

The knight looked at him. 'Master?'

'That woman's doing charity work at the hospital.'

'Looks that way.'

Jasim turned to Farid. 'Are you hungry? I believe there's an inn opposite the infirmary.'

'I'm always hungry.' Farid grinned. 'Lead on, Master.'

Nodding farewell to the knight, Jasim and Farid strode down the street and entered the square opposite the hospital. A well head stood in the centre of the square and the inn was set to one side. The inn appeared popular, tables had been set up outside and they were filling fast. Jasim eased on to a bench next to a palm tree.

'Farid, see if they have wine, will you? And ask for cheese pastries. Fruit. You have whatever you want.'

'Very good, Master.'

After Farid had gone into the inn, a faint noise caught Jasim's attention. Across the square, the infirmary shutters were open and inside someone was playing a lute. A gentle melodic tune that was new to him hung in the air. It was soothing. Calming. Whoever was playing was incredibly talented.

Was it the young woman? It must be. While

Jasim waited for Farid to return, he gazed blindly at a cat stretched out in the sun and allowed the music to float through him. He'd never heard anything quite like it; it was plaintive, filled with yearning and utterly beautiful. If it was the girl in grey, she played like an angel.

A couple of knights rode past and the clop of hooves drowned out the music, and after that Farid returned and Jasim turned his attention to the cheese pastries. He forgot about the girl.

As the shadows fell back, the tavern's customers spilled into the square. Every now and then a servant from a nearby house came to the well to draw water. Some tradesmen joined them and stood in clusters talking idly to one another. One had a willow cage at his feet, a few pigeons were shifting about inside it.

The sun rose ever higher, and the heat built. The infirmary door opened. It was the young woman, surrounded by her entourage.

Jasim found himself wishing she wasn't wearing that veil. He would have liked to see her face. His gaze followed her as she crossed to the well head. To Jasim's surprise her men fell back and she engaged the merchant with the cage of pigeons in conversation.

That woman, who was she? Sensing a mystery,

Jasim strained to hear her voice. Curse it, there were too many people, and her voice was quiet. As melodic as the music, it was too soft for him to make out the words.

A bellow of laughter drowned her out completely and then, as the laughter faded, that melodious voice reached him.

Spanish? Jasim froze. If he wasn't mistaken, he had caught a snatch of Spanish. Jasim spoke a little Spanish himself, though not half as well as this woman. Why, she spoke like a native.

Thoroughly intrigued, he shifted his attention to the merchant with the pigeons. Every citizen in the Emirate knew that relations between Granada and the neighbouring Kingdom of Castile had soured. Skirmishes at the border were a regular occurrence. Was the man Spanish? What was this? Revolt? It didn't seem possible that this young girl would be involved, but these days...

The tradesman was replying to her in Arabic. Jasim frowned. Had he imagined hearing Spanish? He would swear he had not.

Crumbling the remnants of a pastry between his fingers, he watched the group by the well head like a hawk.

The young woman nodded and smiled as the tradesman picked up his bird cage and passed it to her. Her hand was slim and unadorned, Jasim saw no rings or bangles, which would seem to indicate that she was of no great importance. Yet she had the habit of command, immediately handing the cage over to her maidservant. And the way her escort watched her every move. Who was she?

She gestured and her two other servants handed a pair of covered baskets to the tradesman. She'd accepted a cage of pigeons; Jasim couldn't imagine what these other baskets contained.

Jasim nudged Farid in the ribs. 'Did you see that?'

Farid wiped crumbs from his chin. 'See what?'

'That woman, the pigeons? The baskets?'

But the crowd had swirled around the well and the young woman's guards had her in their midst, she was lost to view. All Jasim could see was the white scarves of her escort as they trooped back towards the street of the armourers.

Curiosity thoroughly aroused, Jasim pushed to his feet. 'Never mind. You've settled up?'

'Yes, Master.'

'Follow me.'

The little procession moved swiftly through the streets. It went past the armourers' workshop and up the tree-lined road to the main city square.

Jasim knew exactly where they were. Unbelievably, it looked as though the young woman and her entourage were heading towards the Alhambra Palace. But if she and her guards had come from the palace, why bother to hide the Sultan's insignia? If someone from the palace was helping in the hospital, why the need for subterfuge? Curiosity strong in him, Jasim continued after them.

'Where are we going, sir?' Farid asked. 'Our horses are the other way, down the hill.'

'I know, lad. Bear with me. I doubt this will take long.'

The hill grew steeper as the small procession hurried up the road. The trees fell back. The lack of trees proved they were indeed headed for the Alhambra. The last time Sultan Tariq had been threatened with insurrection, he'd ordered the trees cut back some distance from the palace walls.

And there, sure enough, a great wall loured over them, stones gleaming red in the sunlight. In the sky above, swifts were screaming to one another as they sliced through the air.

The young woman's party hurried past the first gate, took the road skirting the edge of the wall and continued. Jasim was determined not to lose sight of them, but he kept his distance. There was no saying what might happen if those guards realised his interest. That young woman's charity work might be a cover for something more sinister. Whatever she was doing was surely clandestine.

'Isn't that the palace?' Farid asked, a worried frown appearing. 'Are we going inside?'

'Not today.'

The anxiety on Farid's face reminded Jasim about the warning the knight had given him earlier. With Jasim's parentage, the Sultan might well question his motives for entering the tournament. He shot his squire a quick look.

'You're afraid the Sultan will resent my entering the tournament? There's no need. I have it in writing that my entry is valid. The steward sent word I would be welcome.'

Farid mumbled beneath his breath, but Jasim was too busy staring up at the palace to hear him.

Ahead, two great buttresses leaned out from the walls. Between the buttresses was an unremarkable iron-banded door with a small grille. One of the guards in grey marched up to it and rapped on the wood. A spy hole appeared behind the grille, the door opened smoothly, and the girl and her party slipped through.

Thoughtfully, Jasim turned away. He knew that the door was unlikely to lead directly into the palace or its grounds. There would be a series of linked corridors, followed by innumerable doors and gates, all of which would be carefully watched and guarded. There would be barracks, and guardhouses and armouries.

As he and his squire made their way back down the hill towards the city proper and their horses, Jasim couldn't stop thinking about the mysterious young woman. Even though he would shortly be in the palace himself, he was unlikely to see her again.

Which was a pity, for she fascinated him. A woman from the palace had been playing her lute in the city infirmary. For what reason. Charity? Or was it something more sinister? Could she really be hand in glove with the Spanish?

Farid huffed out a breath. The boy was still worried.

'Why the long face?'

Farid jerked a shoulder towards the palace. 'You're truly going to enter the tournament?'

Jasim stopped walking. 'Farid, I enrolled months ago, you know I am. I'm not going to change my mind.' He searched his squire's troubled face and swore softly. 'My uncle's been talking to you, I see.'

Farid chewed his lip and didn't bother to deny it. 'Master, the Governor is extremely concerned about you fighting in front of your father's old enemy.'

Jasim's eyebrows lifted. His uncle, Ibrahim ibn Osman was a cautious man, and Jasim believed he understood his reservations, though he didn't agree with them. As Governor of Madinat Runda, his uncle's decision to hold the Sultan at arm's length had been disastrous for local trade. Madinat Runda had suffered because of it. And it would go on suffering until some sort of accord was made between the two districts.

Jasim would be the first man to admit that the Sultan was difficult, and he was all too aware that the trouble had started when his father had made his noble but ill-judged attempt to challenge him on the matter of taxes and tariffs.

He set his jaw. He was confident that the people of Madinat Runda would benefit from closer association with Granada. By entering the tournament, Jasim hoped, in his small way, to bridge the distance that had developed between the districts. 'My uncle told you to speak to me, didn't he?'

'Aye. The Governor wishes you to withdraw from the tournament.'

'I can't do that.'

Farid looked earnestly at him. 'Master, the Governor has your interests at heart. He doesn't trust the Sultan an inch.'

His uncle was concerned for him? It was far more likely he was fretting over the possibility of new tariffs and taxes. Jasim smiled inwardly. There was much of the merchant in his uncle.

He made his voice stern. 'Whose squire are you, mine or my uncle's?'

'Why yours, of course.'

'Fine. Now we have that straight I'll hear no more talk about withdrawing from the tournament. We'll be moving into our lodgings in the palace at first light. I need your support, Farid, and I trust that I have it.'

'Yes, Master, always,' Farid said, his face relaxing. 'I knew that would be your answer. I told the Governor you wouldn't be persuaded, but he made me promise to try.'

Jasim clapped him on the back. 'And so you have. Objections duly noted.'

As they made their way back to the stables,

the calling of swifts gave way to the chattering of sparrows and house martins. Temporarily, the mysterious young woman was forgotten.

Chapter Three

Zorahaida yawned and stretched. She was in the habit of breaking her fast early in the courtyard at the bottom of her tower. Usually she rose when the sparrows started cheeping in the myrtle bushes outside. They were already cheeping, and light was edging into her bedchamber. It was time to get up. Wondering why no one had come to assist her, she dressed herself and went downstairs. Hunter rode on her shoulder, gently gripping her hair.

The courtyard below was cooled by a fountain. Zorahaida enjoyed sitting near it, because when the doors to the adjoining chambers were open, light came in from all angles. Oddly, the courtyard was filled with shadow, the doors were firmly closed.

'Maura?' Zorahaida called. How strange that no one had come to help her dress. Where was everyone? 'Sama?'

Except for the sparrows in the myrtles, all was quiet. There was no sign of her handmaids. Nor, save for a bowl covered with a cloth on a shelf, was there any sign of her breakfast.

How very peculiar.

Pulling the doors open one by one, Zorahaida went into the adjacent rooms and opened the shutters. Hunter bounced off her shoulder and scampered back to the central courtyard. Having let in as much of the morning light as she could, Zorahaida returned to find him perched on the shelf. He had whipped the cloth from the bowl which was full of dates and dried fruit. Eagerly, the monkey helped himself to a date.

'Hunter, you are a naughty boy. You are supposed to wait until I feed you.'

Ever since Alba had gone, Zorahaida had been trying to train him. In the main, she had succeeded. Hunter no longer used the gilded bird-cage as a swing, he no longer raced around the tower like a mad thing, leaping on anyone who came near. But as far as food was concerned, she was fighting a losing battle. Hunter ate what he liked. And he loved dates and dried fruit.

Zorahaida went to the window facing the palace grounds and frowned. Why was it so quiet?

A door thudded shut and she heard a swift foot-step. Maura hurried in, basket in hand.

'Forgive me, Princess,' Maura, said. 'The kitchens are overwhelmed. It's utter chaos. There were plenty of grapes, but I had to wait for a fresh batch of honey bread to come out of the oven.'

Zorahaida blinked. 'They never run out of honey bread.'

Maura set the basket on the table. Her face was lit up, clearly, she had interesting news to impart.

'They do when your father has invited every knight in the kingdom to take part in a tourna-ment,' Maura said, watching Zorahaida for her reaction.

'What?'

'A tournament. Your father the Sultan, peace be upon him, is hosting a tournament. Knights are arriving from all over the Emirate and be-yond. The kitchens are struggling to keep up with demand.'

'A tournament,' Zorahaida breathed. Her inter-est was well and truly caught. She knew a tour-nament was a practice battle, a competition held to hone warriors' skills. Such mock battles were usually run according to ancient laws of chivalry.

All Zorahaida knew about chivalry was that

her sisters Leonor and Alba had had the good fortune to run away with two of the most chivalrous men in the Kingdom of Castile. She did, however, know that not all knights were Christians living in the Spanish kingdom. There were knights in the Emirate too. Moslem knights who, like their Christian counterparts, had been trained to fight according to chivalric rules such as those practised in Spain. Educated, noble men, they swore to fight for justice, give aid to the poor and protect those less able to defend themselves.

'Maura, do you know where it will be held?'

Maura smiled. 'Right here in the palace.'

'Here?' Zorahaida felt a pang go through her. 'I'd love to see it.'

Firmly, Maura shook her head. 'Oh, no. All those strange men. You won't be allowed anywhere near.' An expression of revulsion crossed her face. 'Besides, tourneys are battles, are they not? Blood will be shed. You won't like it.'

Zorahaida sighed. 'Maura, the fighting isn't real. Tournaments are mock battles, a practice of sorts.'

'In this instance, I think you will find you are wrong, Princess. Particularly since Sultan Tariq has announced that the overall champion will receive several caskets of gold and the finest gem in his collection. Men have fought to the death for less.' Maura gestured Zorahaida toward a cushion and offered a plate of bread and grapes. 'Here, you must be hungry. The bread is still warm.'

Zorahaida reached absently for some bread, so wrapped in thought that she barely tasted it.

The Sultan had offered the finest gem in his collection to the Champion? It was hard to believe. Of late, her father had taken to retiring to the treasury more and more. She'd been told that he liked nothing better than having a strong box unlocked so he could run his fingers through the best of the jewels. He was often open-handed, but long ago Zorahaida had come to realise that his generosity was calculated.

'I wonder what he wants,' she murmured.

Maura, pouring a cup of juice, snorted. 'You know the answer to that.'

'Father wants prestige,' Zorahaida said, quietly. 'He wants the world to know how powerful he is, how indomitable, how rich. He wants every district in the Emirate to bow to his authority.'

'No doubt he wants to impress the Spanish King too.'

'No doubt.'

Maura picked up the jug. 'Do you care for orange and pomegranate juice?'

'Thank you.' Zorahaida sipped thoughtfully, aware her heart was beating faster than it had in some time.

News of this tournament was exciting and somewhat unnerving. Life in the palace had a certain rhythm, everything ran like clockwork. Her father liked it that way. He liked to know where he stood. That he was choosing to host a tournament spoke volumes about his insecurity. And when her father felt insecure, Zorahaida noticed that someone else usually suffered.

First Yamina, she thought. Who would be next?

The idea that the Sultan might take it upon himself to host a tournament simply for entertainment was ludicrous, particularly since it was being held inside the palace walls. The gates wouldn't be open to all. Only the most trusted counsellors and servants were allowed anywhere near.

No, her father was up to something. Was he planning war against the Spanish Kingdom of Castile? Was this an attempt to rally the troops, as it were?

The thought made her queasy. Since Leonor and Alba had fled to Castile, their father seemed to have forgotten that their mother, Lady Juana, his beloved Queen, had herself been Spanish. The Sultan had become so bitter. In the immediate aftermath of what he termed her sisters' defection, Zorahaida had withstood his ill temper and changeability. She'd given him the benefit of the doubt again and again, certain that in his heart he loved all his daughters. Her father was hurting, she told herself. She'd been sure that time would heal him.

Unfortunately, it hadn't. She took a deep breath. What was he planning? Murder? War?

'Maura, I don't suppose any of the contestants are Spanish, are they?'

'I'm sorry, my lady, I have no idea.'

Zorahaida had to find out more about the reasons behind this tournament. Asking her father directly was simply not possible. He invariably took questions as a threat to his authority. Briefly, it occurred to her to consult her uncle, Prince Ghalib. But, no, the Prince's ever-growing family was already in danger, thanks to her father's resentment of his brother's prowess in fathering children. Her uncle's favourite concubine was expecting yet another child. Would it be a boy? If it was a boy, the baby would be a potential claimant to the throne because the Sultan himself had no sons. Sultan Tariq only had three daughters, two of whom he saw as deserters.

Father has not sired a boy. Prince Ghalib is his successor.

Was that what this was about?

Heavens, she must tread carefully. The last thing she wanted was to put another cousin, or indeed the women in her uncle's harem, in danger.

She put down her cup, ate a grape and stared blankly at the honey bread. She couldn't let this lie, she had to act. Today, her father would be busy welcoming his guests. He'd greet them either in the Court of the Lions or in one of the audience chambers. As soon as she'd finished breakfast, she would change into her maidservant's disguise and head that way. She'd done it before, admittedly when her father was in a more lenient frame of mind.

Maura was nibbling a bread roll. She wouldn't tell Maura, she would only fret. Besides, it wouldn't do to put Maura in the firing line.

I need to be subtle. For the sake of everyone in the palace, I must find out what Father believes this tournament will achieve.

* * *

Dressed as unobtrusively as possible in grey servant's garb and with her face hidden by her veil, Zorahaida walked carefully towards the Court of the Lions. She had planned her mission with care.

Experience had taught her the best way to walk to avoid being noticed, so she kept her head down in a meek and modest posture. She walked as though she had a definite objective in mind, she must look as though she was engaged on an errand. She didn't run and she didn't dawdle.

The Sultan's Guard was out in force. A troop was stationed around the Court of the Lions, making it plain that Sultan Tariq was receiving his knightly guests in a chamber adjoining the courtyard. Zorahaida's heart lifted. So far, so good.

At the centre of the courtyard, water streaming from the lions' mouths glistened in the sun. Zorahaida's path led across two sides of the square, in the shade of columned arcades. She headed quietly for the shadows next to the most sumptuous of the receiving chambers, where another of her father's thrones was placed.

Now for the risky part. Zorahaida's objective was the curtained alcove reserved wholly for the

Sultan's concubines. An ornamental vase that was tall as a man stood on a stand in the corridor outside. If the alcove was empty, she would only have moments to conceal herself. And if it was not empty…

Praying that her father was so distracted by his guests that he hadn't thought the comfort of a concubine would be necessary, Zorahaida held her breath. She slipped past the curtain.

God was good and the alcove was empty. Straightening the curtain, she breathed again. Decorated tiles covered the walls and a plump cushion took up most of the floor.

Ignoring the cushion, Zorahaida shifted to the other side of the alcove, where she could hear and see a little of what was going on in the audience chamber. In the gap between the curtain and the wall she could see more guards standing at either side of the entrance to the audience chamber. Beyond the guards stood a group of turbaned men, presumably some of the knights who were her father's guests. The visiting knights were facing her father on his throne, so they had their backs to her. They looked to be unarmed, which wasn't surprising, since only the Sultan's Guard bore arms in the Sultan's presence.

Her father was speaking. Zorahaida couldn't

make out what he was saying but his tone was curt. Angry. She bit her lip. That didn't bode well for the knights in that chamber.

Twisting sideways, half-leaning against the vase on the other side of the curtain, she eased herself into a position where she could see a little more. Her father's face was taut and fierce, and his voice was easier to hear.

'You are the son of Ismail ibn Osman of Madinat Runda.'

Zorahaida's stomach knotted. That had sounded very much like an accusation. Who was Ismail ibn Osman? The name wasn't familiar. He must have crossed swords with her father in the past. The Sultan had a long memory for grudges.

The taller of the men bowed. He was wearing a blue robe belted at the waist. 'Indeed, Great King,' he said, in a calm and measured voice. 'I am Jasim ibn Ismail of Madinat Runda.'

The Sultan's fists opened and closed. 'Jasim ibn Ismail, I am astounded at your effrontery.'

'Great King, should a man be judged only by his parentage?' the knight said coolly. 'I am not my father, as I hope to prove to you.'

The Sultan's frown deepened. 'And I am to take your word for that? The son of a known rebel?'

'I am a knight. I have taken knightly vows.

That was good enough for your steward, Great King, when I enrolled in the tournament. He was happy to take my word.' He bowed again. His calm courtesy made a marked contrast with the Sultan's brusqueness. 'But if you wish to deny me the chance to prove my worth, I shall of course relieve you of my presence.'

Silence. No one moved, it was as though they were all watching the workings of an ugly spell to which there could only be a grim ending. Zorahaida's heart thumped. By behaving so reasonably, this knight had contrived to back her father into a corner. If the Sultan took against this Jasim ibn Ismail with these other knights as witness, he would be made to look a fool. And the Sultan would never forget it.

God save that knight, Zorahaida thought. No one crosses my father and gets away with it.

The Sultan's nostrils flared. When his fists bunched, Zorahaida jerked, knocking the tall vase so it rocked on its stand. In the appalled silence, the noise was horribly loud.

Footsteps approached and the curtain rings rattled. A guard stood looking at her.

Praise God, it was Captain Yusuf ibn Safwan, Zorahaida had helped his family more than once.

Swiftly, the Captain pulled her out of the alcove, making it appear, bless him, that she had merely been standing in the corridor. It wouldn't do to be caught eavesdropping in the place reserved for the Sultan's favourite.

'Captain?' Her father's voice reached her, angrier than ever. 'Is someone there?'

Zorahaida grasped Yusuf's sleeve. 'Yusuf, it's me,' she whispered.

Yusuf lifted an eyebrow and kept his reply soft. 'I didn't imagine it would be anyone else. Princess, you must take more care.'

'What's going on? Who is that?' Her father pushed to his feet, his expression stormy. 'Captain, bring that woman here.'

'My apologies, Princess.' Yusuf took her by the elbow and marched her, veil still in place, before her father. There were more guards inside, they lined the walls like statues, obscuring much of the flowing script on the patterned wall tiles. 'Great King, it is only a passing maidservant.'

Zorahaida dropped to the floor in full obeisance as the knights and guards looked on. Never before had she been the focus of so many eyes. Men's eyes. She realised she was trembling, and it wasn't through fear of the men. Strange men as Maura had called them.

The bruises she had received at the hand of

her father throbbed a warning and she braced herself.

'Rise, girl.' The Sultan was wearing white robes again with a dazzling jewelled belt. The ruby in his turban glowed as bright and baleful as a dragon's eye and the golden scabbard of his dagger was shaped like a leopard's claw. 'Who are you? What were you doing?'

Head lowered, Zorahaida got to her feet. 'A thousand apologies, Great King,' she whispered, in the hope that her father wouldn't recognise her voice. 'I am just a servant. I missed my way.'

'You missed your way? Come closer.'

Swallowing hard, she braced herself and obeyed.

Her father lifted his hand, seemed to recollect where he was and with whom, and his hand fell.

'Captain, remove this woman. She almost broke a valuable vase. Proper discipline is needed. See to it, personally.'

Yusuf bowed. 'At once, Great King.'

Gaze fixed firmly on the floor, Zorahaida walked out of the audience chamber, Yusuf at her heels.

Uncomfortable, Jasim watched the girl go. The vase hadn't broken, yet Sultan Tariq had been about to strike her. It was yet further proof that his terrible reputation was well earned. What had he meant when he had said she needed 'proper discipline'? Would the guard beat her?

Guilt tightened inside him. Jasim was uneasily aware that his presence, being an unwelcome reminder of his father, had been what had upset the Sultan.

The Sultan had wanted to strike him rather than the maidservant. If he hadn't been here, she would probably have been let off more lightly. He had to make sure the guard didn't maltreat her.

'Great King.' Jasim bowed. 'I apologise if my presence here offends you. With your permission, I shall withdraw.'

The Sultan directed his dark gaze on him, and though he knew he should not, Jasim held that gaze.

'You are withdrawing from the tournament?' the Sultan asked, frowning.

'If it is your will.'

The Sultan tucked his thumbs into his belt and took a slow, deep breath. His gaze flickered to the other knights standing before him. Faint colour stained his cheeks. It was almost, Jasim thought, as though the Sultan regretted having lost his temper.

'I spoke hastily, sir knight,' the Sultan said. 'Your personal reputation precedes you. I agree with my steward, you may compete in the tourney.'

'Thank you, Great King. You are most generous.'

Jasim bowed again and before the Sultan had time to change his mind, he backed out of the chamber and strode into the Court of the Lions.

There was no sign of the maidservant or the Captain. The marble courtyard was full of other guards, but not the one Jasim wanted. He went down one arcade and then another; he passed through an antechamber and found himself blinking into the sun.

There they were, walking slowly through a square filled with orange trees. The Captain had released the maidservant, who was walking quite freely at his side. They were talking in undertones. Jasim increased his pace, determined the woman shouldn't be punished on his account. As he caught up with them, something about the way she walked reminded him of someone. He shook his head, the resemblance remained elusive.

'Captain?'

The man's hand shot to his sword hilt and

he swung round to face him. Not only was the guard bristling with tension but Jasim couldn't help but note how he had placed himself protectively before the maidservant. She stood, perfectly submissive with her head down, a couple of paces behind.

Interesting.

'A word, if you please,' Jasim said. He spread his hands. 'As you see, I am unarmed.'

The guard regarded Jasim warily, and after a moment he seemed to accept that Jasim presented no danger to the servant girl for his hand lifted from his hilt.

'You must have missed your way, Jasim ibn Ismail,' he said softly. 'The barracks lie in the other direction.'

'I haven't missed my way, I wanted to speak to you.' Jasim nodded towards the maidservant. 'I would like your assurance that this woman will not be harshly punished.'

Behind the guard, the veiled head lifted, she was listening to him.

Jasim continued. 'She knocked into a vase which wasn't broken. I believe it was my presence in the audience chamber that angered the Sultan and I am afraid that led him to demand a harsh punishment for a light transgression.'

Reaching into his purse, he scooped out a handful of silver. 'Please, take this, the Sultan's displeasure is surely punishment enough.'

The Captain came a couple of paces nearer and to Jasim's surprise he shook his head and leaned in. 'That will not be necessary, Master. I can assure you that I wouldn't dream of harming a hair on her head.'

Jasim felt himself relax. 'Good man.' He slipped the coins back into his purse.

The servant girl cleared her throat. She was toying with her veil, rolling the edge between thumb and forefinger and Jasim saw that her hand was fine-boned and cared for. Whatever her role in the palace, she didn't do manual work.

'Peace be upon you, Jasim ibn Ismail,' she said, softly. 'Your kindness does you much honour.'

Jasim felt his jaw drop. No wonder he'd thought her familiar! That melodious voice belonged to the woman who walked about the city with an escort and took a lute into the infirmary. He opened his mouth to say more but found himself staring at her back. They were walking away.

Wryly, he shook his head. He had been dismissed. As he watched the pair of them cross the tree-filled square, he could hear them talking easily to each other. Who was she and what was her role in the palace?

Clearly, she was far more than a simple servant.

Each of the competing knights had been allocated space in the barracks hall to assemble their gear and for the rest of the day, Jasim was fully occupied preparing for the tournament. He and Farid stationed themselves by a trestle table, giving his equipment a final check.

Jasim slid his sword back into its sheath. 'Well done, Farid, this has a fine edge.'

Since arriving at the palace, Jasim had felt naked without his sword. He'd known what to expect but he didn't have to like it. Within the walls of the Alhambra only the Palace Guard and the Sultan's household knights bore arms. An exception would be made for the tournament.

The Sultan lived in fear. Assassination was ever in his mind. Given the bloody history of the Nasrid dynasty, it was understandable. Several of the Sultan's predecessors had died at the hand of a brother or relative, eager to seize the throne.

Before entering the Alhambra, Jasim had hoped that Sultan Tariq's reputation for cruelty and self-serving was exaggerated. He had felt

confident that his hot-headed father had precip-
itated the argument that had caused the rift between Madinat Runda and Granada.

He was no longer so certain. Having seen first-
hand Sultan Tariq's violent reaction to the dis-
covery of the maidservant near the audience
chamber, it was plain the Sultan trusted no one.
Had it been the Sultan rather than his father who
had caused the rift between the districts?

Grimacing, he shook his head. Given Sultan
Tariq's reaction when he had realised Jasim was
Ismail ibn Osman's son, there was no tactful way
he could enquire about that particularly difficult episode in history. He would probably never
know the answer. What was clear was that Sultan Tariq lived in fear and crushed anything he
considered a threat.

'What a way to live,' he murmured.

'Master?'

Jasim kept his voice low. 'This tournament is
the Sultan's way of reaching out to his allies yet
see how we are watched.'

Farid was an intelligent lad. His gaze skimmed
over the guards lining the wall and he nodded.
'I had noticed, and I don't think much of it. It
makes me feel as though I have done something
wrong, and I haven't, Master, I swear it.'

'I know that.' Jasim smiled. 'The tournament will be over soon. With luck, we'll be on our way home in a couple of days.'

Jasim prided himself on his easy-going nature. Yet he'd not been in the palace above a day and the atmosphere was making even him edgy.

Guards everywhere. Watching eyes at every turn. To be sure there was luxury too, but he could do without that. Everyone here was walking on eggshells.

He had entered this tournament bent on being crowned champion. Was it worth it?

Of course it was. For years Jasim had wanted to repair the damage wrought by his impetuous father, if indeed his father was to blame.

Jasim's father, like Jasim, had been a second son. Ismail ibn Osman had been belligerent, impetuous and brave. Those qualities had served him well on the battlefield, but they had made him unsuitable for the role of Governor. Governors needed tact. Governors needed to be diplomats. And governors were usually chosen on merit.

There was no doubt that Jasim's uncle, Ibrahim, was the perfect governor. Or he would be, if he would only assert himself over the lapsed trade agreements.

Jasim curled his fingers into a fist. In a sense the cause of the rift between Madinat Runda and Granada was irrelevant. It had gone on for far too long. Jasim's goal hadn't changed. If he did well or could win the tournament, he would attempt to broker a deal with the Sultan. It was vital that trade between the districts improved and even the Sultan must see that improved relations would be to everyone's benefit. Jasim would repair the damage caused by the rift between east and west. And if at the same time he could show his uncle the Governor that Jasim ibn Ismail could be relied upon, so much the better.

This will be worth it, he thought, trying not to scowl at the guard watching his every move.

He didn't envy that poor maidservant her position here. Given that he'd seen her in the city, it seemed likely that she served one of the harem favourites. She clearly had some influence, though in all probability she would have no choice but to obey her mistress.

What must it be like to run the gauntlet of mistrust and irascibility every day of your life? That guard in the orange grove had said he wasn't going to chastise her, and Jasim had believed him. For a palace guard to place himself in jeopardy by contravening the direct command of the Sultan himself, she must serve someone important.

'You're happy with these, master?' Farid asked, gesturing at a row of blue and white lances laid out for inspection.

'As long as they are ash with weakened tips, as we discussed, they are fine,' Jasim said, weighing one in his hand. 'This is a competitive joust not a battle; it wouldn't do to spear someone.'

'I was assured the lances will break when you score a hit, master. And the points have been blunted.'

'It was you who painted them with my colours?'

'Yes, master.'

Nodding approval, Jasim tested a vambrace designed to stop his hand sliding up the lance on impact. It held firm. He moved on to his saddle, checking the padding, the girth, everything. Stirrup straps, bridle…

At length he looked at his squire. 'Everything is in order, well done, Farid.'

Farid grinned.

'Come, let's head to the jousting field. I need to remind myself of the position of the sun. It's best to work out where one might be blinded and where the shadows will fall.'

Chapter Four

Zorahaida entered the chamber at the top of the tower, thinking about Jasim ibn Ismail of Madinat Runda. Standing in the alcove by the audience chamber and prostrating herself before the Sultan, Zorahaida had not had a chance to see his face. Her first clear sight of him in the orange grove had snatched her breath away. What a strong-looking, handsome man. With those amber eyes and that red-gold beard, he put her in mind of a warrior angel. Even unarmed, he came across as fierce and determined.

She remained wary. There were many classes of angels, evil as well as good. Jasim ibn Ismail had followed her into the orchard, supposedly to ensure Yusuf didn't beat her. None the less, he was bound to be dangerous. Why, even her father had been concerned about him entering the tournament.

His looks were certainly unusual. He had

pleasing, regular features and she'd been close enough to notice that his beard was threaded with gold and russet.

At court, there was a fashion for men to adopt such colouring—her father's vizier used henna to dye his beard and the effect was harsh and flat, startling rather than pleasing. Jasim ibn Ismail's amber-coloured eyes seemed to suggest that God had made him that way. His beard looked entirely natural. She found herself speculating on whether, beneath his turban, his hair was the same red-gold as his beard.

Irritated by what was a most unseemly train of thought, Zorahaida shook her head. The man baffled her. Jasim ibn Ismail had come after her and she couldn't understand it. Why would a knight from the west care whether a lowly maidservant took a beating? Could he really have been concerned for her or did he have ulterior motives?

Hunter scampered into the chamber, chattering. He was followed almost immediately by Maura.

'There you are,' Maura said, huffing out a breath. 'I've been looking for you everywhere. How is that bruise? Would you like me to apply more salve?'

'No, thank you, Maura. I can manage.'

Maura looked her up and down, a pleat in her brow. 'Princess, you are dressed as a servant again. What have you been doing?'

'Nothing much, I was walking in one of the orange groves,' Zorahaida said lightly.

A ball of guilt formed in her stomach. It was unpleasant being evasive with Maura, but what else could she do? If Maura worked out that she'd been eavesdropping on the Sultan and had almost been unmasked, she would be terrified. It would serve no purpose.

Happily, Maura took her at her word and went on to tell her, in great detail, about the new fish that were being homed in the palace ponds.

Zorahaida nodded and said something non-committal, even as she was wondering where she could find the best vantage point from which to watch the jousting. She had been fortunate that morning. Her father hadn't recognised her. She would take more care tomorrow, there would be no creeping about the lists for her. Bearing in mind Maura's nervous nature, she had best say no more about her interest in the tournament.

Not for the first time, Zorahaida found herself wishing she lived elsewhere. In Spain, where her sisters had gone, ladies often attended tourneys. They had ladies' stands giving full view of the entire competition. The ladies would know many of the knights, and they would offer favours or tokens to their favourites, so the knights went into their mock battle with a lady's scarf fluttering bravely from their sleeve or lance. Chivalry in the Kingdom of Spain appeared to be far more romantic than chivalry in Al-Andalus.

Admittedly, it sounded rather frivolous, but it also sounded, Zorahaida thought wistfully, as though it might be fun. With a jolt she realised that she couldn't remember when she'd last had fun. Of late, life in the palace had become so very dark.

When her sisters had gone, they'd taken the Princesses' Spanish duenna, Inés, with them. Before that though, Zorahaida had asked Inés to explain what went on in Spanish tourneys. That was how she knew that in the Christian kingdoms, one of the ladies would be chosen as Queen of the Tournament. It was the Queen of the Tournament who awarded the prizes and crowned the Champion.

Imagine—a woman handing out tourney prizes, instead of a man! That would never happen here. Much as the Sultan prided himself on being conversant with the rules of chivalry, much as he wanted the world to know how cultured he was, he would never countenance such a thing.

Chivalry in the Emirate was more intellectual than chivalry in Spain. Here, knights were strong and ruthless in battle, as were their Spanish counterparts. They were also well versed in poetry and the arts. But as to being cheered on by smiling ladies waving from their stand, as to the handing out of favours and flirting. No. It would never be permitted.

Did the Sultan know about these more relaxed traditions? It was possible, the word was that he had been more open-minded in his youth. Had he discussed the differences between chivalry in Spain and chivalry in Al-Andalus with his Spanish Queen?

It suddenly occurred to her that the Sultan might belatedly realise the identity of the clumsy handmaiden caught lurking near the audience chamber.

'Maura, do you know if the Sultan wishes to see me?'

'No, Princess. He is taken up with the competition tomorrow, I am sure.'

Zorahaida let out a slow breath and stared blindly at the fairy-tale fretwork on one of the shutters. She longed to watch the tournament, but never in a thousand years would her father give her permission. Even if she wore her veil, palace protocol wouldn't allow her to set foot in a stand. Tomorrow, the audience would be made up entirely of men. Counsellors and courtiers, knights and guards and possibly a handful of foreign diplomats.

The tournament was for men. That being the case, she must find her own way of seeing it.

Captain Yusuf could take her up to one of the watchtowers above the lists, she would have a good view from there.

As Zorahaida planned how best to manage it without putting her small household in danger, she found herself wondering whether Jasim ibn Ismail, the knight with the amber eyes, would win any of the bouts.

Jasim steadied his lance and narrowed his eyes against the sun. Since his last pass from this end, the sun had moved. It was blinding and burningly hot; sweat was soaking into the padded tunic beneath his armour. No matter. His opponent would be suffering from the same challenges when they changed ends and, thus far, Jasim was ahead on points with several direct hits to his credit and a man unhorsed. He was enjoying himself.

As the herald moved into position, Jasim's black destrier, Blade, jerked his head. Excited by the action, Blade was jumpy enough to race down the list at the drop of a pin. Jasim held him firmly.

'Steady boy.' Highly bred, strong, fast and brimming with energy, Blade was the perfect horse for a tournament. If kept in check.

Squinting through his visor, Jasim kept his opponent in the centre of his vision and waited for the signal.

A horn blared. Jasim gave Blade his head, his gaze never wavering from his target.

Hoofs pounded. Sawdust and soil spewed out from beneath the horses' hoofs. Men shouted in the stands.

Jasim braced himself for the jar of impact, swayed and sat firm. He had his opponent's measure. Breathing thanks to God, he wheeled Blade about and took up his position at the shady end of the lists. The other knight had remained seated, but barely.

Jasim fixed his eyes on his target. He would win this bout.

* * *

At the top of the watchtower, Zorahaida was being discreet. Truth to tell, the jousting was something of a disappointment. Peering through a crenel with her veil on, she couldn't see as much as she'd hoped. The knights were wearing helmets, and since she didn't know their colours there was no telling one from the other. Not that she had met any of them, of course, save for Jasim ibn Ismail.

'Captain, who is the knight in blue? He seems to be doing quite well.'

Yusuf stared down at the lists. 'The knight on a black destrier with a silver shield?'

'Aye, that's the one, his shield has wavy blue lines on it.'

'I couldn't say, Princess. There are so many men competing, I am not conversant with all their devices.'

Light footsteps came hurrying up the stairs to the parapet and the door scraped open.

'Princess,' Sama said, voice tight. 'When Maura told me she didn't know where you were, I guessed you might be here.'

Sama's hands were trembling and she sounded completely distraught. Zorahaida's insides turned to water.

'My father knows I am here?'

'No, thank God. But please come with me. The Sultan has summoned you. You are to distribute the prizes.'

Zorahaida's knees went weak, she had surely misheard. 'What? That's not possible.'

'Princess, hurry. *Please.* He is waiting, they will all be waiting.' Sama wrung her hands. 'God have mercy, the Sultan will have my head on a platter if you go before those knights in that grey servant's rag.'

Zorahaida glanced down at herself. 'He would be humiliated.' And there was nothing her father disliked more. She went to the head of the stairway. 'Sama, why does he want me to do this?'

'A delegation has arrived from the Spanish court. Diplomats, I believe.'

'That explains it.'

A cold dread crept over her as she flew down the stairs, Sama at her heels.

The world of the palace was generally so small. Since her sisters' departure, Zorahaida had worked tirelessly to spare its inhabitants the worst of her father's excesses and during that time her sense of self-worth had grown by leaps and bounds. She wasn't completely helpless. She had some influence within the palace walls, but she sensed that lately something had changed.

Her mind raced. The Sultan was using this competition to impress both his knights *and* the Castilian delegates. He owed the adjoining kingdom of Castile much money in tribute. Did he think to escape paying it by following their traditions? Was that why he suddenly wished her to act as Queen of the Tournament?

Zorahaida glanced back at Sama and, pushing her thoughts to one side, made her voice calm. Light. 'I am going as fast as I can.'

'Princess, you will need to wear silk,' Sama said, breathlessly. 'You'll need gold bangles. Rings. And to preserve your modesty, I think a dark veil covered in seed pearls. Everything is laid out in your bedchamber. Hurry, I implore you.'

Trumpets blared. Zorahaida stepped on to a stand that lately had been filled with cheering men. A faint odour of male sweat lingered. Ignoring it, she joined a handful of other veiled women. Their jewellery gave away their identities.

'Anya,' she murmured, nodding at her father's favourite concubine and her maid. 'Najina.'

Veiled heads dipped in acknowledgment, but since none of the other women spoke, Zorahaida had no way of knowing what was going through their minds.

Sama followed her and made a great show of arranging her mistress's veil.

The Nasrid red and gold standard hung at either side of the next stand, where Sultan Tariq was sitting. His gilded chair was shaded by a crimson and gold awning to match his colours and he was surrounded by his right-hand men. The Spanish dignitaries, marked out by tunics emblazoned with the Castilian coat of arms, had been given the privilege of watching from the Sultan's stand. They'd even been offered a cushioned bench, set slightly to one side.

Zorahaida made a show of facing her father's stand. She put her hands together and gave a deep obeisance. She knew what was expected of her, her father's vizier had explained the protocols as she had hurried from her tower to the tiltyard.

At no time was she to remove her veil. On no account was she to touch the contestants. All she had to do was wait for the successful knights to ride up, then she would nod her permission and a steward would hand out the prizes. She was permitted to offer her congratulations. In a modest voice, naturally. The prize-giving would begin with the minor prizes, the overall champion would come last.

As Zorahaida had received her instructions, she had been glad of the veil that hid her smile. She was certain that the Spanish delegation was more likely to be amused than impressed by the prize-giving ceremony as devised by her father.

The sun beat down. Again, the trumpets sounded. The herald made an announcement and the first knight rode up, his horse lathered and snorting through wide nostrils. The knight had removed his helmet, which was slung over his saddlebow, and was wearing a simple head-cloth. She didn't recognise him, so he wasn't one of her father's knights. He had black eyes and a dark beard.

Zorahaida bowed her head and gestured towards the prize chest. She murmured her congratulations and the prize, a small purse, was handed over. The herald called another name and a new knight rode up. And so it went, with the prizes handed out by the steward gradually becoming grander and more ostentatious.

She felt ridiculous and very out of place. This prize-giving was a farce, she was no Queen of the Tournament. Knight after knight collected his prize, some she recognised, most she didn't. Some were bruised and battered, others had cuts on their faces. Finally, after much fanfare the overall champion was called.

The champion had amber eyes and a red-gold beard. Her breath caught. As he rode up to the stand and came before her, a smile formed behind her veil. Jasim ibn Ismail had won the tournament.

A bruise was darkening on his cheekbone. With his black horse and silver shield, she recognised him as the knight who had caught her attention earlier. The wavy blue lines on his shield must represent the River Guadalevín which ran through Madinat Runda. His squire stood by his stirrup and the boy had obviously had time to rub his master's horse down, for the black flanks, though glossy, were free of foam.

Her smile faded. How very frustrating. She had been torn away from the watchtower too soon, she would very much have liked to watch him win. And then, to her horror, she said exactly that.

'Congratulations, Jasim ibn Ismail. I am sure you are a worthy champion. I only wish I could have seen you win.'

Jasim ibn Ismail blinked several times. He frowned. Briefly, he looked as though he had seen a ghost.

Hastily, Zorahaida gestured at the steward. 'Give the champion his prize, if you please.'

'Princess Zorahaida?' Jasim murmured, unable to believe his ears. That voice belonged to the maidservant he had seen at the city infirmary and in the orchard yesterday. She was the Sultan's daughter? It seemed impossible, yet this was surely the same woman. She had the same melodious voice. She was of the same height, and she had the same build—slender, yet womanly enough to make a man dream.

She bowed her head. 'Congratulations, sir knight.'

Discreetly, she stepped back, leaving Jasim with an absurd desire to break every convention. He wanted to talk to her. He wanted to find out whether Sultan Tariq was aware she went into the city. He was curious as to what she'd been doing outside that audience chamber near the Court of the Lions. Had she been spying on her father? Would she dare?

Of course, his questions could never be asked, never mind answered. He would be skewered on the spot if he engaged the Princess in conversation. Besides, whatever she'd been doing outside the audience chamber, she wouldn't thank him for giving her away.

Fascinated, he stared at the pearls sewn on to her veil. If only he could see her.

Jasim had never wanted to see a woman's face more. Would her face be as delicate as the womanly body he was sure was concealed beneath all that silk? He shook his head. His thoughts were wildly out of hand, yet they would not stop.

The palace was known to be a hotbed of intrigue. It was common knowledge that that Sultan Tariq and his brother Prince Ghalib had filled the Alhambra with spies. They didn't trust each other. The Sultan was desperate to remain alive and so, too, was his heir the Prince.

Despite himself, a smile formed. Clearly, the Sultan and his brother were not the only ones with secrets. Impossible though it seemed, Princess Zorahaida had them too. He had first seen her taking her lute into the infirmary. And, later, in the orchard when he'd chased after her, she'd been talking quite comfortably with the Captain. Further, Jasim had received the distinct impression that the Captain hadn't had the remotest intention of punishing her. That man had been prepared to run the gauntlet of the Sultan's displeasure because he respected her.

No, that captain felt far more than respect. Princess Zorahaida was adored. Plainly, she had a heart of gold.

'Master?' The steward interrupted his flow of thought. The man was struggling to present him with a weighty-looking golden casket overflowing with coins. 'You wish your squire to take charge of your prize?'

Jasim spared the casket a brief glance. Princess Zorahaida was far more intriguing than the Sultan's entire treasury. A woman like that could surely work miracles. An idea came to him. A bold idea he had no business thinking. And yet...

He held up his hand. 'One moment. There was talk of the champion choosing a gem from the Sultan's collection.'

The steward grimaced, trying again, to offer the casket. 'This casket will be more valuable than any one gem, Sir Jasim.'

The pearls gleamed on the Princess's veil, she was watching him, he was sure. Was she as fascinated with him as he was with her? Would she forgive him for what he was about to do?

His cautious half was screaming warnings whilst his more reckless half was urging him on. If he succeeded, his uncle, the Governor of Madinat Runda, would, once he had got over the shock, realise the wisdom of what Jasim was trying to achieve.

And if he failed, well, his uncle would doubtless thank the stars that he no longer had to worry about what his scapegrace nephew might do next.

God help me.

Jasim cleared his throat. He was careful to hold the steward's eyes, though he pitched his voice loud enough to carry to Sultan's stand. 'I seem to recall the finest gem in the palace was offered as part of the prize.'

The steward nodded. 'As you wish.' He cleared his throat. 'Though you must understand, this casket will not be as full.'

Jasim dismissed the casket with a negligent wave. 'Forget the casket. I simply require the prize that was offered, the most precious jewel in the Sultan's possession.'

The lists had fallen uncharacteristically quiet. On Jasim's right, the tinkling of harnesses told him that other knights were nudging their mounts closer, straining to hear him. Out of the corner of his eye, he saw men on the stands leaning forward to discover what was happening. Others crowded up to the wooden railings.

The steward sent a bewildered glance towards the Sultan. The Sultan gave a curt nod and the steward relaxed.

'Very well,' the steward said. 'It is agreed. You may have the gem your choice. Once you have disarmed, you will be escorted to the treasury.'

'My thanks, but that will not be necessary. I have made my choice.'

He looked directly at Princess Zorahaida. The other ladies, who until then had remained motionless as statues, suddenly seemed to understand what he was about. One took a firm hold of the Princess's arm. Whether she was offering support or attempting to control her wasn't clear. The other ladies moved to surround her.

Apart from the whisper of Granada silk, there was silence.

'I choose the Princess Zorahaida,' Jasim said. 'She is the finest gem in Al-Andalus. I wish to claim her for my bride.'

Chapter Five

Jasim ibn Ismail's request was so preposterous, Zorahaida was sure she had misheard. He was claiming her as his prize? He actually thought he would be allowed to marry her?

His arrogance robbed her of breath. Jasim ibn Ismail must see that it was impossible. She was the Sultan's daughter. He wasn't a prince; he'd merely won a tournament. How dared he?

Her place was in the Alhambra, where she was needed. It was her home. If she were to marry this man, she would have to leave. Who would watch over the servants? And what about the hospital? The city beggars?

Shifting her head to see past the encircling ladies, Zorahaida glared at him from behind her veil. She fought to think past her shock. This wasn't about her, it couldn't be. During their brief interaction in the orange grove, Jasim ibn Ismail had struck her as intelligent. To risk rousing the Sultan's fury by claiming her instead of a chest crammed with gold and silver was the act of a madman. But this knight was far from mad.

What was he up to?

When hiding in the alcove outside the audience chamber, Zorahaida distinctly recalled the Sultan saying that Jasim ibn Ismail came from Madinat Runda. She might live quietly, but she took pains to find out what was going on inside the Sultan's kingdom. Madinat Runda had been disadvantaged when her father had increased trade tariffs to punitive levels. The entire district desperately needed to amend their trade agreements with Granada. If not, it would slide deeper into poverty.

Zorahaida also knew that Jasim ibn Ismail's uncle was the Governor of Madinat Runda. From what she had overheard in the audience chamber, it appeared that Jasim ibn Ismail's father had offended the Sultan. Had that been the reason for her father raising the tariffs? It must have been. One way or another, Jasim ibn Ismail's father had crossed the Sultan.

Her insides quivered as fear replaced shock. How would her father respond? This knight, whatever his father might have done, came from an influential and honourable family. At this moment though, his bloodlines were irrelevant. As champion of the tournament he was owed a glittering prize, but for him to ask for her hand in marriage—it was outrageous. She prayed the Sultan didn't respond with violence.

If Jasim ibn Ismail thought claiming her hand would bring his district a step closer to prosperity, he was about to be given a hard lesson. The Sultan would never agree. It was out of the question.

The silence stretched out. None of the onlookers knew how to react, they watched in fascinated horror.

Zorahaida wrenched her gaze from the champion of the day and glanced at the Sultan. Beneath his turban, her father's face might have been carved from stone. The lines between his eyebrows and around his mouth were deeper than ever. Her heart thudded. Everyone who knew him would realise that Sultan Tariq was blindly, dangerously angry.

His daughter was not an object to be given away as a prize in a tournament. Since Zorahaida's sisters had flown, they had been disowned, in effect making her Sultan Tariq's only child. She liked to think that he loved her, the last reminder of Lady Juana, the woman he had made his Queen.

What a nightmare. This could only have one ending and it was likely to be bloody.

The Sultan would, she prayed, control his anger sufficiently to set Jasim ibn Ismail right. Zorahaida might be astounded that Jasim ibn Ismail had the temerity to ask for her as his prize, but she didn't want him dead. He had followed her to the orchard, intending to spare her a beating. He couldn't be all bad.

The Sultan rose. Benches scraped and clattered on the stands as everyone scrambled to their feet. To remain seated when the Sultan was standing would be a grave insult. When the noise had died down, the Sultan gave the Spanish contingent a smile—his false one—and turned to the steward.

'Take my daughter back to her chambers.'

The summons to attend the Sultan came, as Zorahaida suspected it would, shortly after she had returned from the bathhouse. Her father would want to tell her how he had dealt with Jasim ibn Ismail. She felt alarmingly jumpy. Whatever had prompted Jasim ibn Ismail to make his preposterous proposal, she didn't want him killed.

The sun had set, and the gardens were grey

in the twilight. Zorahaida would know her way through the grounds blindfolded, none the less she accepted the assistance of a torchbearer to lead her along the paths and through the courtyards. At the entrance to the audience chamber, the torchbearer bowed and melted quietly into the dark.

Taking in a breath to calm her nerves, she passed through the door. Lamplight illuminated the flowing script on the wall tiles and the fragrance of frankincense drifted in the air. The Sultan was seated on his throne with the usual array of household knights.

How strange, a small table and two chairs were positioned immediately before him. Confused, Zorahaida blinked at the chairs. Other than the Sultan's thrones, there were very few chairs in the palace. She couldn't begin to think why these were in here. The table was spread with a beautifully embroidered silk cloth.

The Sultan gestured her forward and, even more strange, as she was about to make her usual obeisance, he shook his head.

'No need for that tonight, Daughter.' He waved her towards a chair. 'Be pleased to sit.'

Feeling as though she was dreaming, Zorahaida took the nearest chair and watched in disbelief as the Sultan dismissed most of his guards.

Her mouth went dry and a sinking feeling in her stomach warned her that something unheard of was about to happen. Something over which she would have no control.

Bending her head modestly, she managed to look about her. Never had she seen her father with so small a guard. Only a few household knights remained. The Spanish delegation stood in a corner. And...

'Jasim ibn Ismail, be pleased to step forward,' the Sultan said. Though his words were courteous, he sounded as though he was speaking through clenched teeth.

God have mercy. What was her father about to do?

Jasim bowed deeply at both the Sultan and Princess Zorahaida and took the other chair.

His gamble had paid off. Amazingly, the Sultan had agreed that he could marry his daughter. Jasim was wryly aware that if the Spanish envoys hadn't been present, his request would have been turned down in no uncertain manner.

As matters stood, however, the Sultan couldn't afford to show weakness before the Spaniards.

He had made a public declaration and thanks to his twisted sense of honour, felt honour-bound to stick to it. Jasim's assessment of the Sultan's character—that he had too much pride to consider retreat—had been correct.

Jasim's proposal of marriage had stunned more than the court. Jasim had stunned himself. In truth, ever since he'd learned of his father's failed attempt at diplomacy, he'd been living under a cloud. His plans, which had once included marriage, had been shoved aside. What decent woman would want to ally herself with a knight whose father's actions had brought misery to Madinat Runda?

In truth, until the prize-giving, the idea of marrying the Princess hadn't even occurred to him. And then, flushed with success, he'd been unable to think of anything else. He'd imagined he'd come to terms with not marrying. Apparently not. He wanted to marry. And his desire to marry was driven by more than ambition. He wanted this particular woman. Princess Zorahaida.

Oddly, rather than feel elated by the success of his gamble, Jasim remained tense. It was no use reminding himself that once he was married to the Sultan's daughter, his uncle would no longer be able to ignore his counsel. He had yet to get home.

He didn't think much of what he had seen of the palace, the entire court seemed to be permanently on tenterhooks with everyone watching each other. The sooner he and his bride were on their way home, the sooner he could relax.

He smiled at the Princess, aware of a new complication. Women of her status rarely had any choice in their marriage partners. They married every day according to their fathers' wishes. Princess Zorahaida would have little choice but to accept the Sultan's decision. Even so, she was bound to be shocked. And now the moment of truth had arrived, Jasim found he wanted a willing bride. His stomach churned. How would she respond?

'Daughter, you doubtless heard this man's request at the tournament,' the Sultan said, briskly.

The veiled head dipped. 'Yes, Father.'

Wishing he could read her expression, Jasim frowned at her veil.

'You should know that I have agreed. You will marry this knight.'

The Princess sprang to her feet. 'No, Father. No!'

Jasim went cold. Slowly, he rose. He had feared

the Princess might object, but he was determined to win her over. He would marry this woman. Fresh trade agreements must be made between Granada and Madinat Runda. He would rid himself of the shame caused by his father's disastrous political meddling. When he went home he would return a hero.

He held out his hand to her. 'Princess—'

'No touching,' the Sultan barked. 'There is to be no touching. Daughter, be seated.'

The Princess didn't move. Her chest was rising and falling, and Jasim couldn't help but note that her hands had fisted in her robes. 'Father, I don't want to marry this man! I won't do it. You can't make me.'

Jasim grimaced. He'd known his proposal would shock her, but he hadn't expected such vehemence.

The Sultan snapped his fingers and two household knights moved to stand at either side of the Princess.

Jasim stopped breathing. He'd asked for her hand on the spur of the moment. He should have thought it through. And now the Sultan was bullying her, it wasn't pleasant to watch. He poised himself to defend her.

'Daughter, I think you will find that I can.'

The Princess held her ground.

'Father, I don't want to marry him.'

Her veil shifted with every agitated breath and Jasim thought he heard her muttering. For a moment, the Sultan looked as though he might strike her. Finally, she took her seat and the household knights returned to their posts at the Sultan's side.

Jasim's guts twisted. The Sultan's display of force had confirmed all his fears. The man was a tyrant and a bully. Did the Princess want to live in the palace for the rest of her life? When he'd realised she was the same woman he'd seen taking a lute into the city infirmary, he'd imagined she would be glad to escape. Was he wrong?

That was the trouble dealing with women outside the family. They usually wore veils, and it was impossible to read their faces. All you had to go on was actions. And the Princess, though her father might not know it, had been wandering about Granada. Jasim would bet his life that the Sultan had no idea what she was up to.

'You too.' The Sultan threw him a dark glance. 'Be seated. You may address my daughter directly now.'

Jasim sent the woman behind the veil a careful smile. 'Princess, I have asked Sultan Tariq for your hand in marriage and he has agreed. I would be honoured beyond measure if you would accept me.'

If she agreed, protocol declared that the Princess would lift her veil so he could see her face. Jasim was looking forward to that. At least it might grant him some insight into her thoughts. He hoped she was pretty, but that, he reminded himself, was irrelevant. Character counted for more than beauty. Besides, he wanted this marriage for political reasons.

Princess Zorahaida didn't reply at once. She paused long enough for the sweat to break out on Jasim's brow. There was even time for him to notice a moth flying drunkenly towards one of the lamps. Well, if she did refuse him, at least he had done his best for Madinat Runda. He only hoped that his uncle understood what he'd been trying to do.

'Very well, Father.' Her voice wobbled. 'If it is your wish, I will marry this man.'

The Sultan jerked his head at his household knights and they and the Spanish envoys all filed out. For the next part of the betrothal ceremony, Jasim, the Sultan and his daughter would be alone so Princess Zorahaida could lift her veil.

The other men must leave as traditionally they were not permitted to see her without it.

When the door closed behind the last of the household knights, Princess Zorahaida threw back her veil.

Her eyes were heavily lined with kohl, but no amount of kohl could hide the fact that her face was bruised and swollen on one side. Shocked rigid, Jasim could only stare.

Someone had struck her hard enough to give her a black eye. Only one person would have the gall to hit the Princess, her father, may the devil take him. Fortunately, Jasim knew better than to accuse the Sultan of brutalising her. It took effort, but he kept his gaze on the Princess and spoke softly for her ears alone.

'You're hurt.'

She focused on the embroidered cloth. 'It is nothing.'

Seeing her face sent Jasim's reservations about asking for her hand flying to the four winds. His misgivings, the uneasy realisation that marriage to him would mean he might be stealing her away from everything she knew and loved, could be dismissed.

He must separate her from her father, and quickly. This could not go on.

Princess Zorahaida will be safe with me.

He would overcome her objections. It should be easy. Why would she choose to remain here, in the control of a father who mistreated her, when she could establish her household in Mondragón Palace, with a husband who would guard her with his life?

'Nothing?' he said, in an undertone he hoped only she could hear. 'It is not nothing.' *It is monstrous, it is a travesty. The Sultan does not deserve to be a father.*

He studied her, making the most of the few moments she would be without her veil.

Princess Zorahaida had hair as dark as midnight and eyes to match. The table Jasim was gazing across was small, and they were close enough for him to tell that the eye that wasn't swollen had astonishing depths. Her mouth was trembling. It was prettily curved and, when she saw him taking inventory of her features, it edged up into a lop-sided smile. Her teeth were as white as pearls.

She was, or she would be when her bruises faded, extremely comely. Jasim found himself staring at her mouth, wondering how she would respond to a kiss, and felt a rush of desire.

Hastily, he lifted his gaze. 'Princess, whilst I

have breath in my body, I will protect you. You will want for nothing.'

'Thank you.'

The Sultan's foot tapped. 'That is enough. Daughter, cover your head.'

The Princess drew her veil back, the Sultan clapped his hands and his knights tramped back into the chamber. A servant followed with a casket that was the twin of the one that Jasim had rejected at the tourney. The servant placed the casket in the centre of the table and effaced himself.

'For you, Daughter. I would not wish you to arrive in Madinat Runda like a beggar.'

'Thank you, Father. May I ask when the marriage will take place?'

'In two days' time.'

Jasim heard her swallow, though she said nothing, merely dipped her head. Outwardly, her rebelliousness had vanished.

And inwardly? What was going through her mind? That wretched veil, Jasim loathed the thing. The one glimpse he'd had of her face had shown it to be extraordinarily expressive.

A ruby glinted as the Sultan dismissed her with a flick of his wrist. 'Return to your quarters, Daughter. Your attendants will be furnished with silk cloth for your bride clothes. Damasks, velvets, choose whatever you like.'

'Thank you, Father,' the Princess said meekly.

She rose, bowed carefully to the Sultan and walked gracefully from the chamber. Jasim couldn't help but note that he, soon to be her husband, received no such courtesy.

Shortly afterwards, as Jasim followed a torch-bearer back to his quarters, he realised he had underestimated his betrothed.

Princess Zorahaida was clearly an extremely resolute young woman. Jasim had barely exchanged a handful of words with her, yet he already knew she was capable of defying the Sultan. She colluded with the Palace Guard in order to leave the palace at will. She spied on her father. She was a woman with a mission—perhaps several missions—and she was set on carrying them out, heedless of the consequences.

As he made his way back to the barracks, he glanced guiltily towards where he believed the Princess's tower was sited. He had offended her. He didn't believe it was because she had taken against him personally. Rather, her anger stemmed from the fact that his proposal had knocked her plans awry.

It wasn't the best way to begin a marriage.

Jasim sighed. He would simply have to find a way to put things right. Like her father, the Princess was proud. And with her father's insistence the marriage went ahead, she must feel she'd been backed into a corner.

If Jasim offered her a way out, she might be more amenable to his proposal. If she realised she had a choice. Yes, that might serve...

It was odd, he had proposed the alliance in the flush of victory, the instant he understood that his desire to marry hadn't gone away. He'd thought it fortuitous that the Princess intrigued him. He'd suddenly seen a way forward for both Madinat Runda and his personal ambitions. In marrying the Princess, he could kill two birds with one stone.

He'd been a fool, an arrogant fool. He would have to win her over.

Having seen the Princess's face, Jasim wanted the marriage more than ever. Politics be damned, the idea of leaving her behind at the mercy of her violent, irascible father was unthinkable.

And if she insisted on staying here?

It was a risk.

He sighed. There was nothing for it, he must offer her a choice. Hopefully, she would see sense. Life in Madinat Runda, where she would have his protection, had to be better than life in the Alhambra where she was brutalised.

Meeting the Princess before the marriage ceremony wasn't going to be easy. The Sultan saw no necessity for the two of them to see each other before then. It was possible he might change his mind, but even supposing Jasim was permitted to meet her, their every breath would be watched.

Jasim had to find a less orthodox way of talking to her. And soon. He would make her understand she would be safe with him. Then, whatever she decided; he would respect her decision.

Getting to see the Princess on her own would be something of a challenge.

Alone, Jasim didn't stand a chance of arranging a private meeting with her. He needed help from someone who knew their way about the palace. Someone brave enough to break the protocols and fiercely loyal to the Princess.

The captain he had met in the orange grove sprang to mind. The man hadn't hesitated to aid the Princess after she had been caught wandering about near the audience chamber. If Jasim could track him down, he might be prepared to help.

As Jasim reached the barracks, he turned to the

torchbearer. 'I need to speak to one of the officers. Would you kindly direct me to the guard-house?'

Zorahaida's betrothal turned her maidservants into madwomen. The ink was barely dry on the marriage agreement before bolts of cloth began piling pile up in the antechamber at the foot of the tower. Everyone except her seemed thrilled.

'Princess, look at this velvet,' Maura said. 'I believe it comes from France.'

'No, no, this cloth of gold is finer by far,' Sama said, shaking out a length of glittering fabric. 'It's from Cathay.'

Delicate veils were dragged from great iron-bound chests. A spray of purple flowers arrived from Prince Ghalib. Her maidservants discussed the merits of velvet slippers, beaded with fresh-water pearls. They admired kidskin riding boots that had been dyed red to match the Nasrid colours. They squealed and talked non-stop.

Even Hunter caught the excitement, he leaped from chest to chest, unearthing yet another veil and chattering almost as loudly as her maids.

It was too much. Maura and Sama were never usually so excitable. They kept exchanging glances with one another and eyeing her in the most extraordinary manner. If Zorahaida didn't understand they were over-excited about her marriage, she might suspect they were up to something.

I am going to marry a stranger from the west.

When Zorahaida could bear no more, she gave Sama and Maura instructions that she was not to be disturbed and took refuge up in her bedchamber. She left Hunter below. Save for the songbirds, whose cage was covered in a cloth to encourage them to sleep, she was alone.

It was a warm evening, so she put on a gauzy silk nightgown and went to lie on her feather bed. The shadows created by a lamp danced about her chamber. She wouldn't sleep. She just needed some peace.

I have been given away as a prize in a tournament!

The cheek of the man. The nerve.

Her head pounded. She lay on her bed, gently rubbing her temple. She wanted to think about the man she was to marry before she could begin to contemplate silks and satins and leather riding boots dyed with the Nasrid colours.

A door thumped decisively downstairs, and she heard the snap of a bolt being thrown.

Then, blessed relief, quiet. Maura and Sama

must have retired, they would be sleeping in a chamber below.

Rising, Zorahaida padded to the window facing the mountain. Kneeling on a cushion in the embrasure, she pushed at a shutter which stuck a little before opening.

The heavens were filled with stars and below them was the dark outline of the mountain. In Zorahaida's mind, this window opened out to more than a view of the snow-capped Sierra Nevada and she often found comfort gazing out of it. This window reminded her of her sisters, of the time the three of them had been serenaded by three Spanish knights. Shortly after that, her sisters had flown from her life and her father had made it plain that he would never let her go. Not for a moment had she believed he would change his mind.

Now he had. She was to marry a knight from the west, Jasim ibn Ismail. Would it actually happen? Her father had declared it before witnesses, but her father was unpredictable, to say the least.

Releasing her breath in a sigh, she leaned her head against the shutter and wished she knew more about Jasim ibn Ismail. When he'd believed her to be a maidservant he'd hurried after her in order to prevent her from being beaten. He had compassion. The trouble was, she'd made the mistake of speaking to him. He'd heard her voice. And since he'd heard it again at the tourney, he would know that she was in the habit of wandering about the palace in the guise of a maidservant.

Crucially, he didn't seem to have told her father what she was up to.

What else did he know? Could she trust him not to say anything about her being the clumsy maidservant?

She closed her eyes and the small night sounds washed over her. The rustle of a tiny creature in the undergrowth, the cry of an owl. Her mind drifted. She thought about the warmth of Jasim ibn Ismail's smile, of his extraordinary amber-coloured eyes...

Down in the gully, a twig cracked. It was astonishingly loud. Zorahaida stilled. A man's voice reached her.

Who could be in the gully at the bottom of the palace wall? The Palace Guards?

When she placed her hands on the cool of the windowsill, she saw something had been fastened around the central pillar. It was hard to make it out in the weak light, it felt hard and rough. It looked and felt like...

Rope! A rope was tied to the window.

Heart thumping, she crawled on to the low sill and leaned right out. The rope snaked down, seemingly to the bottom of the tower, to where two men, blurry shapes in the night, were standing. It was so reminiscent of the time when Zorahaida and her sisters had sent food down to their Spanish knights, that her eyes stung.

'Who's there?' she hissed.

'Be calm, it is only your betrothed.'

Jasim ibn Ismail was down there? What madness was this? If he should be seen by the guards patrolling the wall walk…

The rope creaked. One of the men, Jasim ibn Ismail presumably, set his hands to the rope and began to climb.

Zorahaida's eyes widened, she couldn't believe what she was seeing. The tower was tall, if he fell, he would break his neck. Heart in her mouth, she watched him. He didn't rush, he was careful. Hand over hand, one foot ever twisted in the rope, he came slowly, steadily nearer. At one point his headcloth fell off but he never missed a stroke. On he came. Relentless.

Goodness, he was strong. Her pulse thudded.

The rope shifted. Fibres groaned. As he reached the top, Zorahaida leapt back as though scalded.

Broad shoulders eased through the opening and he jumped lightly into the chamber. He shoved hair out of his face—red-gold, beautiful hair—and gave her a courtly bow. He was slightly out of breath.

'Don't be alarmed, Princess.'

'I'm not,' she said, disconcerted to realise it had never occurred to her to call for help. Edging cautiously round him, she stuck her head out. His companion remained where he was, staring up at her. 'Who is the other man?'

'Captain Yusuf ibn Safwan.'

'My captain helped you?'

'Aye, he arranged for the rope to be secured whilst you were busy with your maids. He was most obliging.' Jasim ibn Ismail smiled and it did strange things to Zorahaida's insides. It wasn't unpleasant, but it was unsettling. 'He told me that your sisters spoke to their suitors from the top of the tower.'

Zorahaida swallowed. 'That is true, but my sisters' husbands were in chains at the time. They never climbed up here.'

Jasim shrugged. 'Yusuf never told me that. I assumed—'

'You might have been killed.' She hesitated,

speaking softly so no one would hear. 'You still might be, if you are discovered.'

He stepped closer, his hair glowing rose gold in the lamplight. His hair, she thought vaguely, was truly magnificent. She had the most astonishing urge to touch it.

'Princess, I needed to speak to you urgently and in private. I could think of no other way that didn't involve palace protocols and us being watched.' He laid his hand on his heart. 'Besides, I had a yearning to see your face again.'

He was too charming; he couldn't possibly be sincere. Zorahaida gave him a stern look. 'If you think flirting will win my heart, you are mistaken.'

An eyebrow shot up. 'Flirting? Princess, we are strangers to one another. A woman in a veil has a certain allure, I'll not deny that, but I had a mind to know your thoughts. Since I've not learned to read you from your voice, I needed to see your expression.'

'Oh.'

When he glanced her up and down, Zorahaida realised, somewhat belatedly, that her filmy nightgown was a little too revealing and he seemed interested in far more than her expression. Snatching up a shawl, she draped it round her. 'You will keep your eyes on my face, that is shocking enough.'

His smile grew. 'Apologies, Princess. I meant no insult.'

'My father the Sultan, will kill you if he finds out you have come here.'

'We shall converse quietly, if you agree. Otherwise I shall leave.'

That he had gone to all this trouble to speak to her and was prepared to leave should she wish it settled the matter. In any case, Zorahaida was burning to hear what he had to say.

Coolly, she nodded, gesturing for him to take a seat on one of the cushions. She took the next cushion, noting that he didn't sit until she had. He appeared to be naturally courteous towards women. It was yet another point in his favour.

'Very well, Jasim ibn Ismail, what is so important that you must risk your life to discuss it?'

Chapter Six

Save for the chilling bruises, the Princess was so beautiful, Jasim struggled to find words. He could hardly believe his good fortune. If God willed it, this beguiling woman would be his.

Was frankness the best way to handle her? Perhaps he should keep his personal desires out of this. Did she know anything about statecraft? As a princess, she might be more sympathetic about his political targets.

'Princess, I should like to be honest with you. I asked for your hand on impulse.'

'I guessed as much. May I ask why?'

'As you are aware, I am from Madinat Runda. My father's foray into politics—'

'I know about that,' the Princess cut in. 'Your father overstepped himself and my father the Sultan took his anger out on the entire district.'

Jasim nodded. Once again, she had surprised him. Everything in this tower bedchamber—

the honeycomb plasterwork ceiling, the decorated wall tiles, the silk cushions and, yes, even that gilded birdcage—spoke of the ultimate in luxury. The Sultan was the most contradictory of parents. He treated his daughter with cruelty and harshness, yet he appeared to shower gifts upon her. She was waited on hand and foot…

In similar circumstances, how many women would trouble themselves to learn about what went on elsewhere? Not many. Yet this one went about dressed as a maidservant; she crept out of the palace to visit the hospital. She fascinated him as no woman before.

A satin ribbon was loosely wound into her hair, holding it back for sleep, and a few stray tendrils framed her face. Jasim wanted to touch them, to twine a glossy lock about his finger. Was her skin as soft as it looked? A pulse throbbed with want and for the first time in his life he was gripped by the most primitive of urges.

This woman is mine.

With a glance at her bruises, Jasim held himself back. Her father's brutality must have given her an abiding mistrust of men. He swallowed. He must tread carefully. His body was more than a little interested in her person. He didn't want to alarm her.

He cleared his throat. 'It came to me that a marriage with the Sultan's daughter could improve relations between Granada and Madinat Runda.' He smiled ruefully. 'I hoped to undo the damage caused by my father's foolhardiness. Many go hungry and—'

'You wanted to make amends. Do you truly believe such an alliance will bring prosperity to your district?'

'Aye.' Jasim leaned forward, resting his forearm on his knee. 'My uncle is Governor of Madinat Runda. He has no sons.'

'You hope to win favour with him. This is not only about trade, you have ambitions.' Long eyelashes fluttered down, briefly shielding her eyes. 'I understand and I thank you for your honesty.'

So, she valued honesty. In that case, he would tell her all.

'Princess, there is more. I think you should know that having seen you, I find you attractive, no, it is more than that.'

Her eyes widened; tiny green sparks glimmered in their depths. She touched her bruise and her pretty mouth twisted.

'You must be blind, sir knight.'

'Not so, you are a desirable, beautiful woman.'

Jasim's hand was inches from her. He could

practically feel her body heat. All he had to do was reach out. He reminded himself that she was a Nasrid princess. She would be pure. Untouched. And she was at this moment frowning, her dark eyes filled with uncertainty.

'Sir knight, you risked much to be here tonight. I confess I am not sure why you came.'

The shawl the Princess was using as a shield had slipped a little, taking with it what passed as a nightdress. Her naked shoulder was in plain view. Further, she was lying on her side, legs half-curled beneath her. She had pretty feet and the shape of her calves was visible through the fabric of her nightgown. It was very distracting. Jasim eased back into his cushion and tried not to look at her beautiful, sinuous body.

'Princess, I need to know your will. I came to tell you that if you wish, I shall withdraw my request to marry you.'

Silence.

When she lifted an eyebrow, he ploughed on. 'I do not need an unwilling wife.'

'Jasim ibn Ismail, it is a pity you did not consider this before you asked to marry me. You must be aware that if you withdraw now, after the formality of our betrothal, my father would construe it as a grave insult.'

'It's possible.'

Princess Zorahaida shifted towards him, and he caught the scent of roses. Her dark eyes were intent. 'Not possible, sir knight, but a certainty. Father will kill you. That and that alone was why I agreed to your proposal. I am not unwilling.' She bit her lip. 'It is just that—'

'Your life is here,' he murmured.

She shot him a startled glance. 'Indeed. I have duties here and only I can undertake them.'

'Only you?' He thought about her charitable expedition into the city. 'Surely one of the other ladies could help?'

'There are some things only I can do. I have a vital role in the palace.'

'If you accept me, you will have a role in Madinat Runda. I shall not interfere with your interests. Believe me, there is plenty of opportunity for charitable work in our infirmary.'

The colour drained from her face. 'You know about that?'

He gave her a gentle smile. 'I saw you by the hospital. I was at the tavern.'

'The one by the well?'

'Just so. Naturally, I didn't see beyond your veil, but I heard your voice. I recognised it later in the orange grove, where I mistook you for a maidservant. Even then I didn't realise your true identity until you spoke at the tourney.'

And her voice, Jasim realised, had somehow prompted him to ask for her hand. Why, he had no idea.

She stared at him, face ashen. 'Father mustn't know about my visits to the infirmary.'

'Of course not.' Jasim reached for her hand in reassurance and as soon as his fingers closed on hers, a frisson of awareness ran through him and reassurance was the last thing on his mind. He wanted to draw her close, he wanted to feel her body melt against his. 'Of course not,' he repeated, even as he was wondering how she would respond if he attempted to steal a kiss.

'Father mustn't find out about my masquerading as a maidservant either.'

'On my honour, I won't breathe a word.' Throat dry, he swallowed. 'Princess, I should warn you, I am about to break convention.'

She blinked and to his surprise and delight, laughed.

'Break convention? That doesn't surprise me, sir knight, you seem to be a past master at that. You rejected your prize at the tourney and asked to take me in marriage instead; we are not supposed to meet, and you climb the tower and appear in my bedchamber. Worse still, we are conversing in my bedchamber whilst I am un-veiled. Are there any conventions you haven't broken?'

He felt himself smile. 'One or two. Princess, with your permission, I am going to touch you.'

Carefully, Jasim slid his hand up her arm. For-tunately, their cushions were close, and it was an easy matter to draw her towards him. Uncertain as to whether she would resist, he prepared to pull back at the first sign of alarm. Happily, there was not a trace of alarm and no resistance. She allowed him to draw her closer.

'You are beautiful,' he murmured.

She lowered her eyelashes, they lay like dark crescents against her cheeks. He rather thought she was studying his mouth.

'You are going to kiss me.' Her voice was soft and husky. 'I find that pleases me, very much. I have often wondered what it might be like. Please, sir knight, continue.'

Jasim's pulse gave an excited thump. Was this truly the nervous Princess who had stayed be-hind when her bolder sisters had left the palace? There was no sign of nervousness in her tone and certainly no fear.

'With your permission, Princess.'

She leaned invitingly towards him. 'If you would. I am most curious.'

That did it. Jasim slid his hand around her neck and set his lips to hers. She gave a small jolt, so he kept it gentle with tiny, nibbling kisses. He kissed her mouth, her cheeks and returned to her mouth. It was warm and soft. And again, there was the subtle scent of roses. Roses and sweet, warm woman.

Princess Zorahaida moaned softly. Fearing he was rushing her, Jasim relaxed his hold and drew back. She lay against him as though born to be there. Her eyes were closed, and her cheeks faintly flushed. Her shawl had fallen away completely and the outline of her body—an extremely womanly body—was plainly visible. The beautiful curve of her breasts made him ache for more intimate contact. His gaze lingered on the swell of her hip, and much as he longed to caress her there too, he would go no further. It was too soon. Desire beating hard in his veins, he forced himself to ease back even as he realised that this was what he had climbed up her tower to discover. He'd wanted to find out if they were compatible as bedmates.

Well, he had his answer. Princess Zorahaida was deeply sensual. With the right man, she would be a joy to lie with. Jasim must make her his.

Those dark eyelashes lifted, and she gave a languorous sigh that had Jasim's blood heating all over again.

'Thank you, sir knight.'

His mouth twitched. 'You are most welcome, Princess.' It flashed in on him that the stories he had heard about the timid princess who had stayed behind in the palace whilst her bolder sisters ran off with their Spanish suitors were very wide of the mark.

Timid? This woman was a lioness.

'Before my sisters went away, I dreamed of marriage,' she said, touching her lips in a dreamy fashion.

Jasim struggled to order his thoughts. He wanted nothing more than to go on kissing her. To uncover every tempting curve, to kiss every inch. The need to make her truly his was burning so brightly it was in danger of eclipsing rational thought. He couldn't afford to let that happen tonight. It would be akin to signing his own death warrant.

He linked his fingers with hers and kissed her knuckles. 'You must miss your sisters.'

Her eyes filled with shadows. 'Every day. I

fully intended to go with them.' She shrugged. 'I changed my mind.'

'Why was that?'

'I couldn't imagine being married.' She gave a reminiscent smile. 'The Spanish knights who bore my sisters away had a comrade. I was ready to go with him. I am not sure why I didn't; I can only set it down to instinct. At the beginning, everything had been so romantic. We had three knights serenading us from the bottom of the tower. We were angry with our father who had confined us in here, and it was intoxicating to know that we were defying him.' Her eyes were pensive, she was focused on the past. 'I made the right decision, for I found out later that my cavalier never intended to marry me.'

Jasim searched her expression for any indication of distress. He couldn't be sure, but she seemed more resigned than distressed. 'He misled you.'

'He was already married.' She blushed. 'I don't know how much you know about Spanish marriage customs, but in Spain, Christians only take one wife, and he'd never mentioned her. I felt foolish when I found out. All he wanted was... Well, it's pretty obvious what he wanted, only I was too naive to realise. Since then, I have discovered that he was in the habit of enjoying many ladies and it didn't trouble him whether they were willing or not.'

'That knight was a dog, he didn't deserve you,' Jasim muttered.

He stared at Princess Zorahaida, his mind turning. This conversation was extraordinary on several levels. The Princess was an innocent in the sense that she was untouched. It had been an honour to be the first to kiss her. In other ways though, she was probably far from innocent.

She had the run of the palace, and she was apparently so determined that for her nowhere was out of bounds. The way the Sultan's concubines had closed about her at the tourney proved that those women knew her and knew her well. In Jasim's experience women talked, usually without cease. The Princess would have been told, in great detail, how a concubine was expected to pleasure her master. She would know how a wife was expected to behave. To be sure, her knowledge would be academic. She would have no real experience.

He shifted as desire burned anew. He fully intended to be the one to teach her the joys that might be found between a man and a woman.

Another thought came to him.

'You say the knight was already married?'

'Apparently.'

How had she found that out? Someone in the palace must have told her. It could be almost anyone, several parties were competing for dominance. That was why you couldn't walk two yards without having the sense that you were being observed.

The Sultan would have his faction, he was desperate to ensure that his brother and heir Prince Ghalib didn't make trouble. And Prince Ghalib would doubtless have his, for self-preservation, if nothing else. And since knowledge was power, each party would have its ways of learning what was happening in the neighbouring Kingdom of Castile.

Jasim watched the Princess's breasts gently rising and falling beneath that delicate and all-too-revealing silk. She was the most intriguing of women. It would never have occurred to him that the Sultan's daughter would have so much freedom, freedom she appeared to have won for herself and exercised in secret.

Her father didn't know the half of it. She commanded loyalty from soldiers like Captain Yusuf ibn Safwan. Doors and gates opened to her all over the palace. She went in and out at will.

How far did her influence extend?

'Do you write to your sisters?'

He didn't miss the way her eyes evaded his. 'How could I? My father the Sultan banished them on pain of death, did you not hear? They are barred from setting foot in Al-Andalus. It is even forbidden to talk of them. I am aware they have married.' She sighed. 'I used to think that life was poorer without them.'

Jasim thought he understood. 'You took up charity work to fill the void.'

Dark eyes flashed; he'd said the wrong thing.

'I took up charitable work, sir knight, because there was great need.'

Jasim glanced meaningfully at her bruises. 'Your father is a harsh master.'

'I cannot deny it.' She huffed out a breath and the anger left her eyes. 'Father was always prone to rages. I stayed behind, in part because I mistrusted that Spanish knight, but also because I hoped that over the years Father would mellow. I was certain that in his way, he loved us. We, the three Princesses, are his only children. I couldn't bear the thought of him thinking that we had abandoned him.' Silk rustled as she turned earnestly towards him. 'I thought I could help him.'

'You hoped to change him.'

'Exactly.' Sadly, she shook her head. 'I have failed dismally, sir knight.'

'You have done admirably, in my view,' Jasim said. 'You have survived.' And given her father's volatile temperament, that was no mean feat. 'Princess, I need to know, are you truly content to marry me?'

'Surprisingly, I am.' She gave him a direct look. 'I reacted badly at first because, frankly, your proposal came as a shock. However, provided you agree that we can remain in the Alhambra until I have handed over my responsibilities to someone else, I am content.'

For a moment, Jasim hesitated. He didn't want to deny her, but he loathed it here. Beautiful though it was, the place reeked of intrigue and betrayal. Brother had warred against brother for generations and much innocent blood had been shed. Perhaps, he thought soberly, it was known as the Red Fort not simply because the walls had a reddish cast to them, but also because of the blood that had been spilled inside it.

As far as Jasim was concerned, another day in the Red Fort was a day too long. However, it wouldn't do to rush her. After this meeting he really wanted her. Not to mention that coming home with a Nasrid princess as his bride would encourage his uncle to take him more seriously.

'All shall be as you wish.' Lifting her hand to his mouth, he kissed it and glanced meaningfully towards the window. 'Princess, I ought to take my leave. It is peaceful out there, but that could change.'

'You are right, sir knight. There is danger everywhere.'

More reluctant than he would have thought possible a few hours ago, Jasim pushed to his feet.

'Sir knight?' She rose and came to stand before him, bruised and beautiful and incredibly desirable. Her dark hair was glossy in the lamplight. Lightly, she touched his hand.

Jasim's heart missed a beat. It was the smallest of gestures, subtle as the touch of a butterfly's wing, yet it meant much. Princess Zorahaida would not be in the habit of initiating contact with a man. It was a good omen, he was making progress. 'Aye?'

'Thank you for your thoughtfulness, it is more than I hoped for.'

Closing his fingers on hers, he tugged. Silk trailed across the floor tiles as she came to stand before him. She barely reached his shoulder.

'A farewell kiss for my bride,' he said, tipping her head towards him.

He kept it brief and chaste, only allowing himself the pleasure of feeling her mouth soften against his and of hearing her gentle murmur. He disengaged before the temptation to carry her back to those cushions became unbearable. 'Princess, after I have gone, I'd like you to untie the rope and let it fall. I would hate to think anyone else might disturb you in your nest.'

'Very well.'

With a bow, Jasim went to the window, happier than he had believed possible with his betrothal. 'Farewell, then, until our wedding day.'

Heart aching, Zorahaida watched Jasim ibn Ismail slip lithely through the window. When he had gone, she poked her head out to follow his progress. He moved swiftly and with great efficiency and was soon standing on the gully floor. Yusuf handed him his head-covering, and Jasim glanced up at her.

'Princess?' Jasim's voice, though low, carried up to her. 'Untie the rope, if you please.'

Zorahaida wrestled with the rope, tearing a nail in the process. His weight had pulled it fast. 'I can't, it won't shift.'

'Very well, draw it up out of sight. It will be removed in the morning.' Jasim bowed, white teeth flashed, and he and Yusuf walked away. The night swallowed them, and it was almost as though she had dreamed the entire meeting.

Almost. His kisses stayed with her long after he'd gone. Zorahaida sat in the breeze on the window ledge, fingering her mouth, wondering why she was filled with such sadness. When he had claimed her as his prize at the tournament, she'd been outraged. That initial fury had ebbed away, all she felt now was unbearably sad. Why, she had no idea.

There was no need for sadness, she had learned much from their meeting. That kiss had transported her. When she had talked with her uncle's concubines and wondered what it would feel like to kiss a man, she'd no notion it would have such power. Those kisses had been magical; her mind had emptied of everything except the warmth of Jasim's body and his gentleness. His scent had been musky and male and incredibly enticing, she'd breathed it in and for a wild moment it was as though their souls were dancing together.

She grimaced, all too conscious that Jasim's personal charm put her in danger of deluding herself. Souls couldn't dance. She was being far too fanciful. And at what point in their unexpected and unorthodox meeting had he become Jasim to her, rather than Jasim ibn Ismail, knight at arms?

Wryly, she shook her head. Jasim didn't love her. Why, he didn't even know her. By his own admission, he'd seen an opportunity to marry for political and personal advantage and he'd seized it. At least he'd been honest, it was far better to have an honest husband than a dishonest one. None the less, despite what she'd told him, she wasn't entirely happy.

Three years ago, she'd made the decision to stay in the palace in order to help as many of her father's people as she could. She'd known that meant that the door to marriage would be closed for her and she had few regrets. Sir Enrique de Murcia meant nothing to her. She'd certainly made the right decision as far as he was concerned. Enrique de Murcia had misled her from the start. He was a liar and an abuser of women.

It was hard to fault Jasim. He'd been honest. Not only that, but he'd given her a tantalising taste of pleasure, and Zorahaida knew how rare that was because when she'd told the women in the harem about Sir Enrique de Murcia, his behaviour hadn't surprised them.

The concubines had warned her that a man who took pains to please a woman was rare. A man like that was to be treasured, the women had said, for in the main when a man and woman lay together, it was the woman's duty to give pleasure to the man.

Zorahaida had had no difficulty accepting what she'd been told. After all, it was common knowledge that her mother, Lady Juana, had been a Spanish captive. The Sultan had fallen in love with her and when she had begged to be allowed to return home all her pleas had fallen on deaf ears. In the end, Lady Juana had had no choice but to marry the Sultan. As his Queen she had spent the rest of her days in Al-Andalus. Beloved by the Sultan, living in the most sumptuous apartments, Zorahaida's mother had lost her freedom for ever.

Jasim's bright hair shone in Zorahaida's mind's eye, like a beacon of hope. Firmly, she told herself not to pin any dreams on him. Her soon-to-be husband might be a rarity among men, but he didn't love her. She didn't know him. He might appear to be honourable and kind, but she had learned that appearances could be deceptive. She would remain wary.

She frowned darkly at the cushion which carried the imprint of his strong warrior's body. He had certainly turned her life upside down. If she truly was to marry him—and with her father liable to change his mind on a whim, the marriage was by no means certain—she had much to do.

Tomorrow, she must make some changes. She couldn't bear it if anyone were to suffer because she had gone to Madinat Runda.

Sama was her most capable maid, Zorahaida would have to leave her behind. Sama knew who to trust and she was discreet. Yusuf too would be worth his weight in gold, he and Sama could work as a team. The purple flowers from her uncle caught her eye and she found herself wondering whether Sama and Yusuf might, at a pinch, take Prince Ghalib into their confidence.

She fingered her bruise. No, she couldn't risk it. After Yamina's near drowning, the enmity between her father and his brother had come to a head. Who knew what Prince Ghalib might do?

And Maura? Maura was far too nervous to be entrusted with anything hazardous. She would give herself away in a heartbeat. Zorahaida smiled. And that was all to the good, because she would need a personal maid in Madinat Runda. Maura would be perfect.

Her head was beginning to ache again. Rubbing her temples, she rose and headed back to bed.

Before she fell asleep, she found herself wondering when the rope could have been fastened to the window. It must have been done before she retired. Recalling the knowing glances Maura and Sama had exchanged earlier, she huffed out a breath.

Her most trusted companions had conspired against her so that Jasim ibn Ismail could enter her bedchamber. They seemed certain she would wish for this marriage.

If only Zorahaida shared their certainty.

Chapter Seven

The Sultan had decreed that the marriage ceremony would take place in the Chamber of the Ambassadors, a cavernous room with a double row of arched windows. Every inch of the intricate plasterwork was covered with flowing inscriptions and symbols. Nasrid mottoes sat cheek by jowl with writings from sacred texts.

Other than the location of the ceremony, Jasim had little idea what to expect. The Sultan was a law unto himself and Jasim's prospective father by marriage was clearly not happy about his daughter's marriage. It had even occurred to Jasim that he might not be alive in two days' time. A dagger between his shoulder blades seemed a strong possibility. That it hadn't happened already was, he felt sure, thanks to the restraining presence of the Spanish contingent. Once they left for Spain, Jasim suspected anything might happen.

He was prepared to take the risk because, despite his misgivings, his clandestine meeting with the Princess had strengthened his desire to marry her. God willing, he would soon be wed.

It seemed that fortune was with him for the two days passed swiftly and without mishap and his wedding day dawned.

As was the custom, Jasim was to bring two witnesses to his wedding. He had chosen Farid as his first witness. Finding a second witness had been trickier, but his luck had been in. A handful of knights had yet to leave the palace, and one of them was happy to support him. The witnesses were there to ensure that the exchange of vows had been properly made and that the marriage agreement was valid.

The bride herself did not have to attend, a tradition which had always struck Jasim as odd. Instead, as long as she sent witnesses to watch proceedings, the marriage was binding.

Unsurprisingly, the Sultan was the Princess's main witness although, rather astonishingly given the animosity known to exist between the brothers, Prince Ghalib had been appointed as her second witness.

Jasim very much hoped that Princess Zorahaida would attend in person. Since he'd climbed down from her tower, he hadn't caught as much as a glimpse of her. He'd wasted too much of the previous night, wondering whether she would attend in person.

Shortly before the time set for the ceremony, Jasim went with Farid to the Court of the Myrtles where he and the knight he'd chosen as his second witness exchanged greetings. Then he and his witnesses strode past what must have been an entire regiment of guards and arrived in the Chamber of the Ambassadors.

The vast hall was practically empty. There didn't appear to be anyone save the Sultan, his brother and one other man, presumably the celebrant.

Today, the Sultan's throne was monumental, it dominated the square room, dwarfing the thrones Jasim had seen on previous occasions. There was almost too much gilding. Shafts of light cut through coloured panes of glass in the upper windows, seeming to set it alight. It was as though the Sultan was sitting on a fiery chariot, an illusion which was probably intentional. The Chamber of the Ambassadors was, as its name suggested, where Sultan Tariq met governors from the various provinces and diplomats from neighbouring kingdoms. Treaties were signed here; alliances were formed and dissolved. Doubtless, the Sultan imagined that if he presented a warlike appearance, he would gain the upper hand in any negotiations.

Prince Ghalib stood stiffly at the Sultan's right hand.

The Sultan nodded brusquely at Jasim. Prince Ghalib inclined his head and smiled. Bowing deeply, Jasim and his witnesses stood to one side.

At the edges of the Hall, several columned arches opened out into side chambers. Looped-back curtains signalled that they could be screened for privacy. Today, most of the curtains had been tied back, revealing them to be unoccupied. One was curtained off. As Jasim looked towards it, his heart lifted. Princess Zorahaida was behind that closed curtain, he knew it.

Sure enough, when the Sultan clapped, the curtain parted. With a rustle of silk and the light chime of bells, the Princess appeared.

Relief made him smile. The Princess's appearance in person was surely a good omen. He hoped it meant that she bore him no animosity for tearing her from her home. Politics and personal interest aside, the urge to remove her from her violent father was irresistible.

For her marriage, Princess Zorahaida had chosen a veil and gown in a subtle shade of blue, lavishly embroidered with gold thread. As she came towards him, beams of light from the upper windows flickered as she passed through them. Briefly, her clothes appeared to shimmer with every colour in the rainbow. A king's ransom in pearls was wound about her wrists. When she came to a halt a few feet away, the bells fell silent. Jasim glanced down. She was wearing an anklet of silver bells. His mouth dried as he thought about what lay beneath the all-enveloping blue robes. He already knew the Princess had a body made for love. Surprisingly, it was her smile he remembered most. It hinted that perhaps, one day, there might be more to their union than politics.

Sensing her gaze was trained on him, Jasim looked warmly towards her and bowed. Curse that veil. What was she thinking? What was she feeling? He burned to know.

For himself, he felt uncharacteristically uneasy. He had rushed her into this. Had their illicit meeting allayed at least some of her fears? It had certainly helped him. The physical side of their marriage appeared more promising than he had dreamed possible.

As Jasim took his place facing the Sultan, he

congratulated himself on what he had achieved thus far. This was the first time in many years that a representative of Madinat Runda had been inside the Chamber of the Ambassadors on official business. His uncle, Governor Ibrahim ibn Osman, had never set foot in Granada, never mind the Alhambra Palace.

Jasim's gamble at the tournament had paid off. If everything went smoothly, his uncle must finally agree that as far as the Sultan was concerned a policy of appeasement was useless. Direct action was the key to successful negotiation with the Sultan.

When the celebrant cleared his throat, Jasim forced himself to concentrate. It was vital that everything was done according to the conventions. This marriage must be legal. He would take home a Nasrid princess as his wife and a new era would dawn for Madinat Runda. One of peace and prosperity.

Zorahaida was uneasy about this marriage, torn in so many ways. She studied the grim set of Jasim ibn Ismail's mouth with a sense of foreboding. He looked as though he was attending a funeral rather than his wedding, although she had to admit he had taken pains with his attire.

Jasim's tunic was one a prince might wear, cloth of gold silk with blue and white motifs embroidered on to it. From this angle, Zorahaida couldn't make out the detail, though the overall impression was magnificent. A jewelled belt glittered. Was this finery for her? It seemed far more likely Jasim wished to impress her father. He was representing Madinat Runda, after all. His turban was a spotless white with a large sapphire nestled in the centre. Blue again, like his colours at the tournament.

Had he noticed that she had tried to honour him by wearing his colours? He was so focused on the celebrant, she couldn't be sure. Where was the gallant knight who had entranced her with his kisses?

She swallowed. It was too late to back out. Not that Jasim or her father would permit her. They were both set on this marriage.

The celebrant was reading Holy Script. In a moment she and Jasim would exchange their vows. She would be married. As to her future—she had no idea what to expect. Seldom had she felt so unsettled.

Heart thumping, she listened with half an ear to the reading and struggled to reconcile the difference between the charming knight who had climbed into her tower and the stony-faced diplomat currently beside her.

All too soon the ceremony was over.

When Jasim took her hand, her father watched, white about the mouth. 'Take care of my daughter,' he growled.

Jasim bowed. 'I will, Great King.'

The Sultan looked at her, face inscrutable. 'Are you ready to travel, my dove?'

Beneath her veil, Zorahaida blinked. 'Today? Father, if it pleases you, I need a few more days to prepare myself.'

Sultan Tariq's face relaxed. Rising, he came towards her and pinched her chin through her veil. She managed not to flinch.

'Not ready to leave me, Daughter?'

A husband had control of his wife in much the same way as a father. It was entirely possible that when she left the palace, she would merely be exchanging one form of oppression for another. What did her father expect her to say?

'Father, I am not fully packed. There is much to prepare.'

The Sultan nodded. 'Very well.' He turned to her husband. 'As proof of my goodwill, Jasim ibn Ismail, you may lodge with my daughter in her apartments until she is ready to leave.'

Her husband bowed, took her hand in a fierce grip and they left the Chamber of the Ambassadors together.

Suma and Maura were appalled by the new arrangement and Sama wasn't the least bit shy about saying so.

When Zorahaida arrived back at the tower with her husband, Sama hastily donned her veil and took her mistress to one side. Happily, Jasim was still on the steps outside, apparently instructing his squire to fetch their belongings from the barracks.

'Your father the Sultan, blessings be upon him, has commanded that you share your apartment with your husband?' Sama hissed.

'Yes, Sama, he has.'

'Princess, it's not right. Jasim ibn Ismail should have his own quarters, then he can summon you whenever he requires you.'

Jasim stuck his head through the door. 'No.' The sapphire in his turban flashed as he shook his head. 'That will not be convenient. The Princess and I shall share the upper chamber. Farid can bed down on the lower floor, near the stairwell. I assure you our presence will not cause difficulties.'

Sama's foot tapped and she muttered under her breath.

He sighed. 'Your name is Sama, is it not?'

'Yes, Master.'

'Sama, we will only be here for a short while, would you be so good as to enlighten me as to what is troubling you.'

'Very well,' Sama's chin inched up. 'Jasim ibn Ismail, Maura and I have served the Princess loyally for many years and this has always been a house of women. We do not wear veils. With you and your squire taking residence with us—'

His face relaxed. 'Is that all? Sama, until I leave Granada, this tower is to serve as my home. You need to understand that in my household, women are not required to wear the veil unless we are entertaining strangers.'

Sama put her head to one side. 'Truly?'

'Truly. Know that whilst you are within these walls you will be respected.' Broad shoulders lifted. 'If you wish to wear a veil, fine. If not, that also is fine. Please understand that as one of the Princess's handmaidens, I consider you part of my household and thus you are entitled to my protection.'

Sama hesitated, and in a sweeping movement,

dragged off her veil. 'Thank you, Master.' She left the chamber smiling and calling for Maura.

Zorahaida faced him. 'I too may lift my veil?'

He smiled. 'I wish you would.'

Zorahaida couldn't remove it completely. Weighed down with her headdress and thick gold embroidery, dozens of pins were keeping it in place, but she lifted the hem and tossed the veil back.

Her husband's squire sent her a curious, assessing look and she felt herself flush. After years of struggling to remember to always wear her veil, it was odd to be without one. Even before a young boy.

'Ignore Farid,' her husband said. 'He is as harmless as his master.'

Her husband believed himself to be harmless? Zorahaida wasn't so sure. Jasim ibn Ismail had braved her irascible father to ask for her hand, he had overridden her every objection and against all the odds they were married.

'Off with you, Farid,' Jasim said. His amber gaze captured hers. 'Princess, I swear to you, that whilst there is breath in my body, neither you nor your maidservants will come to harm.'

As the door closed behind his squire, Zorahaida stared at Jasim, bemused. He was unlike any man she had ever met. One moment stern and forbidding, and the next all charm. The charm was very much in evidence now. He had got his way, she supposed. He could afford to be charming.

'Come.' Eyes glittering, he caught her hand and made for the stairs. 'You can show me the rest of the tower.'

She hung back.

He tugged on her hand. 'Princess?'

'How am I to address you?'

'I was wondering when you'd ask that.' He pulled her closer and dropped a kiss on her nose. 'Jasim, I hope. I also hope that I might address you as Zorahaida.'

'Thank you, I should like that.'

His smile lit his eyes and she couldn't look away. She saw them darken and watched his gaze drop to her mouth. A muscle clenched deep inside.

Was he thinking of kissing her? She rather thought he was. This last couple of days, she had spent far too long thinking about kissing him again. Something about him drew her and she'd been afraid that marriage might change that. Would kissing be as pleasant as it had been before—when he'd been trying to win her over?

Now they were man and wife he need not take care to ensure her pleasure. He could assert his husbandly rights whenever he wished.

'Zorahaida, I thank you,' he said, voice warm. An eyebrow lifted. 'I shall take that as permission.'

'Permission to do what?'

He swept her into his arms and Zorahaida found herself gripping those muscled shoulders. Sama must have returned for she heard a startled gasp and footsteps hastily retreating. Astonishingly, there was no room for embarrassment, for all of her, every fibre of her being was bent on discovering whether his kiss would be as devastating as before.

She lifted her mouth and her stomach swooped. His kiss was tender, gentle. Agonisingly sensual. Her knees buckled and his arms tightened. His tongue traced her mouth. She knew what he wanted. He hadn't done this last time, but the concubines had told her what to expect. She opened her mouth, heard his throaty groan and felt the determined sweep of his tongue on hers.

Her body came alive. It was as magical as it had been. Better, if that were possible. She hadn't been wrong about Jasim, he would never hurt her. Longing swept through her and fleetingly, she found herself wishing that he had wanted her for herself, and not simply as a means to an end.

He shifted his stance and lifted his head. They were leaning against the wall at the bottom of the stairwell and Zorahaida had the strong notion that he was as moved as she. Perhaps it didn't matter that he was marrying her to further his ambitions. The palace concubines had told her that the most she could expect from a man was a little consideration, she would be foolish to hope for more.

'Save me, Zorahaida, you are beyond tempting,' he said, voice hoarse as he stroked her cheek. He frowned. 'Where's your handmaid?'

Zorahaida blushed and eased back. At some point during their kiss, her hands had crept up around his neck and she was mortified to realise that she'd been sliding her fingers under the white cloth of his turban, with a vague notion of freeing his hair. She longed to touch it. 'Sama? She'll be hiding somewhere. I believe we embarrassed her.'

He drew her back, kissed her ear and murmured, 'Sama will have to get used to our being affectionate.'

Affectionate? The word stole Zorahaida's breath before common sense reasserted itself. He wasn't declaring a fondness for her; they hardly knew each other. He was simply being polite. The fire that flared between them came, she was sure, from an instinct far baser than affection. This was lust. Her body attracted him just as his attracted her. It was better than nothing.

Was it a foundation upon which to build a good marriage? She would have to pray that it was, for although she wasn't entirely sure what made a good marriage, she realised she wanted one.

The light in the entranceway was better than it had been in her bedchamber a couple of evenings ago and his eyes, she now saw, weren't pure amber. They were rimmed with grey, with streaks of silver near the centre.

'We are man and wife,' he said. 'Come, show me the rest of your domain.'

Somehow, they made it up the next flight of stairs, though it quickly became apparent that Jasim wasn't interested in looking at any of the chambers. That insistent tug drew her past the living quarters, past a chaos of fabric and half-made clothes, of packing cases and jewel boxes. On up another flight, until at length they were at the top.

He guided her through the bedchamber door. The shutters were closed against the heat of the day, and the floor was covered in starry splashes of light formed by the piercings in the wood. The songbirds were singing.

Jasim stopped before the cage and stared at them.

'The singing disturbs you?' Zorahaida asked.

She was feeling incredibly shaky. And incredibly self-conscious. The concubines had been keen to educate her, in lurid detail, about what went on in the marriage bed. Their blunt recitation of who did what to whom had been far from reassuring. What on earth would it feel like? Dear God, she'd never felt so edgy. Obviously, whatever if felt like, she must do her best to affect pleasure. Men had such pride.

She swallowed. 'Jasim, I can cover their cage if you wish.'

'Leave them, I like it. Come.' He led her unerringly to the bed and sat down, taking her with him. He lifted an eyebrow at her. 'Your maidservants won't disturb us?'

Her cheeks scorched. 'I believe they understand your intention.' Just then she heard a familiar chattering sound and jumped up sharply. 'Oh, no.'

Jasim rose. 'What's amiss?'

'Hunter's in here. He must be hiding.' Half-expecting anger, for the concubines had warned her that men could be impatient if denied their marriage rights, she gave Jasim a shaky smile, lifted the cloth from a platter and picked up a date. She began to search. Behind the birdcage, no. Under the side table, no. Behind a heap of tasselled cushions, no. 'A thousand apologies, Jasim, I thought he was downstairs. We shall have to get him out.'

'Hunter?'

'A pet monkey. Your presence must have startled him.'

Jasim looked at her, face unreadable. 'You have a pet monkey.'

'Aye. He belonged to one of my sisters, I care for him now.' She went back to the bed, dropped to her knees and peered underneath. 'Hunter, come here.'

Beady eyes gleamed from the shadows. 'Come on, boy.' She held out the date. Hunter snatched it from her and allowed her to lift him out.

'Good boy. You are not really alarmed, are you? This is Jasim, my husband.' Cheeks hot with embarrassment, Zorahaida sent Jasim a wobbly smile and hoped he didn't think she was deliberately delaying their union. 'I... I am sorry, Jasim. He will get used to you, I am sure.'

She opened the door and put Hunter firmly outside. When she turned back, Jasim was sitting on the bed, a crooked smile on his face.

'You're laughing,' she said, bemused and intensely relieved.

'Not at you, my sweet, never at you.' He held out his hand. 'Come here, wife.'

Moments later, Zorahaida was sitting on his knee as her husband studied her. 'You're nervous,' he murmured. 'You have no need to be.'

Her chin lifted. 'I'm not nervous.'

He kissed her cheek, murmuring. 'Don't lie to me, Zorahaida. You are as nervous as I.'

She frowned in disbelief. 'You're not nervous.'

'Am I not?' He shrugged, and the lights danced in his amber eyes. 'Believe what you will, I do not make a habit of this.'

Zorahaida felt her jaw drop. 'You are innocent? You have no harem?'

He laughed. 'I am not innocent, though I do not have a harem.'

Jasim reached up to gently remove her veil and headdress.

He didn't have a harem. As he carefully examined her headdress, Zorahaida's mind worked. That didn't sound as though he had other wives. It occurred to her that one of the subjects they had not touched on was whether Jasim was already married. Concubines aside, Zorahaida knew that many men had more than one wife. If a man had the means to keep several wives, and if he swore to treat them all equally, he could have as many as he wished.

Her skin chilled. It was a shock to realise that the idea that Jasim might already be married didn't sit well with her. She knew she didn't love him, but since she was his wife, she wanted to be the only one. She wanted what her sisters had in Spain: a husband who would cherish her all her life. A man who wanted her to cherish him in return.

She felt herself smile. Apparently, life with her father hadn't succeeded in erasing the Spanish side of her character. The part she had inherited from her mother remained intact.

'There are pins keeping this in place?' Jasim asked. He was entirely focused on removing her veil and headdress.

'Aye, start at the crown of my head and behind my ear.'

Did Jasim have other wives?

He kissed her cheek again, and a flash of awareness went through her. It was fortunate that she found his touch reassuring. As he deftly set to work on the pins, she noticed his fingers weren't quite steady. He had spoken the truth, he was nervous. Clearly, this wasn't the moment to ask him whether he was already married.

Oddly, she was feeling less shaky. He was handling her with such delicacy. Unfortunately, the same couldn't be said for her silver hairpins, she could hear them tinkle as they hit the floor. She studied him as he worked. How handsome he was. His amber eyes were framed with thick eyelashes. They were simply stunning. His nose was well defined and beneath his beard, his jaw was strong. His skin fascinated her. It was so much paler than hers. His looks told her that, like her, he had mixed ancestry. Did he inherit his looks from his mother?

He had finished with the pins. With a quiet smile, he eased off her headdress and veil and Zorahaida rubbed her scalp with a sigh of relief.

'Thank you, I wasn't very comfortable.'

His smile grew as he reached about her and brought her hair over her shoulder. 'I don't imagine you were; it is far too hot to wear such things. And your hair is too glorious to hide.'

Zorahaida found herself frowning at his turban and before she knew it, she boldly reached for it. 'Is this hot too? Where does it undo?'

She heard his sharp intake of breath and watched dark colour run into his face. She saw something else. Stark hunger. Whatever Jasim's reasons for marrying her, he desired her. She was not going to let shyness and naivety mess this up.

This was going to be perfect.

He guided her fingers to the sapphire in the centre. 'First, remove this brooch.'

Carefully, Zorahaida unfastened the pin and set the sapphire on a nearby ledge. Jasim shifted slightly beneath her and she became aware that his breathing had changed. It had deepened and she received the impression he was struggling to control it. He was caressing her back with one hand, keeping her firmly on his knee. And, inexperienced though she was, she knew enough to recognise that he was fully aroused. She mustn't disappoint him.

She reached up with both hands and slowly, holding her breath, unwound his head-covering. Waves of glorious rose gold tumbled out and she did what she had been aching to do, she slid her fingers into it, teasing it out, releasing the faint fragrance of sage mingled with a scent she already recognised as being unique to Jasim. Her mouth dried. His hair was silky and—she hid a smile—so beautiful. Fire and gold.

'Now this,' she murmured, 'is truly glorious.'

He gave an inarticulate murmur, pressed his face into her neck and somehow, she ended up lying on the bed with Jasim half on top of her.

'Zorahaida, my wife. With your permission...?'

She gave a shaky nod and watched his eyes darken.

Their mouths met in the gentlest of matings. She loved that he was handling her gently. He stroked her clothes aside, his touch determined, yet as light as gossamer. The mix of resolution and subtlety was incredibly arousing. For her part, she was less gentle with him. She dragged up his tunic and almost tore it from him. When she finally bared his chest, she was stunned into silence and simply stared. She had no idea a man's muscles would be so pronounced. Or so attractive. She yearned to touch, to taste. Dazzled with desire, she bit her lip, wrestling with a rush of embarrassment that this new husband of hers, a man who was virtually a stranger, could elicit such a powerful, visceral response.

His amber gaze met hers. 'Don't think, my princess. Follow your instincts.'

As one, they reached for each other. He caressed her flank, waking her body to more heat and more sensation. Her breasts ached, her womb clenched. Shocked by the intensity, half-fearing she'd lose herself in a storm of passion, she took his hand and kissed it.

He had elegant hands. Long, strong fingers, with callouses from swordplay. A small scar ran up his inner arm. 'You have the body and the scars of a warrior,' she murmured, kissing the callouses before running her tongue along the length of his scar.

His breathing quickened.

'You like that, husband?'

He let out a choked laugh. 'It is unbearable. Don't stop, I beg you.'

She kissed his mouth and was unable to pull back. Their kisses were hot, open-mouthed kisses, drugging in their intensity and when they had finished their clothes had gone. As she kissed his shoulder, she was delighted to discover that Jasim seemed bent on matching her kiss for kiss.

He was kissing her everywhere. When he kissed her neck, she felt the sensation in her breasts. She smothered a gasp.

He lifted his head. Warm amber eyes met hers. 'All is well?'

She managed a nod. 'The concubines didn't tell me everything. I feel as though I'm melting.'

His eyes glittered. 'Excellent.'

Was it? 'It's hard to breathe too, that can't be right.'

'Zorahaida, that sounds perfect. I can't breathe either.'

He caressed her stomach, tracing gentle circles on her skin with his fingertips and her breasts ached. She wanted his touch there too. The desire was so powerful, she frowned.

He noticed, of course, that intent gaze didn't miss a thing. 'Zorahaida, what's amiss?'

She hesitated. The women in the harem hadn't said anything about asking one's lover for more caresses. She should be the one pleasuring him, not the other way about.

'I… I should be giving pleasure, not receiving it.'

'Nonsense,' Jasim said. 'We should both have pleasure.' He was lying naked beside her, one leg slung possessively over hers. He was leaning his head on his hand and when he moved, that incredible rose-gold hair brushed her shoulder, sending tingles everywhere. 'In any case, you are giving me more pleasure than I'd dreamed possible.'

Zorahaida swallowed. He was certainly fully

aroused, she could feel him, hard and hot against her hip. She knew what she should do…

Cheeks burning, she eased back. 'My friends in the harem told me a husband would welcome my touch everywhere. Especially here.' Boldly, she reached for him.

He jerked in her hand and hissed out a breath.

Tentatively, she began stroking him. 'Tell me how best to please you. Like this?'

His face went tight and his throat worked. Gentle fingers closed on hers. 'Only if you want to.'

'I want to.' Surprisingly, that was the truth. When Zorahaida had listened to the concubines talking, she'd been baffled, never imagining for a moment she could do such a thing. With Jasim, she could do anything. Which reminded her, there was more. The women had advised her to use her mouth on him. Men, the women had insisted, loved it. They'd warned her to mask her distaste. 'Master this,' they'd said, giggling knowingly. 'And you master the man.'

Well, that was an intriguing idea.

Using her free hand, she nudged and pushed him on to his back.

'Zorahaida?'

'Lie still. I want to try something.'

She kissed his chest and ran her tongue over

the fine golden hairs running down his body. A choked moan urged her on. His scent surrounded her; musky and masculine, it both aroused and reassured. So far, she'd not felt any of the distaste the women had mentioned. Perhaps she never would.

'Zorahaida, no, this can wait until we know each other better.'

Despite his words, his voice urged her on, it was thick with what she recognised was desire. He was lying against the pillows with his eyes closed, a dark slash of colour across his cheekbones. His face was tight with expectation. She had no doubt that he wanted this. She shifted over him to give him the most intimate of kisses.

'Zorahaida, that's…'

His voice faded and she felt his hand on her head, carefully guiding her.

It wasn't as she expected. He tasted salty. The intense silence told her she was doing something right, all she could hear was the thud of her heart. She had the impression he was struggling for control.

Covering him with kisses, she took him fully into her mouth. The harsh intake of breath and the tightening of his muscles were her guide. She kissed, she licked, she did everything the women had talked about, until…

His chest heaved and the fingers tightened on her scalp. 'Enough.'

He hauled her into his arms, took her mouth with his and gave her a mind-numbing kiss.

She pulled back, breathless. 'I dare say I need practice.'

'Practice?' He huffed out a breath, he was laughing again. 'You are a natural.'

Zorahaida smiled. Laughter was the last thing she'd expected when bedding her husband. It was wonderful. Such a blessing. They were strangers and laughter gave her hope that one day they might become friends.

'Your turn.'

Jasim eased her on to her back and nuzzled her breasts. As his hair trailed across her, she trembled with need. Friendship? Beautiful though this was, it was dawning on her that with this man, friendship might not be enough. He took turns in kissing first one breast and then the other. Tiny, tantalising kisses that had her arching encouragingly towards him.

He fondled and kissed her so tenderly that she barely noticed when he pushed her legs apart.

A light touch made her jump.

'Relax. Let me pleasure you.'

Confused and slightly embarrassed at the intimacy, she gave a jerky nod.

'Jasim, what are you doing?'

'I hope to give you joy.'

Deft fingers sent shivers of delight running through her and she jerked again. Why had no one mentioned this? What he was doing was positively indecent. It was fabulous. She'd had no idea her body was capable of feeling this way.

The tension was winding tighter and tighter. Zorahaida was getting hotter and more restless by the moment. She moaned and wriggled. She wasn't so innocent that she didn't know what she was asking for. The girls in the harem had aroused her curiosity long ago, and one evening, after returning to her lonely bed in the tower, she had begun to experiment. She knew what her body liked. And what she had learned paled into insignificance as compared to what Jasim was doing to her.

'Jasim, please.'

'Relax, my sweet.' His voice warmed, taking on that slight edge of humour. 'I am doing my best to ensure that you want me as much as I want you.'

That did it. The instant she realised that her

pleasure was important to this man, the sweet moment of oblivion swept her away. Blind with bliss, her body convulsed.

In a haze of pleasure, she was vaguely conscious of Jasim kissing his way back up her body and of that strong body settling between her legs.

In a distant part of her memory, she recalled the concubines mentioning that there was likely to be pain, the first time. Entirely unafraid, she met her husband's gaze. If anyone could take away the pain, she thought, it would be Jasim.

'I will be gentle, I swear,' he said. 'Trust me.'

Thankful he could control himself and that he cared about her well-being, she nodded. Pain? Perhaps. He was so much larger than her, in every way. She could feel him against her thigh, fully aroused.

Bedclothes rustled as he bent over her, kissing her breasts, toying with them, suckling even as his hands moved down her belly, exploring, both teasing and tempting.

The ache inside returned, stronger than before. His every stroke had her trembling all over again. She shifted impatiently and when he positioned himself, she moaned in relief.

He entered swiftly, she felt a slight pinch and he braced himself on his arms and looked at her.

'Zorahaida? All is well?'

She smiled and nipped his shoulder and he pushed fully in. It was a strange sensation, not at all as she had expected. 'We are one,' she murmured.

'Aye.'

He rocked out a little and then back in. The pinching sensation had gone. The pain had been negligible, likely because he'd taken care to arouse her.

Jasim was a fine man. Zorahaida's last thought as she gave herself up to more sensation was that nothing she'd been taught had prepared her for Jasim.

With Jasim, reality was better.

Chapter Eight

The rest of the day was filled with earthly delights.

Zorahaida and Jasim made love countless times and in countless ways, breaking apart to sip wine from Venetian glasses they discovered on a ledge by the bed. Sama or Maura must have prepared well earlier, for there were pastries too, delicate almond pastries that melted in the mouth, and fat black grapes.

At length, a soft footfall outside the door reminded them of the world outside. Jasim left the bed, padded to the door and opened it a crack. Zorahaida lay where she was, wrapped in bliss, and admired her husband's well-formed body. Her gaze took in that wild mane of hair, those wide shoulders, that slim waist and the sensuous curve of his buttocks. His legs were incredibly long, no wonder he was so tall. The man was perfectly proportioned, he made her melt just to look at him.

The concubines hadn't told her the whole. None of them had ever hinted that sharing your body with a sensuous, attractive man could be so addictive.

Zorahaida had no illusions about love. This wasn't about love for either of them. Notwithstanding, that didn't stop her wanting him. All over again. It was not a sin to enjoy one's husband. And how blessed she was, for he seemed to be genuinely kind.

Jasim went out on to the landing. There was a brief pause before his voice floated back to her.

'How hungry are you, my love? Someone has left us some rice with spiced chicken.'

'I'm hungry,' she said, as he came back in with another tray.

He'd called her his love. She reminded herself that it didn't mean much, that it was simply a phrase lovers used.

Jasim set the tray next to the wine, bright hair gleaming. He was a lion, a beautiful golden lion. Her lion.

Her stomach clenched. Was he hers? In the rush of joining with him, she'd still not found out whether he was already married.

Since Zorahaida's sisters had gone, she had set aside her dreams of marriage, though in her heart she'd often wondered what she might be missing. Never in her wildest dreams had she imagined that God would see fit to bless her with a husband who wanted her satisfaction as well as his own. Against all the odds, she had married one. It was such a blessing. A blessing she didn't want to share. Theirs wasn't a love match, was it wrong of her to want him all for herself?

He'd said he had no harem, but he might have a wife.

'Jasim?'

He was busily spooning rice and chicken on to a plate and looked up. 'Hmmm?'

Uncertainly, Zorahaida twisted a strand of her hair. She was well versed with what went on inside the Alhambra, other households might be different.

'There is something I meant to ask you earlier.'

Plate in hand, he came back to the bed and the mattress dipped as he sat on the edge. 'Go on.'

'Men of our faith are permitted more than one wife. Do you have other wives?'

He was filling a spoon with the chicken, and his eyebrows lifted. 'Other wives? Why do you ask?'

Zorahaida felt some of her joy ebb away. Of

course he was already married. He might claim to be relatively inexperienced, but a man who knew his way about a woman's body as well as Jasim was bound to be married. She shrugged, as though the matter was of little import. 'I was curious, that is all.'

He held out the spoon to her and she allowed him to feed her. When he said nothing more, but kept on feeding her, she eventually held up her hand.

'Enough, I thank you. Jasim, your other wives…?'

'My other wives,' he murmured thoughtfully before breaking into a smile and leaning forward to kiss her cheek. 'You need have no fear, Zorahaida. You are my princess and as such will outrank all other women.'

Zorahaida swallowed and when he offered her a spoonful of rice, she shook her head. Her appetite had gone.

Jasim was already married. And if life at Madinat Runda was anything like life in the palace she dreaded going there. The intrigues and jealousies between women in a harem were as dark and bitter as the intrigues between her father and uncle.

Jasim was a kind man. He was. He would never be cruel.

Aware of a sudden melancholy, she studied his profile, terribly afraid that kindness on its own meant little. After all, her father had, on many occasions, been kind to her. He overwhelmed her with gifts. He called her his dove. Yet not once had she felt any sense of intimacy with him. Her father's kindnesses were based on calculation.

She caught her breath. She wanted more than kindness based on calculation from her husband. She and Jasim had been intimate physically, and pleasurable though it had been, she felt as alone as ever.

She wanted more than physical intimacy with Jasim, she wanted a genuine meeting of souls. Was that possible?

As one day slipped into another, Jasim grew increasingly frustrated. Not physically, there he had no complaints. Each night, he and the Princess came together in a blaze of passion. Zorahaida was the perfect bedmate. Her sensuality amazed him. At night, she was pure delight.

By day, it was another matter. The Princess was too busy to talk to him. She spent hours with her maidservants. Jasim even saw her by one of the bathhouses, talking earnestly to Captain Yusuf ibn Safwan. At his approach, they fell silent. Every blessed time. If Jasim hadn't known from their wedding day that the Princess had come to him untouched, he might conclude that she and the Captain were indulging in an affair.

Even so, Jasim found himself asking Farid to make a few discreet enquiries. He was startled by the rush of relief when Farid informed him that Captain Yusuf ibn Safwan was happily married, his loyalty to the Princess was purely professional. Thank God.

So why the delays? Each day his wife tested his patience by conjuring a new reason for putting off their departure. Why? Theirs wasn't a love match, Jasim had no illusions on that score, though he was reasonably certain she liked him. Surely no woman could be so relaxed in bed with a man she didn't like. Was she afraid she would miss her father? The man had abused her, he was a tyrant. Jasim had assumed she'd be eager to get away, and he'd assured her that she would have more freedom at Madinat Runda. He'd told her that Mondragón Palace, where he lodged with his uncle, was scarcely a hovel. What was the problem?

The Sultan had to be at the root of her reluctance to leave. The human mind was a strange and complicated thing and Zorahaida's relationship with her father was bound to be conflicted. Jasim recalled his uncle telling a story about a slave in Madinat Runda who had won his freedom. The slave left his master's house a free man, only to crawl back a few months later, weeping and tearing at his clothes. He'd begged to be taken in, on any terms. He was prepared to work as a servant and, yes, even as a slave. The poor wretch had been part of the household so long; it had become his home. He'd been desperate to return, under any terms.

Well, that wasn't going to be Zorahaida's fate, Jasim wouldn't allow it. When women married, they left their families behind them, irrespective of whether they loved them or loathed them. Nor did it matter what they thought of their husbands. It was the way of the world that women went to live with their husbands.

God had seen fit to give him Zorahaida for his wife. Come what may, she was going to share an apartment with him in Mondragón Palace.

None the less, Jasim was all too conscious that their budding relationship was fragile. He didn't want to begin his marriage with an argument. He would have to be patient. His wife was a sensual woman, and if he kept that part of her nature satisfied, all should be well. He'd give her another week, though he would warn her their departure would be soon.

That night, after they had made love, Zorahaida was lying softly in his arms, as she did every night. Her bruises were fading, she was growing more beautiful by the day. He wound a dark strand of perfumed hair round his finger and gazed up at the light flickering over the lacy plasterwork ceiling.

'My love, we have been married almost a sennight. Are you ready to leave?'

It was impossible to miss the way her body stiffened.

'Soon, my husband.' She lifted her head and long-lashed eyes sought his. 'My clothes, you understand. One or two garments need final adjustments.'

'We have seamstresses at Mondragón Palace.'

She smiled and lifted herself on her elbow. 'I am sure you do.'

'They will be delighted to help.'

She pressed a kiss to Jasim's chest, and her hair swept across him in a way that never failed to awaken his baser instincts. 'My father has also promised me a jewelled girdle from a goldsmith in Granada. It is not yet finished.'

Her comment gave Jasim pause. He held back a frown, he hadn't thought Zorahaida was a woman to place much importance on new clothes and jewelled belts. Then she ran those careful, knowing hands up and down his flanks, a quiet, seductive smile on her lips. She was trying to distract him. He was ruefully aware that she was succeeding. He gritted his teeth against a troublesome surge of desire and pressed on.

'Madinat Runda has plenty of goldsmiths,' he said. 'It is not a wasteland. When we get there, you may have as many jewelled girdles as you wish. If it pleases you, you may design them yourself.'

'You are generous, my husband.'

Zorahaida's voice was pure seduction and her hand—her hand moved inexorably, tantalisingly, lower. Then clever fingers closed firmly around him and Jasim's mind clouded. The subject wasn't closed, he told himself, surrendering to pleasure. They would discuss it on the morrow.

Late the following afternoon, Zorahaida and Sama were alone in the bathhouse. As Zorahaida emerged from the water, Sama reached for a drying cloth and began patting her dry.

Zorahaida shook her head and wrapped the cloth firmly about her. 'Thank you. Sama, but we have important matters to discuss. I shall dress presently. Come, sit beside me.'

She went to the couch at the side of the bathing pool and Sama, who over the years had listened to countless confidences and helped make many plans, took her place beside her.

'Sama, I hope you know how much I value your counsel.'

Sama dipped her head. 'You are kind, Princess, it is my pleasure to serve you.'

Zorahaida gave a crooked smile. 'I hope it is more than that. Sama, I count you as the dearest of friends.'

Sama's face lit up. 'I am honoured. I feel the same.'

Zorahaida hesitated. 'You must also be aware that I would love you to come with me to Mondragón Palace, but I fear that will not be possible. I need you in the Alhambra, to keep an eye on my father.'

Blinking rapidly, Sama looked swiftly away. 'I understand,' she murmured in a choked voice.

'Sama, I am sorry if my decision comes as a shock.' Zorahaida reached for Sama's hand and squeezed it. 'I would give anything to have you with me, but I can't risk it. I trust you more than anyone.'

'And that is why I must stay?'

'Exactly.'

Sama gave her a puzzled frown. 'Princess, when you told me that Prince Ghalib witnessed your wedding, I hoped that meant that he and your father...'

'You think they are reconciled?' Zorahaida thought of the pink rose and the jewel box her uncle had sent her and shook her head. 'That is far from true. I suspect my uncle attended to support me, rather than my father. Believe me, the rivalry between them has never been so keen.'

'You fear more violence?'

'After what happened to Yamina, I'd say it was a certainty.' Zorahaida stared blindly at the couch on the other side of the pool. 'Sama, my husband is impatient to go. I shall take a basket of Imad's pigeons with me so that I may contact you. Unfortunately, you won't be able to reply until I have smuggled a basket of Madinat Runda pigeons back to Granada. Yusuf knows my mind on this, he will alert our sentries to allow the Madinat Runda pigeons into the palace.'

Sama nodded. 'So you and I will use the same method of communication that you have been using with your sisters?'

'Exactly. When the pigeons from Madinat Runda arrive, please give them to Imad. He will look after them until you need to send me a message. The instant anything goes awry, I'd like to know. I am not sure what I shall be able to do from Mondragón Palace, but I would like to be informed.'

'Very well.' Sama frowned and looked her squarely in the eye. 'Princess, your husband appears to be most understanding, will you tell him—'

'No.' Aware she had spoken sharply, Zorahaida moderated her tone. 'I hardly know him. Later, perhaps, when Jasim and I are no longer strangers.'

'I understand.' Sama smiled in her calm way and reached for the box of perfumed massage oils. 'Come, my Princess. Let us make you ready to greet your husband when he returns to the tower.'

Zorahaida gave Sama's hand a grateful squeeze. 'Thank you, my friend.'

* * *

The light had gone, the lamps were lit and there was no sign of Jasim. It was the first time he hadn't appeared for the evening meal. Zorahaida put her hand on a covered dish. He was so late it was barely warm.

'My husband is usually here long before this,' she said, her heart twisting. 'Maura, do you know where he is?'

'I am afraid not, Princess.'

Had Jasim tired of playing the ardent suitor? As Zorahaida had told Sama earlier, she hardly knew him. What she hadn't said was that she longed to know him better. True intimacy must be more than the meeting of two bodies in bed. Had the warmth she had felt been a mirage? Over the past few nights she had begun to wish that one day she and Jasim might share more than physical pleasure.

It was a wish that was taking her into dangerous territory. She wanted Jasim to want her not for political reasons, nor because he found her physically attractive. She wanted him to want her for herself.

If only she didn't think this way. It was confusing and upsetting and, worst of all, it gave him far too much power. As her husband, he already had power over her person. She would not grant him power over her soul. The problem was she liked him. More than liked him.

A door slammed downstairs and Zorahaida and Maura exchanged glances.

'Princess?' Farid called up the stairs. His voice was tight and anxious. 'Princess, come quickly!'

Zorahaida and Maura flew down the stairs.

Jasim was slumped against the wall by the door. Zorahaida's breath froze. His face was pale as death and his skin was bathed in sweat.

She reached his side as he lifted his head. His eyes were glassy, he didn't seem to know her.

'Farid, what happened?'

'We were in the barracks, Princess,' Farid said, even as Jasim began to slide to the floor.

Hastily, the boy put his shoulder beneath his master's to prop him up. Zorahaida moved to help, and she and Farid edged Jasim to the foot of the stairs. She caught a distinct whiff of wine and her nose wrinkled.

'Is he drunk?'

They struggled up the first flight of stairs.

'I doubt it, Princess. The master never overimbibes.'

'That is something to be thankful for.' Jasim's face was unnaturally pale. It made no sense. 'He must have eaten something that has disagreed with him. Of late it's been very warm; the food could have gone bad.'

Farid shook his head. 'We ate from the same dish. I don't think it's that.'

'Well, it is most odd, he looks as though he's drunk himself into a stupor.'

Somehow, they manhandled Jasim up to the bedchamber and on to the bed. He lay there groaning, a hand to his belly. Zorahaida picked up his wrist to take his pulse. She was no doctor, but she'd learned a little on her visits to the infirmary and Jasim's pulse was so weak, she could hardly feel it. Heart in her mouth, she pressed her fingers to his neck and got the same result. He was very sick.

'Farid, how is this possible? He was strong as an ox this morning.'

Farid looked at her, eyes stricken. 'I know. Princess, it is most unusual. My master never gets sick.'

He never gets sick.

Zorahaida removed her husband's headdress and was horrified to find it drenched with sweat. The way he was groaning cut her to her core. He was writhing in pain. What could it be?

'He was well earlier,' she muttered, heart

cramping as she remembered the way his gaze had softened as he'd bidden her farewell. 'Come, Farid, help me with his clothes.'

All at once, it was as though her father the Sultan was in her bedchamber, for she heard his voice in her head, repeating what he'd said immediately after the marriage ceremony. He had pinched her chin, and said, 'Not ready to leave me, Daughter?'

Ideas crowded in on her, grim ideas that pushed all others aside. After the marriage ceremony, Sama had been shocked when Jasim and his squire had moved into the tower. It had been unusual, though Zorahaida hadn't questioned the change of lodgings. She'd been too busy wondering what it would be like to bed a stranger.

Why had her father suggested the move? The tower was some distance from the other residences; the harems were reached by walking through orange groves and along myrtle-lined pathways, and it was even further to her father's apartments. As for the palace guest houses, they were close to the barracks, at the other side of the grounds.

Had the Sultan sanctioned Jasim moving into the tower because of its isolation? Had murder been on her father's mind, even during the marriage ceremony?

If so, her father might have decided the tower was the best place to house him. At the edge of the palace grounds, there would be few, if any, witnesses should anything untoward happen.

My master never gets sick.

The Sultan had encouraged Jasim to move into her tower because he never intended him to return to the west. Zorahaida's throat dried, she didn't want to believe it, but the image of little Yamina sinking beneath the water lilies was clear in her mind, and even now she could feel the imprint of her father's hand on her face.

Her father was a violent man. Had he ordered Jasim poisoned?

'Poison,' she whispered. Jasim had been poisoned.

Maura let out a keening sound.

'Maura, you don't think Father—?'

'Don't say it, Princess,' Maura said. 'Don't even think it.'

Zorahaida couldn't think of anything else. The Sultan hadn't wanted her marriage, he'd only agreed to it because the entire court had witnessed him declaring that the overall champion could take the best gem in his collection for his prize. Zorahaida's marriage had been forced on him and there was nothing the Sultan disliked more than to be forced into anything.

'There is no proof,' she murmured. And then she realised that proof was irrelevant. All that mattered was Jasim. 'Jasim must not die. We have to leave. Farid, am I right in thinking that the Spanish party set out for Castile this morning?'

'I believe they did.'

Aghast, she closed her eyes. Her father had been eager to impress the Spanish. Their presence at court must have stayed his hand. That was why he had chosen this moment to strike. This was her fault. If she hadn't delayed their departure, Jasim would be safely on his way to Mondragón Palace.

Zorahaida clenched her jaw. Her father was not going to kill Jasim. They must escape, and for that to happen, Jasim needed a little doctoring.

'Maura, I need you to go to my uncle's harem. Ask for Naima, she is a gifted herbalist.'

Maura's eyebrows rose. 'Wouldn't the palace doctor be better?'

'No! Maura, we have to be discreet. The doctor would go straight to Father. Besides, Naima is extremely knowledgeable.'

Laying her hand on Jasim's brow, Zorahaida frowned. He was hotter than before, and his eyes were glazed. He looked to be losing consciousness. She felt his wrist; his pulse was frighteningly uneven. The poison had to be expelled.

'Farid, has he been retching?'

Farid shook his head.

She turned back to Maura. 'Very well. Ask Naima for a purgative. You have my permission to tell her that you suspect poison and that the victim is strong. Make sure she realises the poison needs to be expelled quickly. Do *not* name names. Understood?'

'Yes, Princess.'

'Run, Maura. *Run.*'

Jasim spent the best part of a night and a day closeted in the tower with his wife. It was pure hell.

The first night passed in a haze as he floated in and out of consciousness. He felt so wretched, he was barely able to muster a coherent response to Zorahaida's questioning. And she was relentless.

'Jasim, what did you eat?'

He managed a groan. His stomach ached like the devil. As for his wits, he could barely think.

'What did you drink?'

His wife's pretty face was blurred. 'Zorahaida, what's going on?'

She gave him a bitter draught and afterwards he was vilely ill; at one point he'd thought he'd lose his innards.

'Are you trying to kill me?'

'No, you fool, I'm trying to save you.'

When she attempted to give him more of the stuff, he feebly waved it away. At which point his pretty wife became quite brutal.

'Farid, lift him higher on the pillow and hold his shoulders. Firmly now. Don't let go.'

Farid, the wretch, did exactly as she bade him. Then Zorahaida, wearing a ruthless expression that reminded him uncomfortably of her father, took firm hold of his nose.

Jasim held his breath until his lungs ached and when, inevitably, he was forced to open his mouth to breathe, more of the disgusting potion was tipped down his throat.

He coughed and choked, but the stuff went down. He glared at Farid. 'Traitor.'

Farid shook his head, and Jasim thought he mumbled, 'You'll thank me later.' But he couldn't be sure because his stomach cramped, and he spent the rest of that night being most vilely sick.

As Jasim's wits began to return, he realised

that the Princess was guarding him as fiercely as a lioness guarded her cubs. Later, the only other person he recalled from that night was her maidservant Maura hovering solicitously in the background. And Farid, the ingrate.

'Jasim, are you feeling well?' his wife kept on asking. 'Do you care for water? Ale? Jasim, you must drink something.'

Far from trying to kill him, it was evident that she believed someone had poisoned him.

'I've been poisoned?' Why would anyone trouble to poison him?

'Jasim, sleep. You must recover your strength.'

His head ached and his mind was sluggish. At least his wife wasn't trying to kill him. However, after a draught of ale, his eyelids became so heavy, he strongly suspected that she wasn't above drugging him. She had laced his drink with poppy juice.

He had lost track of time and when he next woke, dawn was lightening in the east and his mind was a little clearer. He wasn't exactly fighting fit, but he felt much improved, particularly when he turned his head to see Zorahaida sleeping at his side. He lay there, content to listen to the birds and watch her waken.

She stretched and smiled. 'Jasim!' Cool fingers touched his brow. 'How do you feel?'

'As though I've been turned inside out. My head feels twice its usual size, but generally I'm much better. What happened?'

'I believe you were poisoned.'

His lips twitched. 'Last night you were so fierce, I thought to lay the blame for that at your door.' He sobered. 'Your father?'

She looked down, flushing. 'I am not sure, but I believe so.'

She looked so awkward and guilty that his heart went out to her. 'Zorahaida, it is not your fault.'

'It is.' She took his hand and kissed it; dark gaze firmly fixed on him. 'If I hadn't been so slow preparing to leave, you wouldn't be ill. You would be safely on your way to the west.'

He squeezed her hand. 'Zorahaida, I am not convinced your father is to blame.'

'He is, I know it. Father tried to kill you, and it is my fault.'

'What nonsense. My love, I am not convinced your father tried to kill me, but even supposing he did, you weren't to know what he might do.'

'That isn't true. If I hadn't been distracted by the speed at which we were married, I might have guessed what would happen. You bested him and he hates that.'

'Zorahaida, it is not your fault. It's entirely possible it was food poisoning.'

Thoughtfully, she tipped her head to one side. 'That is your inherent goodness speaking. You are an honourable man; you find it hard to see the dishonour in others. It is an unusual and attractive trait. I like you far more than I thought possible.'

Jasim's breath left him. That little speech had pleased him more than he could say. He opened his mouth to respond, but she dropped his hand and sprang from the bed. She went to the window overlooking the palace gardens and eased open a shutter. He noted that she'd only opened it a crack, just enough for her to see the path that led to the heart of the palace. She peered out, and hurried back, frowning.

'Will you be able to walk by this evening?'

He groaned. 'If I must. Zora—'

She was back at his side, pulling him upright, forcing him out of bed with the determination of a drill sergeant. 'You must. Let's give it a try.'

He managed a few stumbling steps, but his legs didn't feel as though they belonged to him and he toppled back on to the bed. She stood over him, biting her lip.

'I can only pray that you will be strong enough by this evening.'

'Strong enough for what?'

She perched on the edge of the bed. 'Jasim, we leave the palace tonight.'

He stiffened. 'If your father had me poisoned, he can't be allowed to get away with it. I need to speak to him.'

'I thought you wanted to leave.'

'I do, believe me. But your father must be questioned.'

She lifted her chin, eyes suddenly cold and the pleasure he'd felt when she'd confessed to liking him drained slowly away.

'Don't be a fool. No one questions my father.'

'Perhaps that's the trouble. Someone should have done so years ago. My father tried—'

'Your father failed,' she said bluntly. 'You would fail too, everyone does. Jasim, don't you dare think about speaking to my father. He doesn't fight fair.'

Her vehemence was unexpected. Jasim studied her thoughtfully. 'Zorahaida, I am not convinced your father is to blame. He knows exactly where

I am. If he truly wanted me dead, he could have sent an assassin. He hasn't done so.'

'That's because he's waiting for the poison to do its work. Jasim, this is my father's handiwork. He's doing nothing because he's waiting for me to announce your death.'

'You could be wrong.'

'I'm not.' She bit her lip. 'Jasim, don't you want to see your uncle again?'

'Of course I do. However, I'd like to speak to your father first. He should be given the chance to exonerate himself.'

'And if he kills you?'

Jasim's head began to thump. He didn't want to argue, but he felt as though he'd been challenged and he'd never run away from a challenge in his life. 'Is the tower being watched?'

'It's possible.'

'We need to know. Put Farid on watch. Get your man Yusuf involved if necessary. If we see anything untoward, I shall speak to your father. You can say your farewells and then we can leave.'

Zorahaida looked doubtfully at him. 'You'll swear to that?'

He put his hand on his heart. 'On my honour.'

'Very well. Tomorrow, we shall ask Father for an audience.'

'Thank you.'

'Now, if you will excuse me, Jasim, I need to bathe and then I must see that everything is in order for our departure.'

With that, she dragged on a robe and picked up her veil. 'I'm for the bathhouse. Maura will bring up your breakfast. I shall see you later.'

As she left their chamber, Jasim found himself massaging his forehead. He had a pounding headache. Was he imagining it, or was there a mismatch between Zorahaida's vehemence about not wanting to speak to her father and her swift capitulation?

He mulled over his wife's sudden meekness until his headache grew so insistent, he was forced to lie back with his eyes closed. He was soon asleep.

Chapter Nine

The harem herbalist Naima had been correct. In moderation, poppy juice could be very useful. If one masked it with spiced and honeyed wine, a sleepy patient didn't notice.

As a result, Zorahaida was wrestling with guilt. She'd been the one to hand Jasim a cup of doctored wine. The worst of it was that he'd taken it with a grateful smile. He'd swallowed every drop and had slipped into the deepest of sleeps.

Zorahaida wouldn't make her next move until the sun had sunk below the horizon. While she waited, she sat at the bedside, holding Jasim's hand, occasionally caressing his cheek with the back of her fingers.

The fading light brought out the bright glints in his hair. Her throat tightened.

Guilt sat like a cold stone in her stomach. Jasim was asleep because he trusted her. Trust wasn't easily won, and Zorahaida was afraid that by drugging him she might have lost that trust for ever.

Setting her jaw, she reminded herself that it had to be done. Jasim's idea of confronting her father the Sultan was suicidal, she couldn't allow it. They would leave the palace tonight, whilst Jasim was lost in poppy-induced dreams.

She pinched his forearm to test the depth of his slumber and he made not a murmur.

Tonight. Two hours from now.

When she could bear the guilt no longer, she rose from the bedside. She had best make sure that Maura wasn't panicking and that Sama had passed her instructions on to the guards.

Zorahaida had raided several jewel boxes to find bribes for some of the men. For her plan to work, it was vital that her father remained ignorant of their departure for as long as possible. Stealth was needed and tongues must be stilled.

She and Jasim would leave the palace covertly. It was the only way. Jasim's life, she was certain, was at risk if they stayed.

Once outside the city there would be no furtiveness. On the contrary, Zorahaida and Jasim would travel in style. They would have an entourage. There would be uniformed outriders. Guards. Zorahaida wanted the world to know that the Sultan's daughter and her husband were journeying to Madinat Runda. The more people who saw them, the safer she would feel. Her father didn't hesitate to bully those inside the palace, but the palace was a closed world. Outside, where men walked more freely, there would be countless witnesses and her father would be more likely to stay his hand. At least, that was the theory.

In the lower chamber, Zorahaida paused under the arch. It was a relief to see that the chaos was no more. They had been packing all day and the chamber was all but empty. Her clothes had already been secreted out of the palace and sent on to the meeting place by one of the city gates. Hunter had left the palace in his basket. The songbirds too.

In a quiet alley, everything was loaded on to carts and carriages that were hidden beneath sackcloth. Beneath the sackcloth, most of the carts and one of the carriages were emblazoned with her husband's colours. The other carriage, the one in which Zorahaida was to travel, bore the Nasrid red and gold.

Zorahaida and Jasim would soon be gone.

To Zorahaida's dismay, Maura was slumped

on a cushion near a jewel box and the silver lute. She looked exhausted and drained. Terrified.

'It will be all right, Maura,' Zorahaida said.

Maura looked bleakly at her. 'Princess, I am not sure it will. Your father the Sultan, may he live for ever, will be furious. He will chase after us and kill us all.'

'No, he won't.'

'How can you be so sure?'

'Well, nothing is certain, but Sama has ensured we will be able to leave the palace quietly. If fortune is with us, my father won't learn we have gone for some days.'

'If fortune is with us,' Maura repeated in a dull tone. Her worry lines deepened. 'I've learned that it takes a swift horse over a sennight to reach Madinat Runda and you are planning to make a show of it. Princess, a large entourage cannot move quickly. Nor can it hide.'

'Exactly.' Zorahaida smiled. 'Maura, do you remember how my father sent his troops after Leonor and Alba?'

'How could I forget? He set the hounds on them too, if I'm not mistaken. His own daughters!'

'That will not happen with us. Maura, think about it. We shall leave the city in the centre of a great procession. We will travel slowly and with much pomp, ensuring that everyone on our route sees us. The carts carry Jasim's colours as well as my father's. Far from hiding, we are going to proclaim our identity to the world.'

'But—'

'Father's pride will work with us.' Earnestly, praying she was correct, Zorahaida touched Maura's hand. 'Once Father works out that everyone in the realm knows his daughter and son by marriage are on their way to Madinat Runda he will allow us to complete our journey. He will want everyone to believe he approves of our leaving. Two daughters have already fled, he'd look ridiculous if he lost a third the same way. Besides, Father accepted Jasim's proposal before witnesses. Maura, I have no doubt we are safer outside the palace. Inside, Father's word is law. Outside, nothing is so certain. People have eyes. We must put our trust in them.'

'Very well.'

'Maura, as I said, nothing is certain. If you do not wish to come, I shall understand.'

Maura stiffened. 'What, and leave you to fend for yourself in a strange household? Certainly not. You need a personal maid and my duty is to you.'

'Thank you, Maura, I am touched by your loyalty.'

Maura swallowed. 'You are most welcome. When do we set out?'

Zorahaida looked at the sky, it was darkening to purple. 'In about an hour.'

'Will your husband be fit to travel?'

'He will.' Zorahaida pushed aside her guilt and forced brightness into her voice. 'Maura, I can't see the lute case. Where did we put it?'

Someone was groaning and it took a moment for Jasim to realise that he was to blame. 'God be merciful,' he muttered. His head was pounding. He could hear a hollow banging; it was rhythmic and far too loud. What the devil was it? It sounded like battle drums, but it couldn't be.

It was too much effort to hold on to his curiosity, just as it was too much effort to open his eyes, so he lay perfectly still, wondering why he couldn't order his thoughts. They were oddly blurred, and he'd had the strangest dreams. One in particular had been extremely disturbing. Already it was slipping out of reach, but he had a faint memory of Zorahaida smiling at him. And then her beautiful face had been lost behind a swirl of smoke and her delicate features changed.

She stopped smiling. It was as though a djinn had bespelled her. When the smoke cleared, Sultan Tariq stared back at him with soulless black eyes.

Jasim's heart jolted and he scrubbed his face. Such a ghastly dream.

He'd never felt so ill in his life. His bed was rocking from side to side; and if that wasn't bad enough, he must still be hallucinating for the bedchamber was filled with sounds that simply didn't fit. What on earth was that drumming? He was weak as a babe and his throat felt as though it was filled with sand. Swallowing was hideously painful. He could drink a well dry.

'Water,' he croaked, half-hoping that Zorahaida was nearby.

His bed rocked. And then the drumming sound took shape and he recognised it for what it was—hoofbeats. Those were hoofbeats. He opened his eyes and blinked in disbelief.

He was no longer in the tower bedchamber. He was lying on a mattress in what appeared to be a covered carriage. The rocking he'd felt wasn't due to illness, the carriage was moving. The canvas—blue, he noted—was open a little and, though the air was warm, a slight breeze was wafting over him. He was wearing a loose linen tunic. That too was blue, and a cursory glance told him it was emblazoned with his coat of arms.

'Zorahaida? Farid?'

With an effort, Jasim rolled on to his side and his gaze lit on a water bottle. Poison was insidious stuff, for him to feel so weak, it must still be inside him. Deciding it was best washed out, he snatched up the bottle, fumbled at the stopper and drank with desperate greed.

Outside, someone bellowed an order and the rocking stopped.

He waited. At length, the canvas was pushed aside and Zorahaida eased through the opening, dressed like the proudest of queens.

Jasim's jaw dropped. His wife looked magnificent. Her veil was encrusted with gems and she was wearing a gauzy divided skirt and so many bangles, it was a wonder she could stand. Rings glinting, she shoved back her veil and, the action at odds with her queenly attire, stooped beneath the blue canvas as she came towards him.

'Jasim, praise God you have woken.' Her smile was wary. 'Are you feeling more yourself?'

The cart was cramped, and Zorahaida had brought with her the scent of roses, a scent that would be linked for ever in Jasim's mind with the pleasures of the marriage bed. He might feel sluggish, but he could well remember how suited they were. He held out his hand and smiled.

'Zorahaida, what the devil's going on?'

Zorahaida swallowed. Oddly, she wasn't meeting his gaze. It was then that Jasim realised what she had done. Today's malaise wasn't the result of being poisoned. His pretty wife had drugged him.

'You drugged me. God be merciful, you drugged me.' Rousing himself, he caught her wrist and pulled her down to the mattress. Bangles jingled. Flimsy silk rustled. He leaned over her and she flinched. His heart twisted. 'I won't hurt you.'

Troubled dark eyes stared back at him. Her bruises had almost faded, and it occurred to him that she was genuinely afraid. The wariness lingered in her expression, and Jasim hated to think he was the cause. Angry though he was, he wouldn't harm a hair on her head.

'That is good to hear,' she murmured.

'Zorahaida, what have you done?' Jasim eased back and gestured at the cart and the canvas above them. 'What's all this?'

'We are on our way west.' Her lips trembled. 'We are going to your apartment in Mondragón Palace.'

'But your father—'

Her nostrils flared and she stared past him.

He touched her chin, turning her face until she met his gaze. 'You drugged me, admit it.'

She nodded. 'My apologies, Jasim. I could see no other way out.'

He could feel the anger building. They had disagreed and instead of talking it through, she had taken it upon herself to force her will on him. It stung. It more than stung. After the care he had taken to handle her gently, it felt like a slap in the face.

'Zorahaida, my mind is clouded, but I distinctly remember telling you I wanted to speak to your father. The Sultan is a tyrant, he needs to learn that being a ruler does not mean the world is his plaything. He cannot lash out at everyone who gets in his way. Great responsibility comes with great office. Sultan Tariq needs to learn about justice. He needs to learn that because he can take what he wants, that doesn't mean he should. The rule of law must be respected, even by him.' With a sigh, he rubbed his brow. That ghastly dream chose that moment to float back into his mind and he felt a wave of nausea. 'There is more of your father in you than I believed possible.'

She stiffened. 'What! Jasim, I—'

'Hear me out, if you please.' Conscious that the only thing between them and the world outside was a thin layer of canvas, he lowered his voice. 'You didn't want me to seek an audience with your father, so you did all in your power to prevent it. That was wrong. A wife owes her husband some respect. I realise that being a Nasrid princess you are probably used to everyone scrambling to do your will, but if our marriage is to succeed you will have to learn to consult with me.'

She stared. 'And when we disagree? What if I think you are wrong?'

'Zorahaida, I have no wish for a compliant wife who defers to me on all things.' He nudged her shoulder with his nose. 'That would be boring beyond belief. Nor do I wish to control you. However, I won't have our marriage become a battleground. Whatever faces us in the future, we must learn to find common ground.'

Jasim studied her expression. Had he gone too far? Apart from Sultan Tariq, not many people would challenge the acts of a Nasrid princess. But the devil take her, she had drugged him. 'What did you give me?'

Mouth tight, she stared at the canvas beyond his shoulder. 'Poppy juice.'

'Poppy juice.' He sighed. 'That explains the headache. And the thirst.'

Shifting, she reached for the water flask and handed it to him. 'This should help. It's from a spring in the mountains.'

'You shouldn't have done it.'

'Jasim, I didn't want you killed. Is that so terrible?'

Leaning on his elbow, he took another draught of the water. 'I am not questioning your motives, Zorahaida. I am asking for a little respect.'

She bit her lip. 'I am sorry.' She began toying with one of her bracelets, a heavy gold bangle that on its own would be worth a king's ransom. 'Jasim, I don't wish to anger you, but I don't think you should expect much of this marriage.'

His hand jerked and water splashed on to his wrist. 'What do you mean?'

'I doubt I will make a very good wife. As you know, I never expected to be married. Furthermore—'

Strangely chilled by her words, Jasim put his finger to her mouth. 'Enough.' He smiled. 'What's done is done, we shall put this behind us. If you swear never to drug me again, you, my love, will be the perfect wife.'

His head was pounding again. Smothering a groan, he lay back against the pillow. 'How many carts do we take to Mondragón Palace?'

'Six?'

His eyebrows lifted. 'So many?'

'We have a carriage each, six carts, a troop of armed knights, and a wagon for a retinue of servants, most of whom will return to the Alhambra. Oh, and Maura and Farid and your horses, of course.'

'Quite the cavalcade then?'

'Aye.'

'What about your sister's monkey and the songbirds?'

'They are here too; I wouldn't dream of leaving them behind.' She searched his face, voice husky. 'Jasim, I thought it best we made something of a show. When the Sultan realises his subjects assume he has given us his blessing, he will be less inclined to interfere.'

Jasim was silent whilst he thought it through. 'I'll say this for you, Zorahaida, you are certainly a headstrong woman. And you understand your father.'

She pushed to her feet. 'I shall leave you to recover for an hour or so. When you are up to it, it would be helpful if you could show your face. Do you think you could ride?'

'I'm a knight, Zorahaida,' he said, drily. 'I can ride in my sleep so, yes, despite your giving me that filthy potion, I think I could manage it.'

Zorahaida lowered her gaze, gave a curt nod and slipped through the canvas. The carriage tilted as she left it, an order was shouted, and the rocking began again.

Jasim gripped the water flask and closed his eyes. Already he was regretting that parting remark. She had drugged him with the best of intentions. He didn't like it, not least because it put distance between them and ever since their marriage, he'd been telling himself that their physical intimacy and the joy it had given them meant she was learning to trust him. Though he hadn't understood until now, her trust meant more to him than their physical joining.

Clearly, he'd been mistaken. She didn't trust him. What had she said?

I don't think you should expect much from this marriage.

She'd not expected to marry. She was telling him that she regretted it. Well, disappointing though that was, he couldn't afford to dwell on it. Not when he'd come to Granada in the hope of renewing the ancient trade arrangements. Those agreements were vital. In a sense, the impulse that had led him to ask for the hand of the mysterious princess he'd seen visiting the hospital was irrelevant. He'd not come to Granada for her, he'd come to amend relations between Madinat Runda and Granada. His wife's wilfulness might have put all that at risk.

Jasim stared blankly at the canvas above him. It was all very well Zorahaida making a great parade of their departure, but the way she'd arranged it was unpalatable. Drugging him in order to leave without the Sultan's blessing was utterly outrageous. Women weren't usually so self-willed.

Those covert visits to the city infirmary should have warned him that his bride was unusually strong-minded. Until today he'd had no idea that she was also extraordinarily stubborn.

Which was a shame, because if she had alienated Sultan Tariq, Jasim's hopes for renewed trade agreements would lie in tatters. Any chance of proving himself worthy of more than a back seat in the government of Madinat Runda would be gone.

Thanks to Jasim's beautiful, infuriating wife, his future was once again uncertain.

He shook his head as a pang went through him. Women were a mystery he longed to understand. Jasim's mother had died when he'd been born, so he'd never had a chance to know her. The woman he knew best was his cousin, Fatima. Fatima was warm-hearted and caring, Jasim held her in great respect.

After marrying Zorahaida and discovering that they were so well matched in bed, Jasim had found himself hoping they'd be compatible in other ways. He'd wondered if one day his wife would come to mean as much to him as his cousin. He would have liked that.

Thanks to his clouded past, Jasim had been in the habit of keeping lovers at arm's length and until Zorahaida had entered his life it had never occurred to him that he would want it any other way. Zorahaida. His fingers tightened on the water flask. Had she alienated the Sultan for all time? Would the wretched rift between east and west never be healed? After this, Jasim had no idea. He did know that there was a strong possibility that his marriage to Zorahaida would cause yet more trouble. His uncle, peacemaker that he was, would be less than thrilled.

Regret pierced him. Despite his misgivings, Jasim wanted to keep her. She was his wife. And for all that she was likely to be troublesome, she was a delight in the bedchamber. He wasn't ready to leave that behind him. Not yet. Not ever.

He rammed the cork back in the flask and glared at the opening in the canvas.

Rest was impossible. Besides, he was more than a little curious to see their little entourage.

The entire cavalcade halted in a small town whilst Jasim called for Blade. His horse at least was glad to see him, whinnying softly as Farid led him up to the waggon.

Jasim was conscious of townsfolk standing by the roadside, staring, just as Zorahaida had hoped. Some nudged each other in the ribs; others broke into delighted smiles. Jasim overheard several comments.

'It's our Princess!'

'That must be her husband.'

'Husband? I didn't know the Princess had married.'

'My thanks, Farid,' Jasim murmured, taking charge of Blade.

His cares seemed smaller after he'd climbed into the saddle. Riding had that effect on him.

Relaxing, he leaned forward to pat Blade's glossy black neck and review the cavalcade.

His eyes widened. Though Zorahaida had warned him, it was larger than he had imagined. His carriage had his coat of arms painted on the canvas. Several baggage carts also displayed his coat of arms. He had no idea what the carts contained, he hadn't brought much with him, they might be empty for all he knew. A couple of other carts were emblazoned with Nasrid red and gold, they must contain his wife's belongings. Perhaps they all did.

Jasim ran his gaze up and down the line. Zorahaida had accomplished much in a short space of time. There were uniformed knights with fluttering pennons. Squires, servants...

A memory stirred. In Jasim's youth, trading caravans had been common in Madinat Runda. When he was a boy and on better terms with his older brother, Usayd, Usayd had taken Jasim to watch the arrival of the caravan of a wealthy merchant in the marketplace. Jasim had enjoyed that day, and although he and his brother no longer saw eye to eye, Jasim was determined that merchants' caravans would become commonplace again.

Puzzled, Jasim looked down the column.

Where was Zorahaida? His gaze ran past the red and gold carts; past the knights with their glittering helmets; past donkeys laden with covered baskets. It was certainly impressive.

'Farid, where's my wife?'

'The Princess is in the Nasrid carriage, with Maura,' Farid said, pointing. 'You won't be able to see her from this standpoint. She has the canvas thrown back so all may see her.'

'She brought no horse with her?'

Farid shook his head. 'I am not sure your wife rides, Master. She certainly brought no horse.' He grinned. 'Everything else, but no horse.'

How odd, Jasim had been certain sure the Princess would ride. He'd heard tales of her riding out with her sisters on matching white ponies. Tales. They could well be wrong. Perhaps she couldn't ride, perhaps she was afraid of horses, many women were. It might explain why she had stayed behind when her more audacious sisters had left the palace.

He frowned. No, he was doing her a disservice. Zorahaida was extraordinarily wilful, and she was nothing if not audacious. This extravagant progress through her father's lands proved that. It was worthy of the Queen of Sheba.

Aware that the captain at the head of the outriders was looking to him for the signal to continue, Jasim waved his hand. 'Proceed, if you please.'

As the wedding procession of the Sultan's daughter and Jasim ibn Ismail of Madinat Runda rumbled ponderously into motion, a ragged cheer went up. The townsfolk waved and a young girl threw a spray of myrtle into their path. Others were swift to follow her example, showering the dusty road with fresh foliage and flowers.

Jasim found himself smiling. Zorahaida certainly knew how to cause a stir. He set his heels to Blade's sides and headed for the Nasrid carriage.

Maura was sharing Zorahaida's cushioned seat at the front of the carriage. Naturally, both women were veiled, and Maura was holding a sunshade to keep the worst of the heat at bay. A fringe of coloured beads at the edge of the parasol swayed and flickered in the sunlight, like fireflies.

Zorahaida stared blindly at the village they were passing through. She kept nodding and waving, she wanted the villagers to understand that she appreciated the tributes and cheers directed her way. It was hard though.

Inside, she was shaking, and she had no idea why. She'd known all along her marriage to Jasim had been one of convenience and she'd gone into it with her eyes wide open. She'd known there would be disagreements. What she hadn't anticipated was how much they would upset her.

Her father the Sultan often angered her. In truth, the random and unjust punishments he had imposed on her and her sisters had taught her the meaning of rage. Like the time he had locked the three of them up in the tower and had sold their ponies. She'd been blind with rage then, they all had.

Today, however, Zorahaida felt more upset than enraged. She frowned, not at all sure what she was feeling. Whatever it was, she didn't much like it.

'It is absurd,' she muttered.

'Absurd?' Maura asked. 'What is absurd?'

'I disappointed my husband,' she said. 'And I am surprised how much it distresses me.'

'You are falling under his spell.'

'His spell? What are you talking about? I married Jasim to prevent bloodshed. Maura, you of all people, know how it was. He asked for my hand on impulse, backed Father into a corner and once Father had agreed, Jasim couldn't admit he'd made a mistake.'

'Jasim ibn Ismail is blessed with strength and a handsome face. Underneath his ambition, I believe he is more considerate than most men,' Maura said, carefully. 'He might have asked for your hand on impulse, but you married him because you liked him. You want him to like you back and at the moment that is in question.'

'Is it?' Behind her veil, Zorahaida narrowed her eyes. 'You think I have alienated him for ever?'

'I hope not. Princess, giving your husband that sleeping draught got him safely out of the palace, as you desired. But you went against his wishes. It wasn't wise.'

'He wasn't half as angry as I expected. He didn't beat me, although he did say I must learn to consult with him.'

Maura made a choking sound. It was so quickly suppressed, Zorahaida knew she was laughing.

'You find me amusing?'

'Of course not.' The parasol shifted, and the beaded fringe tinkled as it swung to and fro. 'Princess, Jasim ibn Ismail is an honourable man. He is a knight; he is cultured and reasonable.'

'Are you saying he is perfect?'

'Princess, no man is perfect. But he is not a bully. You are used to dealing with a bully. I believe your husband will respond well if you change tactics.'

'And how do I do that?'

'Open your thoughts to him. Talk to him. If handled correctly, I believe your husband will be eager to please you. It's obvious he wants your union to be a true meeting of hearts and minds.'

A true meeting of hearts and minds? Zorahaida wasn't so sure. He'd said he wanted respect.

Hopelessly confused, she frowned at the roadside. A small boy was throwing flowers towards her carriage and without thinking, she inclined her head and waved at him. A cloud of thistledown drifted in the dusty air. She could hear the screech of a hawk and the bleat of a goat.

'I wish I had your confidence, Maura.'

'Be patient, Princess, you need to adjust. Both of you.'

Zorahaida opened her mouth to say more when the motion of the carriage changed, they were slowing down. Hearing hoofbeats behind them, she suppressed a sigh and turned. 'What now?'

Jasim rode up alongside, and her breath stopped. He was dressed in his princely finery.

His posture was confident, his hold on the reins easy and competent. He was impossibly handsome. No one would imagine that not long since he'd been poisoned and drugged.

His smile was cautious, and it struck Zorahaida that Maura might be right. He wanted their marriage to be a success. Her heart lifted.

'Greetings, my husband,' she said softly. 'Is all well with you?'

'Very well, but I lack one thing.'

'Oh?'

'Your company.' He held out his hand. 'Princess Zorahaida, will you ride with me?'

Her jaw slackened. 'You want me to climb on to your horse?' Her heartbeat quickened. 'I can't do that!'

'You fear horses?'

'I adore horses.'

Jasim held up his hand and the cavalcade shuddered to a halt. His mouth went up at the corner.

'I heard your sisters rode with their husbands when they left the palace. I thought, since you have brought half the palace with you, your horse would also be here.'

Her head lowered. 'I no longer have a horse.'

Even to her own ears, her voice was tinged

with regret. Jasim must have heard it, for he leaned towards her, frowning. 'What happened?'

'It—' Her voice cracked, and she shook her head. 'It's not important.'

His expression sobered. 'Not important? Losing a horse can be a matter of life and death.' He held out his hand. 'Come along.'

'I can't ride with you!'

'Why not?'

'It will cause a scandal. It is not done.' Zorahaida spoke firmly, though in truth she had no idea whether riding with her husband would cause a scandal or not. Outside the palace, she was well out of her depth. Life as a Nasrid princess hadn't prepared her for the wider world. For all she knew, what her father found unacceptable might be commonplace elsewhere in his kingdom.

Jasim leaned towards her, his expression unreadable. 'Zorahaida, I wouldn't expect you to do anything you are not comfortable with. I am not asking you to remove your veil.' He shrugged. 'This saddle is large, and I noticed earlier that you are wearing a divided skirt.'

Tempted, she studied him. She liked Jasim, more than she had believed possible. The knowledge that he was upset with her was far too disturbing. Sensing her decision was important, she smoothed the fabric of her skirt. 'This is too delicate for riding.'

'Nonsense.' He smiled. 'Zorahaida, if you sit before me, I won't let you fall. Trust me.'

I won't let you fall. Trust me.

Zorahaida stared at him through her veil. Yes, there was more behind Jasim's request than a desire for her company. This was both an olive branch and a challenge. If she denied him, scandalous though his suggestion appeared to her, his mind might set against her. This was a challenge she must accept.

Several prods in her ribs told her that Maura agreed with her.

'Very well, sir knight,' Zorahaida said. 'If you swear not to drop me.'

He put his hand on his heart. 'I wouldn't dream of it.'

Chapter Ten

Zorahaida leaned cautiously towards Jasim and before she had time for second thoughts, he had plucked her from her seat and placed her before him. Maura smothered what sounded suspiciously like a giggle. Jasim's horse whickered.

'Easy, Blade,' Jasim murmured as, with scant respect for propriety or Zorahaida's dignity, he deftly manoeuvred her so she was riding astride. 'You will be more comfortable like this.'

'Thank you.' Zorahaida gripped the front of the saddle and shot a guilty glance at the villagers gathered by the highway. The men were watching, some guardedly, others looked amused rather than shocked. Furthermore, not all the women were veiled, and the unveiled women were also smiling. She felt herself relax.

'Jasim, look. Not all the women wear veils.'

Jasim eased her closer against him and a muscled arm went firmly about her. 'You will find customs vary from village to village. Indeed, from household to household.'

She fell silent, struck by the extent of her ignorance.

What did she know of life outside the sheltered, imprisoning walls of the Alhambra? They weren't going to leave Al-Andalus, and she had assumed similar conventions to the ones she had grown up with would operate elsewhere in her father's kingdom. Perhaps they didn't.

Zorahaida had scoured the palace library. Eager to learn as much as she could, she had read about wars and trade and border disputes. Unfortunately, none of the scrolls and parchments had shone any light on day-to-day living in her father's emirate. The rules and restrictions familiar to her might not apply everywhere.

Beyond the palace walls, she was a fish out of water. Like it or not, that made her dependent on her husband. It was an unnerving thought.

Jasim raised his hand, heeled his horse in the ribs and their procession rolled into motion. They soon left the village behind.

'Zorahaida?' His breath stirred her veil. 'Tell me about your horse, the one you lost.'

An image of Snowdrop, her beautiful grey pony, flashed through her mind, bringing with it a familiar tug of sadness and loss. Zorahaida rarely thought of Snowdrop. Since the day she'd learned her father the Sultan had sold her, it had been too painful.

Maura's advice echoed through her mind.

Open your thoughts to him. Talk to him.

She cleared her throat and fixed her gaze on the road ahead of them. 'Before my sisters and I were brought to the Alhambra, we lived at Castle Salobreña.'

'How long were you there?'

'Many years. Our mother the Queen had died, and I suspect Father found it too painful to have reminders of her nearby. Mamá's Spanish duenna Inés came with us. She looked after us.'

Jasim's thumb caressed her waist. 'Did you see anything of your father back then?'

'He didn't appear often, though when he did, he was laden with gifts.' She lifted her hand and gently shook her arm, so the bangles and bracelets jingled and sparkled. 'Jewellery mostly. Sometimes he brought sweetmeats, sometimes silver and gold. We weren't that interested; I suppose we were too young.'

'Aye, coin and jewels, though pretty, are not for children. I suspect you would have liked to know your father better.'

She paused, startled by his insight. 'That is true, back then, we longed for our father's love.' She felt her mouth twist. 'We didn't understand until later that he was a stranger to love. He wanted adoration; I think he has always confused it with love. Anyway, on one of his visits he brought the ponies.' She twisted round and even though Jasim couldn't possibly see her through the gauze of her veil, his amber eyes were fixed on her, intent. 'We were given ponies not horses. Three perfectly matched greys with harnesses covered in silver bells. Mine was called Snowdrop, and she was the best of gifts. We were taught to ride and we adored it.'

He laughed. 'I can just imagine the three of you riding accompanied by the tinkling of bells.'

'In our youth, Father was less controlling. Those ponies gave us a taste of freedom. Even so we had an escort, we never rode out without one.'

She felt him nudge the back of her head. A kiss? She couldn't tell. She rather thought he was inhaling her scent. He'd done that a number of times whilst they were in bed. Her cheeks burned, the idea of him doing it whilst out on the public highway was most distracting. And highly questionable. Weren't gestures of affection frowned on, outside the bedchamber? Anyone might see.

He cleared his throat. 'So you were permitted beyond the castle walls?'

'Aye, with our escort. We were still quite young. Father thought of us as children.'

'And then? What happened that Snowdrop is no longer with you?'

'When we grew older, we angered our father.' Her mouth tasted bitter. 'It happened after he had brought us to live in the Alhambra. We assumed our rides would continue as before.'

'Granada beckoned.'

'Just so. We were eager to see the markets. We'd saved all those coins and we thought we'd be allowed to spend them. We couldn't have been more wrong. The Sultan refused to let us out and when we made the mistake of challenging him, he was livid. He locked us up in the tower and sold the ponies. Which only proves that they were never really ours.'

'I agree. A gift is no gift if it can be taken away.' She felt it again, that light pressure on the back of her head. A kiss, it was surely a kiss.

'Jasim, that isn't the end, though I believe you know what happened after that.'

'Your sisters left with their Spanish knights.'

Tears stung at the back of her eyes. Thankful Jasim couldn't see, she bit her lip and nodded, and felt him sigh.

'You are no longer alone, Zorahaida.'

'Thank you.'

Her husband was a kind man. Most likely he regretted his decision to marry her. She'd never intended to, but she had become a burden. Thinking about her father and his rages was making her see that her escape with Jasim was bound to have unpleasant repercussions for Jasim, his family and his district. From his point of view, their marriage had become a disaster.

'Jasim?'

'Mmm?'

'Sultan Tariq is not one to forget a slight. He is bound to view our hasty departure as an insult.'

He huffed out a breath. 'If you are correct about him having me poisoned, he wanted to see the back of me. You would think he would rejoice to see me gone.'

She laid her hand on his forearm. 'Jasim, Sultan Tariq is the most controlling man on earth. Everything that happens is twisted to suit his purposes. By now, he will have forgotten about poisoning you. He will be brooding over the insult of you leaving without bidding him farewell. Further, he will blame you for spiriting me away. As far as he is concerned, I am his only daughter.'

'A daughter he strikes at will,' Jasim growled. 'You are better off with me.'

'All I am saying is that when we get to Madinat Runda, you would be wise to take precautions. My father never forgets a slight.'

'Never fear, precautions will be taken.'

'Jasim, I am so sorry. I am no great bargain. I know you hoped our marriage would unite the districts; it may have the opposite effect. Marrying me will bring trouble your way.' She fiddled with Blade's mane and let out a deep sigh. 'And I think it's worse than you may imagine.'

'Worse? I have stolen the Sultan's daughter, what could possibly be worse than that?'

Astonishingly, his voice was filled with laughter. Releasing Blade's mane, Zorahaida twisted round to stare at him.

'I'm serious. Jasim, you don't understand how ignorant I am. About everything. I've been hedged about all my life.'

He smiled. 'You aren't that ignorant, you got out to visit the hospital.'

'Thanks to my friends, yes. I learned Father's rules and found my way around them.'

'Zorahaida, when you find your feet in your new home, you will regain confidence.'

She touched his forearm. 'I need you to understand that I have little practical knowledge about conventions and day-to-day living away from my father's influence. When we get to Madinat Runda, I am bound to make mistakes.'

'No matter, it will be my honour to help you. Zorahaida, you have a good heart and that will serve you well. You will make new friends.'

She searched his face and saw no trace of anger or disappointment. Only earnestness. With a jerky nod, she faced forward and continued her ride into the unknown. Every now and then she would glance over her shoulder at the road behind them. Whilst sympathetic, Jasim didn't seem to be taking her fears about her father seriously. Were they being followed?

Her father wouldn't let this rest. He would make trouble. And if he realised how much she was coming to admire her husband; he might even come after her. Sultan Tariq had a twisted soul, the very idea of others' happiness enraged him. Much as she might wish it otherwise, she feared that her father was beyond redemption.

Briefly closing her eyes, she relaxed against

her husband's body and allowed herself to enjoy the feel of his strong arm wrapped securely about her.

Apart from the first night, they processed with great pomp through the Emirate, and if Zorahaida hadn't been so concerned that Sultan Tariq's troops might ambush them without warning she might have enjoyed it.

Father won't attack our procession, she kept telling herself. Not before so many witnesses. Unfortunately, no matter how many times she repeated it, she couldn't stop worrying. The knights she'd brought with her had sworn loyalty to her. Would they hold fast if Sultan Tariq's household knights appeared on the horizon? Her gamble, that her father wouldn't attack the wedding party when they had made such a show, might not pay off.

On the first night Jasim appeared to be fully recovered, for when their entourage stopped at an inn to eat, he was well enough to shake his head when she suggested that they spend the night there.

'Jasim, shall we sleep here tonight?'

'I wouldn't recommend it.' He pushed a colourful pottery serving dish to one side and leaned towards her. 'It won't do, not for the Sultan's daughter.'

Zorahaida glanced about. True, it was a little cramped with their knights and servants crowded round the tables, but the atmosphere was friendly.

'I rather like it; they are very welcoming. Jasim, they will be glad of our custom.' She kept her voice down, so as not to upset the innkeeper. 'This is a tiny village; I don't think there is anywhere else.'

He gave a swift headshake. 'There isn't room for all of us inside and I won't have our party split up. You must be properly guarded, the horses and baggage too, and to that end, we'll camp in the open.' He gestured for the innkeeper and took out his purse. He paid generously, if the innkeeper's effusive thanks were anything to go by.

As they made their way back to the horses, she touched his arm. 'Jasim, I apologise if today's sleeping arrangements don't please you.'

He shot her a startled look. 'Zorahaida, you've no need to apologise. I am not your father.'

'Of course not. However, I wanted you to know that for the rest of the journey, our lodgings should meet with your full approval.'

'Oh?'

'When we set out, I sent outriders ahead. They have instructions to solicit lodgings with the governors and village leaders whose towns and villages lie on our route. I couldn't do that for tonight because I wasn't sure exactly when we would arrive. In return for any hospitality, I plan to leave gifts which can be used for the benefit of the townsfolk.'

He blinked at her, and she would swear she had surprised him. Then a slow smile dawned. 'How very organised you are.'

She gave a crisp nod. 'Thank you, I like to think so.'

Initially, Zorahaida had no complaints about the arrangements Jasim made for her night in the open. Beneath a crescent moon, he chose a secluded spot just off the highway and arranged the watch, ensuring that all their men would have rest. A temporary roped paddock was set up for the horses, and the carts and carriages were grouped together.

She slept in the Nasrid carriage with Jasim alongside her. He fell asleep quickly, after a brief, all-too-cursory kiss.

Unreasonable though it was, Zorahaida felt

abandoned. She craved her husband's touch and she'd been hoping he would make love to her, not simply because he took pains to ensure her pleasure but because it would prove he had forgiven her for giving him that sleeping draught.

A small lantern was dangling from a hook on the carriage frame and the light turned his hair to flame. Guards had been posted within calling distance and through the thin canvas, she could hear them coughing and shuffling. They must be able to hear everything that went on inside the carriage. Was the presence of the guards holding him back?

She didn't think so. The presence of the guards might dampen Jasim's ardour, but there was more to it than that. Despite Jasim's continuing kindness, she had angered him by giving him that potion. He understood she had given it with the best of intentions, but he had yet to forgive her. His new aloof manner tore at her heart.

Listening to his steady breathing, she prayed he would forgive her very soon. Above all, she prayed that her father the Sultan would forget all about her and allow her to at least try to make a success of her marriage.

Outside, leaves were rustling. She could hear other noises too, soft night noises, like the ones she used to listen to from her bedchamber high in the tower. Eventually, they lulled her to sleep.

The next day, despite the carriages and baggage carts, they made excellent progress.

Jasim insisted Zorahaida rode before him. He was no longer certain what he felt about her, but he liked to have her close.

Had Sultan Tariq sent men after them? At regular intervals, Jasim glanced over his shoulder to survey the highway behind them. He saw nothing unusual. Unfortunately, every time he faced forward again, that tantalising scent was waiting for him. Warm and womanly, it tempted him every step of the way. His wife's body called to his.

Immediately after their marriage, Jasim had been sure of one thing. He desired Zorahaida more than he had believed possible. And when it appeared that she enjoyed him equally, he'd told himself it was a great blessing. Mutual attraction had been enough. He'd not thought further than that and he should have done.

Zorahaida hadn't been ready for him, not in her soul.

The Sultan's violence against her had horrified him. Jasim had wanted to believe that her spirit hadn't been damaged. He'd taken the ways she'd found to overcome the restrictions imposed upon her as proof of that. She'd gone into the city to help the sick.

And now…

Without warning, just as he'd begun to believe their marriage held promise, she'd drugged him.

Telling himself that she'd gone on to arrange for them to leave the palace in one of the boldest schemes he could imagine didn't help. Nor did the knowledge that she had mustered enough support for them to have a fine escort.

The woman was certainly resourceful. A strategist. It was oddly arousing. Which was probably just as well because despite his disappointment in her tactics, she was certainly interesting. What would she do next?

While he waited to find out what that might be, he wasn't going to let her out of his sight. One thing was certain, she had him in knots. They'd only known each other a matter of days, so it was a mystery why he wanted more than her body. But so he did. It was enough to trouble a man's sleep. And it didn't stop there. He found himself wondering if Zorahaida would ever want him for more than the carnal pleasure he could give her.

He wanted her affection. In short, he hoped for a meeting of minds.

God help him. He'd made a mistake back in that tower. He'd bedded her too soon.

Well, that was easily remedied. He would care for her, he would guard her with his life, but there would be no more bed-play until he could be sure that she felt something for him.

He frowned over the top of her head, confused as to why this mattered, confused by the strange direction his thoughts had taken. No woman had troubled him in this way. Ever. He was becoming a stranger to himself. Well, if he kept his distance, no doubt these unsettling thoughts would leave him.

The sun climbed and almost immediately, Jasim found himself regretting his vow to keep his wife at arm's length. Where she was concerned, keeping himself to himself was well-nigh impossible. Time and time again, he would jerk out of his abstraction to find himself nuzzling her head or finding an excuse to stroke the back of her hand.

Riding with Zorahaida before him was proving such a trial that he heaved a sigh of relief when their party arrived in a village to find a small horse market was underway. The horses stood in awnings, tails swishing.

Zorahaida gripped his arm. 'Jasim, look, horses! May we stop? Please?'

'Very well.' Jasim had no objection, that tantalising scent was driving him to distraction. Moreover, the plane trees planted about the market square offered welcome shade and their own animals needed rest. Not to mention the men. Jasim caught their captain's eye. 'We'll stop here a while.'

'Very good, Master.'

While the knights headed for the cool beneath the trees, Farid came for Blade and Maura appeared with the tasselled sunshade.

Their wedding procession being something of a circus, the entire village turned out to watch. Men and women gathered in doorways; children stared, open-mouthed—everyone seemed eager to bear witness to Jasim ibn Ismail and his Nasrid princess passing through their village. All was exactly as his clever wife had predicted.

The tavern did a brisk trade with food and drink. Serving girls appeared with jugs of ale on trays. Bowls of nuts and olives were put before them and more food ordered.

Jasim's clever wife waved away an offer of refreshment. Her attention hadn't shifted from the horses under the awnings.

'My thanks, but no. Later, perhaps,' she said, turning back to him. 'Jasim, they'll be untethering those horses soon to spare them from the heat. May we look at them before they're led away?'

'If that is your wish.'

Maura and the sparkling sunshade accompanied them as they crossed the square and Jasim's gaze was immediately caught by a grey mare. She was a beautiful creature, with strong legs, well-muscled haunches, a proud arching neck and a flowing mane. Her lines were perfect.

'Oh, Jasim,' Zorahaida breathed. She, too, had seen the mare.

With a sigh of delight, she walked across and was soon deep in conversation with the horse trader.

'Zorahaida, if you like her, I will buy her for you,' Jasim said. 'Though you must try out her paces first. She might be jumpy.' He eyed his wife's divided skirts and was thankful that the fabric looked reasonably robust. The previous day he had surprised her by lifting her on to Blade's back without warning. Today his wife's clothing was far more suitable for riding than the filmy excuse for a garment she had been wearing then.

'That is generous, Jasim. I should like to try her out, although if I like her, I shall buy her myself.' Her voice warmed. 'Remember all those coins.'

He stepped closer. 'Zorahaida, I would be honoured to buy her for you. Think of her as part of my wedding gift to you. But I would see you take a turn about the square; I'll warrant she's feistier than Snowdrop and I've no wish to see you thrown.'

The mare was indeed feisty although Zorahaida proved herself well able to control her. It had never occurred to Jasim that his wife would be so fine a horsewoman, he was impressed. She paraded about the market, testing the grey mare at a walk, at a trot, even at a canter. He could only be thankful she didn't try a gallop, though he could tell she wanted to. She was so taken with the mare that she didn't notice Jasim when he began haggling with the trader over the price. She simply kept on riding, round and round, her veil floating behind her like a jewelled banner, oblivious of the stir she was causing.

It was plain she and that grey mare were going to be inseparable. There would be no more sharing a horse. Perversely, Jasmin felt a pang of regret which he immediately squashed. Given his wife's familiarity with horses, it was only right she should have her own mount.

He turned back to the horse merchant. The price for the mare settled, he went on to bargain for a decent saddle and harness. There were no silver bells, but the leather was of good quality and the tack well made. Zorahaida rode up as he closed the negotiations, and he helped her dismount. They led the mare to the shade near the tavern.

He turned to Zorahaida. 'You will take refreshment now, I hope.'

'Indeed.' Her voice was warm and filled with pleasure. 'A thousand thanks, Jasim, she is perfect.'

Jasim was only glad she hadn't insisted on paying for the animal herself. He liked buying her things, he realised, he would do it again soon. Having seen her seated at a table in the shade, he beckoned for the innkeeper who rushed to bring them ale, savoury pastries, nuts and almond cakes. It was too hot for wine.

Zorahaida fingered the edge of her veil and leaned towards him. 'Jasim, I don't wish to shock the villagers, do you think I ought to retire to our carriage to eat?'

He jerked his head towards the women in the doorway. 'They are not wearing veils, and everyone is being most respectful. I am sure, if you are subtle, the villagers would be honoured if you ate here.'

He handed her a cup of ale and took one for himself, smiling as she discreetly lifted her veil to drink.

'Have you decided on a name for your mare?'

'I shall call her Spirit,' she said, setting down the cup and reaching for an almond cake.

Farid and a couple of knights from the guard had wandered over to where Spirit was tethered and were admiring her. Jasim watched them with a sense of relief.

'It's good to see my squire and your men are on easy terms.'

She glanced across and gave one of her brisk nods. 'Yes, it is very pleasing.'

As Jasim took time to study her knights and servants, he was struck by an unsettling thought. 'Zorahaida,' he lowered his voice. 'Have you thought what will happen to your people when we reach Mondragón Palace?'

She gave a shaky breath and set the almond cake to one side.

'I confess when we left the Alhambra, I was rather distracted,' she murmured. 'It hadn't occurred to me, but they can never go back.'

'My thoughts exactly.'

'Jasim, they are loyal men and they do not deserve to suffer because they aided us.'

He covered her hand with his. 'Nor shall they. When we reach home, I shall speak to my uncle. There is always space for loyal men.'

'Thank you, Jasim.'

She lifted her veil long enough to send him a dazzling smile, and Jasim felt his stomach swoop. What this woman did to him. His need for her was an ache in his belly, he was uncomfortably aware he would desire her until the end of his days. What worried him most was that he was coming to see that desire wasn't the sum of it. Affection might not be enough. He felt utterly baffled.

As Zorahaida turned her attention to a bowl of pistachio nuts, Jasim knew he was in deep trouble.

Each day on their ponderous progress, Jasim discovered more about his princess. Her powers of organisation were impressive, and her reach seemed as long, if not longer than that of Sultan Tariq. How she had achieved this, when 'hedged about' all her life in the Alhambra, as she had put it, was a mystery. After a few days, Jasim learned something else. The Sultan's third daughter was beloved. Everywhere. Her reputation alone opened doors all over the Emirate.

Jasim never asked what her outriders said to the dignitaries and village headmen, he could only guess, but after that first night, news of their progress spread like wildfire. Each stopping place welcomed them with open arms. There were smiles everywhere. He was used to studying faces, and he would swear the delight was genuine.

There were simple households...

'Princess, we are honoured to have you stay with us. You must be tired after your journey, permit my wife to accompany you to your chambers where you may bathe and rest. Your husband shall join you later.'

There were rich merchants' houses, where generations of the same family had built their houses on foundations left behind by the Romans.

'Princess, God is good that He sent you to our humble house. Please come this way.'

The wine was rich in these houses, and the food anything but humble.

They rode through barren wildernesses, where the summer heat had withered the wildflowers at the trackside. Fearsome rock formations loured over them and hawks circled the skies, hunting for prey. At length they were admitted into the fort that housed the Governor of Antequera.

'Princess, Antequera welcomes you,' the Governor said. 'If you desire to see our bathhouse, it is naturally open to you and Jasim ibn Ismail. We have given you and your esteemed husband a set of chambers in the tower. Should you desire to explore the district before you press on to Madinat Runda, my knights will be happy to escort you on the morrow.'

In the tower chamber they looked out on to an ancient landscape the Visigoths would have recognised. A plain stretched into the distance and on the skyline, they found themselves staring at a rocky outcrop that looked, ominously, like the head of a sleeping giant.

After two weeks of such journeying, Jasim's opinion of his wife had grown by leaps and bounds. Keeping apart from her physically was an ordeal he battled with hour by hour, day by day. There were unexpected benefits to his restraint. It helped him see beyond mere physical attraction. Whenever he found himself aching to touch her, which was often, he pushed his desires aside and focused on watching her. On talking to her.

By journey's end Jasim knew he had in his keeping a genuine treasure. Zorahaida was beautiful and clever. She was adored by all who knew her and hundreds who didn't because her concern for everybody was totally genuine, it came from the heart. Despite the restrictions imposed upon her by Sultan Tariq she had a formidable reputation.

When their party reached the southern gate of Madinat Runda, Jasim had lost count of the ways she astounded him.

She had achieved all this from that tower at the edge of the Alhambra?

She was a woman in a million, and he would do all in his power to keep her.

Chapter Eleven

'Not far now,' Jasim said, gesturing at the imposing city gate ahead of them. 'Welcome to Madinat Runda.'

Zorahaida reined in and stared. It was late in the afternoon and the sun still played over the walls and gatehouse. She could tell from shadows thrown by a cluster of palm trees at the roadside that this was the south gate. Madinat Runda was clearly well fortified and, judging by the soldiers patrolling the ramparts and the sentries at the gate, it was as strongly guarded as Granada. Jutting up from behind the city wall, a slim minaret pointed to heaven.

She nudged Spirit towards the gate. She felt queasy, and it was nothing to do with the length of their journey or the food she had eaten. She was apprehensive. So much hung in the balance. The rift between Sultan Tariq and this district had been long-standing. Jasim had mentioned his father's involvement, yet antipathy remained. Was it entirely due to the Sultan? Zorahaida wouldn't be surprised if the Governor refused her houseroom.

'Will your uncle the Governor be in residence?' she asked.

'Very likely.' Jasim's amber eyes crinkled at the corners and his saddle creaked as he reached for her hand. 'Zorahaida, there's no need to be nervous. My uncle will be delighted to meet you.'

Would he? Zorahaida wasn't so sure. Swallowing, she nodded and turned the subject. 'I read that Madinat Runda has been a settlement for thousands of years.'

'That's true, settlers have been here for ever.'

'Because of the cliffs on the western side?' The cliffs and the deep gorge carved in the land by the River Guadalevín were well known.

'Aye. The cliffs are as vital today as they were in antiquity. They make the city easy to defend.'

The Captain of their party spoke to the guards and they were waved through the gate. As they passed into the city, Jasim went on talking. Zorahaida struggled to listen. Her husband had behaved with great chivalry on their journey. They had shared chambers and on occasions beds, but it hadn't escaped her that in all that time he'd barely touched her. It was possible he'd been concerned about them being overheard, but she didn't think that was holding him back. He hadn't forgotten about the poppy juice.

Notwithstanding, he was trying to put her at ease. At heart, he was a kind man.

'Tomorrow, when you are rested, I'll take you to see the gorge,' he was saying. 'There's a zig-zag path down to the bridge at the bottom. I believe the Romans built it.'

'Thank you,' Zorahaida murmured.

They clopped through a military-looking square with a fort and several outbuildings— barracks, stables and storerooms. When they were almost clear of the fort, they took a left-hand fork. Along one side ran a sturdy wall with steps leading to the top.

Jasim saw where she was looking. 'I don't recommend going up on to that wall, the cliff falls away from here. There's no guardrail and the drop is dizzying.'

On her right, Zorahaida saw another minaret and, above the rooftops, another.

They came to a halt by a small iron gate. 'Here we are. Welcome to Mondragón Palace.'

'This looks as though it is part of the fort,' Zorahaida said, puzzled.

'It is close to the fort, but I can assure you this is the Governor's residence.'

Though not entirely comfortable, the next couple of hours were less of an ordeal than Zorahaida had feared. Once inside the palace, Jasim swept her along columned walkways that were paved with clay tiles. She glimpsed many courtyards, some shaded by date palms, others cooled by marble pools or fountains. At last they stepped through a horseshoe arch and stood in a courtyard to rival any in her father's palace. Galleries ran along two sides, supported by marble columns. The arches were decorated with coloured tiles—glossy blue diamonds, bright yellow stars and crimson and blue swirls. Here and there some of the plasterwork needed repair, but the overall effect was stunning. Through another arch, she could see what looked like a water garden.

'This is all part of your uncle's palace? Jasim, it is so like the Alhambra, it is uncanny.'

He lifted an eyebrow. 'You were expecting a hovel?'

'Certainly not, though I am not sure what I was expecting. This is beautiful.'

'I am so pleased you like it,' came a dry voice behind her.

Zorahaida whirled about. Jasim's uncle, Governor Ibrahim ibn Osman, was shorter than his nephew. He was wearing a white turban, a loose over-tunic and soft house shoes. His eyes were brown and thoughtful and his beard grey and neatly trimmed. She couldn't help but note that he had not called her by name. She hung back as Jasim gripped the Governor's arm.

'Uncle, it is my great pleasure to introduce my wife, Zorahaida. As you know, she is Sultan's Tariq's youngest daughter.'

Lips tightening, the Governor spared her the briefest of glances. 'So, it's true?' He turned back to Jasim. 'When the messenger arrived with news of your marriage, I wasn't certain I believed it. All these years, I've been suggesting you take a wife and when you finally do, you marry the Sultan's daughter.'

Jasim frowned and responded curtly, but Zorahaida missed exactly what he said because one thought alone had taken root.

Jasim isn't married. I am his only wife.

She felt a distinct flash of relief. There were no rivals in the harem. And if she had any say in it, there never would be. She wanted him all for herself.

A door latch clicked, and soft footsteps hurried overhead.

'Jasim? Jasim, is it you?'

A young woman leaned over the gallery handrail, her face alight with joy. It gave Zorahaida a jolt to see her without a veil, though Jasim had already mentioned that in his home women were not obliged to wear them. Instead, the young woman was wearing a simple headband and her hair, a glossy mass of dark curls, flowed down well past her shoulders.

The young woman gave an excited little skip. 'Jasim, I am so glad you are back. Don't move, I'm coming down.'

She arrived in the courtyard just as Hunter skittered in. Chattering loudly, the monkey scrambled on to Zorahaida's shoulder. Maura stormed in and, briefly, all was chaos.

'I'm sorry, Princess,' Maura panted. 'Hunter's too fast for me. The instant I opened his basket the little demon was away.'

The young woman watched, her eyes as round as coins. And Zorahaida would swear she saw the Governor's lips twitch.

Hunter gripped Zorahaida's shoulder, trembling all over, still chattering, obviously indignant.

'Hunter, you are exaggerating,' Zorahaida said, ignoring the startled look the Governor gave her. Hunter invariably calmed when she talked to him, she wasn't about to stop when he needed it most. 'You were allowed out every day.'

Small fingers caught at her veil, catching her hair. Zorahaida flinched and reached up to stroke him.

Yes, the Governor was definitely smiling. Let him, she thought. Why shouldn't I talk to Hunter? People talk to their horses, don't they?

'Don't worry, Maura,' Jasim said. 'I dare say Hunter likes confinement no more than the rest of us.'

Maura murmured agreement and stamped out of the courtyard, muttering under her breath.

Jasim turned back to Zorahaida. 'Princess, please allow me to introduce my cousin, Fatima bint Ibrahim. Fatima, this is Princess Zorahaida, my wife.'

Fatima made a small obeisance, so small it was barely noticeable. As an insult it was mild. A challenge? Perhaps. Aware that this was a pivotal moment, Zorahaida kept her head as high as she could, though with Hunter tugging at her veil and hair, she didn't feel remotely dignified. She had no wish for the inhabitants of Mondragón Palace to grovel before her, but if she was going to be happy here, those in Governor Ibrahim's household must learn to judge her on her own merits, and not because she was the Sultan's daughter.

Beside her, Zorahaida felt Jasim tense. 'Fatima,' he growled.

The Governor held up his hand. 'Allow me, Jasim. Fatima, this is the Sultan's daughter and your cousin's wife. You can do better than that.'

Lowering her gaze and bowing deeply, Fatima obeyed. It wasn't a full obeisance, more of a curtsy in the Spanish style, but it was enough.

Zorahaida stepped forward, grasped Fatima's hands and raised her. 'Thank you, Fatima. I am so glad to meet you.'

Hunter chattered and walked down Zorahaida's arm like an acrobat. Beady eyes assessed Fatima, then he jumped.

Fatima squealed. As Hunter clambered on to her shoulder, her expression changed from wary to delighted. 'Hello, little demon,' she said, reaching up to pet him.

'In truth, his name is Hunter,' Zorahaida murmured.

Hunter hopped up and down, babbling and clapping his hands. Fatima grinned at Jasim. The Governor sighed, eyes glinting with definite amusement as he gave Zorahaida a genuine smile.

'Princess, we are an informal household, though pet monkeys are new to us. Since that animal had done his best to remove your veil and you are now family, will you permit us to see you?'

Zorahaida drew her veil over her head and smiled back. Thank God, during the journey her bruises had faded. This wasn't the most formal of meetings, but it would have been dreadful to have met the Governor wearing the imprint of her father's hand. Even so, she was a jumble of nerves.

Taking her by the shoulders, the Governor kissed her forehead and both her cheeks. 'Welcome, Zorahaida, if I may call you that?'

'Governor, I would be honoured.'

'Zorahaida, as Jasim's wife, you have become family. Within the palace, you may address me as Ibrahim.'

'Thank you, Ibrahim.'

Jasim cleared his throat. 'Uncle, where is Usayd?'

'I've not seen him today.' The Governor looked enquiringly at his daughter. 'Fatima, do you know where he is?'

Fatima bit her lip. 'I am not sure.'

The Governor's eyes narrowed. 'He is in the tavern? Again?'

Zorahaida was watching Jasim closely and she saw his smile fade. Usayd? Who was Usayd? Whoever he was, Jasim was disappointed not to see him.

'Never mind, I shall doubtless see him later,' Jasim said. 'Uncle, I need to discuss the Princess's protection.'

'Of course. You have absconded with the Sultan's favourite child and there are bound to be consequences. Come with me.' The Governor paused. 'Fatima, when you have quite finished playing with that animal, perhaps you might show Jasim's bride the bedchambers on the upper floor. She may choose whichever she prefers.'

Fatima gave her father a dark look. 'With the exception of mine.'

'Obviously, you baggage, with the exception of yours.'

Zorahaida's introduction to Jasim's uncle the Governor hadn't gone quite as she had imagined it would, but she thought it would serve. Hunter had broken the ice. He attached himself firmly to Fatima and whilst Fatima took Zorahaida on a tour of the bedchambers on the upper floor, he clung to his new friend like a limpet.

'So, you've seen the chambers set aside for the ladies of the household,' Fatima said. 'Which one will you choose?'

The chamber they were standing in had the most beautiful carpet. It was covered with stylised flowers worked in blue and white. Unsure of her ground, Zorahaida hesitated. In wealthier households, it was usual for the women in the family to be housed on the upper floors where, in uncertain times, they would be safer. Yet she also remembered Jasim telling her that customs varied from village to village and from household to household.

How were matters arranged here? Where would Jasim sleep? Did he have quarters on the ground floor? Would he summon her when he wanted her, or would he join her on the upper floor?

'You are thinking of Jasim?' Fatima said coyly. 'You wish to know where he sleeps?'

Zorahaida smiled. 'If you please. We haven't

really discussed sleeping arrangements, so I have no idea what he expects.'

'Jasim has always slept below, though his chamber is rather cramped. Now that he is married, I expect he would be glad if you chose one of the larger rooms. Then he may join you whenever he wishes.'

Zorahaida felt her face fall. That wasn't exactly what she'd been hoping to hear. None the less, she nodded briskly. 'Very well. This chamber is airy, the carpet reminds me of Jasim's colours, and I like the window opening out on to the courtyard. I choose this one.'

Fatima gave her a wry grin. 'A wise choice, if I may say so.'

'Oh?'

'With it being at the end of the gallery, this chamber has more privacy. Princess, I must apologise for my manners earlier. I am truly pleased to see Jasim married, he is my favourite cousin. He needs some love in his life.' Her mouth tightened. 'However, I must warn you, if you hurt him in any way, any way whatsoever, I personally will ensure you regret it.'

With that, Fatima danced out of the chamber, Hunter in tow.

* * *

Zorahaida spent what was left of the afternoon watching Maura unpack and organise her belongings. The songbirds were brought up and their gilded cage placed near the light. As for the rest, Maura seemed content to make most of the decisions, which suited Zorahaida just fine because she herself was unable to concentrate. She sat on the bed, silver lute in hand, and stared into the distance. Her mind was in a whirl.

'Mistress, I am pleased to have a chamber close to yours.'

'Aye, Maura, so am I.'

Without conscious thought, Zorahaida's fingers began to dance over the strings, and the bedchamber filled with sound. She was dimly aware of Maura shooting a glance in her direction, and was thankful she didn't have to explain herself. Maura had been with her long enough to know how the lute calmed her. Playing helped order her mind.

Zorahaida was unconcerned by Fatima's parting comment. On the contrary, it was heartening to know that Jasim's cousin was such a loyal supporter. With luck, once Fatima realised that Zorahaida had no intention of hurting Jasim, she would become a friend. If Zorahaida was to be happy here, she would need friends.

She was more concerned with how long Jasim would be closeted with the Governor, and with whether she would see him that evening. She feared she might not. Her stomach tightened.

The reunion between Jasim and his uncle would be complicated, they had much to organise. Jasim had recognised the threat posed by the Sultan. He would, Zorahaida was sure, be doubling the watch. He would be ensuring that her escort, the servants and guards who had come with them from Granada, were properly housed. Perhaps he would be giving some of them posts in her new personal guard. She certainly hoped so. She also hoped Jasim and his uncle understood that, vengeful father or no, there was no way Zorahaida would allow Mondragón Palace to become her prison. She'd had enough of all that.

The more she thought about what Jasim and his uncle would be discussing, the more distressed she became. Her fingers flew over the strings. Maura glanced at her and pursed her lips.

It wasn't pleasant being excluded from discussions. Zorahaida had been excluded for most of her life. Her father the Sultan had never consulted her. On anything.

Today, Jasim was making decisions on her behalf. It didn't help to know that he would be making them with the best of intentions. Unlike her father, Jasim was no tyrant. Nevertheless, Zorahaida longed to be involved. She gave a heavy sigh. Unfortunately, with her arrival so recent, she was in no position to make demands. This was Governor Ibrahim's household and she was merely his nephew's wife. The rules she had so painstakingly learned to survive in her father's palace would not apply here.

'Maura, when you next go downstairs, would you enquire as to Jasim's whereabouts? I need to speak to him.'

'Of course, Mistress. The last I heard he was with the Governor.'

As Zorahaida had feared, Jasim didn't come to her chambers that night. Nor was she summoned to his chamber below. She spent a miserable night, tossing and turning on her feather mattress. The songbirds were silent and she didn't have Hunter's friendly presence to distract her. Since deserting her for Fatima, Hunter hadn't come back.

It wasn't that Zorahaida had been neglected. She had luxuriated in a sumptuous bathhouse.

Mouth-watering lemon chicken had been delivered to her chambers on lustrous tableware. She'd been served the finest wine in delicate Italian glasses. Her bedlinen was silk and gently perfumed with rose and lavender. Maura was within calling distance. She had nothing to complain about.

Except...

She wanted Jasim. She missed the sensual comfort he brought her. Immediately after their marriage, she hadn't known him well enough to know whether she trusted him. Despite this, she had taken great pleasure in the marriage bed. And so had he. It had been extremely encouraging.

Unfortunately, since then, Jasim had kept his distance. Zorahaida didn't like it. Jasim was so polite. So formal. Had he set his heart against her?

It wasn't simply that she missed the lovemaking, Zorahaida missed his company. Lately, even when he was with her, she could sense his withdrawal. She felt hollow inside. Lonely.

As the air cooled, Zorahaida lay on her back trying to visualise the position of the stars as they slowly crossed the heavens. She told herself that Jasim would surely arrive before the hour was out. The hour passed. And then another.

He wasn't coming. Why? Was he too busy? Her chest ached. Did he not care? Had she alienated him for ever by giving him that sleeping draught?

As she lay there, she recalled something else. In the courtyard, Jasim had been relaxed until he'd mentioned Usayd. Then his entire demeanour had shifted, he'd looked disappointed. Hurt. Who was Usayd?

The next morning, Zorahaida was again playing the lute when Maura came in.

'Princess, your husband has asked if you would be so kind as to meet him downstairs. The horses are waiting.'

'We're going out?'

'I believe you are to be given a brief tour of the city.'

The lute forgotten, Zorahaida sprang to her feet. She was at the door when Maura called her back, veil in hand.

'Don't forget this, Mistress.'

'Please come this way, Princess,' Jasim said when she reached the courtyard.

He proceeded to guide her, with much formality, towards the palace gate.

In the street outside, a huge escort awaited. It was much larger than Zorahaida had anticipated, at least twenty men. She missed a step and frowned through her veil. Some of the men she recognised, but...

'Jasim, do we need quite so many men?'

'I take no risks with my wife's safety.'

She couldn't argue, not in front of all those guards, but it would be impossible to have a private conversation. It was most unsatisfactory.

Two hours later, Zorahaida was hot and irritable and incredibly frustrated. It wasn't anything Jasim had done, on the contrary, he'd been most solicitous. So much so, she was convinced he was keeping her at a distance on purpose. She ground her teeth and prayed for a chance to speak to him on her own.

Jasim was intent on honouring his promise of showing her the gorge and her chance came when they dismounted. They walked a little way towards an arched gateway.

'The path winds down to the bottom from here.'

Jasim waved at the great chasm in the earth

carved by the river. He was in the middle of an explanation about the strategic importance of Madinat Runda and the part the gorge played in its military defences, when she interrupted.

'Jasim, have I done something to displease you?' Was he still angry about that wretched sleeping draught? She'd made him helpless for a time and men hated feeling helpless. Was that the problem?

He gave her an enigmatic look. 'Displease me? Of course not.'

Not wishing their escort to hear, she lowered her voice. 'Then why didn't you join me last eve?'

'You missed me.' He smiled and reached for her, before drawing back. He, too, was conscious of their escort. 'My uncle and I were talking until dawn. I didn't want to disturb you.'

Forgetting Jasim couldn't see her expression through her veil, Zorahaida returned his smile. 'You had much to discuss, I am sure.'

His mouth edged up at the corner. 'Most of it centred on you. I am determined to ensure your safety.' He gestured at their escort. 'Whenever you want to go out, you will take these men. Ask for Bashaar ibn Suleiman. He captains these knights and they have been assigned solely to you. You will recognise some faces, I'm sure. Many of them came with us from Granada.'

'Aye, so I noticed. Thank you.'

He grasped her hand as they leaned over to peer into the gorge. They were so high; it was like staring into an abyss. Seagulls were flying far below them. Suddenly dizzy, Zorahaida turned away with a shudder.

'It's like looking down from a cloud.'

They were walking back to the horses when a woman caught her eye. Like her, the woman was veiled, so Zorahaida couldn't see her face, but in this case, she didn't need to. Hunter was riding high on her shoulder, so it had to be Fatima. She was standing with a couple of manservants, staring at a rundown tavern.

'Jasim, isn't that your cousin?'

Jasim froze. 'So help me, it is. She shouldn't be anywhere near that hell-hole.'

He took a step towards Fatima, appeared to change his mind and signalled brusquely for Bashaar ibn Suleiman. 'Captain, be so good as to escort my wife back to the palace.'

'Yes, Master.'

Jasim nudged Zorahaida towards the horses and out of the corner of her eye she saw one of Fatima's servants slip into the tavern.

Jasim's swift change of temper was unsettling. He looked so angry. A knot formed in Zorahaida's stomach. It wasn't fear, she knew Jasim wasn't angry with her. However, something was very wrong. What was going on?

'Zorahaida, you must go,' Jasim said. 'Quickly.'

'Yes, but—'

'*Go.* I'll find you later.'

Zorahaida nodded and permitted the Captain to assist her back on to Spirit. She let out the reins and was preparing to ride on when a man staggered out of the tavern. His tunic was stained and his turban askew. Zorahaida had never seen a man in his cups before but she didn't need anyone to tell her that this one was thoroughly drunk. He could hardly stand.

Jasim's hands fisted and his eyes blazed. He looked angrier than the Sultan in one of his rages.

He won't hurt me.

'Who's that?' she asked.

'Usayd,' came the clipped response.

'Usayd?'

'My older brother. When I last saw him, he was honouring a vow to stop drinking.' He rounded on her, amber eyes blazing fire. 'Good heavens, woman, what are you waiting for? Go.'

Chapter Twelve

Disappointment tight in his gut, Jasim propped himself against a wall, folded his arms and waited until the sound of his wife's escort faded. Usayd had seen him, he was certain.

In the past, Jasim's relationship with his older brother hadn't been easy. As the firstborn son of a celebrated knight and his favourite wife, Usayd had carried the weight of their father's expectations for years. He'd found it a heavy burden because their father, Ismail ibn Osman, had made it plain that he expected Usayd to follow in his footsteps.

Usayd had tried his best, long after it became clear that he wasn't born to be a warrior. He rode and fought well, but he didn't excel. Usayd lacked the lightning reflexes and physical decisiveness that his culture required in a knight.

Later, when Jasim—the son of their father's

second wife—proved to be a natural swords-
man, Usayd took it badly. He began haunting
local taverns. He drank too much. Jasim had
hauled his older brother home more times than
he cared to count, particularly after their father's
death, when Usayd had finally lost hope that one
day he would live up to his father's expectations.

There was no question but that their father Ismail ibn Osman had been a demanding taskmas-
ter. Jasim himself understood what it was like to
feel he was a disappointment, for not once, despite Jasim's success on the tourney circuit, had
his father praised him.

Happily, Usayd's fortunes changed when he
took a wife, Aixa. Aixa proved to be the impetus
his brother needed to take charge of his destiny.
Overnight, Usayd stopped drinking and much
of the old bitterness melted away.

And now? Jasim scowled across the square.
Had Usayd fallen by the wayside? He was braced
to storm across and take his brother by the throat,
when Usayd's gaze met his. It blazed with fierce
intelligence and Jasim caught his breath.

Thank God, Usayd was no more drunk than
he was. What was he up to?

Jasim remained by the wall, watching. Fatima

was approaching Usayd, Zorahaida's monkey on her shoulder.

Years ago, the innkeeper and his family had made a fine living from the merchants who'd flocked to the city, these days it was far less prosperous.

Jasim frowned. He would rather Fatima kept clear of this place, although he had a fair idea why she was here. Before Usayd's marriage, Fatima and Jasim had been united in their concern over Usayd's reliance on the bottle. If Fatima suspected Usayd had reverted to old habits, she'd brave this disreputable tavern, hoping to make him see sense.

Even as Jasim watched, Fatima spoke to his brother. Unfortunately, Jasim was too far away to catch what she said. Usayd shook his head at her and make a chopping motion, plainly urging her to leave.

Fatima did so reluctantly, trailing back across the square with the servants, pausing now and then to look over her shoulder at Usayd. She hadn't noticed Jasim, she was entirely focused on Usayd. Who for some God-forsaken reason was hanging about this rundown tavern pretending to be drunk.

But if Usayd wasn't drinking himself into oblivion, what the devil was going on?

Sending Jasim a final penetrating glance, Usayd gave an imperceptible headshake and went back into the tavern.

Well, whatever Usayd was doing, it was apparent he would brook no interference. He was bound to return to the palace soon and when he did, he had some explaining to do.

Back at Mondragón Palace, Jasim washed away the town dust, put on his house shoes and followed a tantalising thread of melody that led him to Zorahaida's quarters. He wanted to make amends for his earlier manner. When he had sent her home, concern for Usayd had made him far too brusque.

Jasim was all too aware that his relationship with his wife was alarmingly fragile. He had no wish to test it to the point of destruction. A wilful, exceptional woman, Zorahaida had already become a vital part of his life—despite her use of poppy juice.

He put his head round the door. 'May I come in?'

Zorahaida was sitting cross-legged on the bed

and the flow of notes broke off. Her lute flickered silver as she set it aside.

'Jasim.' A smile trembled into being, a gentle, welcoming smile. 'God be praised, you are no longer angry.'

'Angry?' Relieved to find her receptive, he strode across and took her hand before he recalled that he had resolved to give her space to get to know him. Still, what could be more innocent than holding hands? 'I wasn't angry with you, my love. My relationship with my brother is complicated.'

She looked up at him. 'You have resolved your differences?'

'Not entirely, but Usayd is not drunk as I feared. I will speak to him later.'

'I shall be pleased to meet him,' Zorahaida murmured.

'And so you shall, of course.'

She patted the edge of the mattress invitingly. 'Jasim, I have a confession to make and a favour to ask.'

Sitting down, Jasim raised an eyebrow. He kept hold of her hand. 'Do I need to worry?'

She laughed. 'I don't think so. Do you recall the baskets of pigeons I brought from Granada?'

'Certainly.'

'They are carrier pigeons, homed in Córdoba. I have been using them to communicate with my sisters.'

Carrier pigeons? Jasim looked thoughtfully at her. He'd never used carrier pigeons himself, but he knew how useful they were. Birds which had been trained in Córdoba, would invariably fly home. You could release them in France or in far Cathay, and it would make no difference. They would always return to Córdoba.

'So that was what you were doing in the square outside the infirmary at Granada, you were collecting homing pigeons.'

'Aye. My sister Leonor sent them. Jasim, I have been using pigeons to carry letters to her for some while. When Leonor has read them, she forwards them to my other sister Alba. I had written so many letters, the pigeon loft in the Alhambra was almost empty.'

Without conscious thought, Jasim entwined his fingers with hers. 'It's an ingenious idea. The Sultan, I take it, had no idea that you and your sisters were corresponding?'

Her smile was crooked. 'Mercifully, he never found out.'

'Zorahaida, you never cease to surprise me. Is

it true that homing pigeons can fly several hundred miles in a day?'

'Yes, pigeons travel faster than a man on horseback. For example, one could fly from here to Granada in a single day.' Her voice broke. 'I miss my sisters, horribly.'

Jasim nodded, he understood something of what she must be feeling. The rift that had formed between him and Usayd had never completely healed and it had often felt like a thorn in his side. How much worse must Zorahaida feel to be separated from her sisters, not by anger or jealousy, but by the whim of a cruel and overbearing father. Banishment, on pain of death no less, was the harshest of punishments. When her sisters had run away with their Spanish knights, Zorahaida must have felt completely abandoned.

She had found ways to console herself. Writing to her sisters had clearly been a lifeline. He stared at her averted face, still learning its contours, and guiltily aware that in taking her to wife, in removing her from all she knew, he had turned her world upside down for a second time. She must feel completely adrift.

'You want to write to your sisters.'

Dark eyes held his. 'Very much.'

'Please, you must write as often as you wish.'

'Thank you.'

When she lowered her eyelashes, Jasim knew she had more to say. He waited, content simply to look at her. She was so beautiful. With her bruises faded, she took his breath away. The dark, lustrous hair, the way her eyelashes curled, the eyes he never tired of looking at. Yet behind the beauty there were shadows. He ached to kiss her, to do something, anything, to chase away the shadows. She simply wasn't ready; it was beyond frustrating.

'Jasim, I would like to do more than write to Leonor and Alba, I would like to see them. It would be wonderful to invite them to Madinat Runda, but owing to their banishment, I wouldn't dream of asking them.'

While she talked, Jasim watched her mouth; he couldn't stop looking at it. The impulse to kiss her was irresistible. Almost. He shifted away slightly. He must wait. Glorious though their joining had been, Zorahaida didn't know him. He would hold back until they were no longer strangers.

She was looking expectantly at him, and he realised she was waiting for his response. What had she been talking about? Ah, yes, her sisters.

'We could visit your sisters in Castile,' he said.

'Then there will no difficulty with their banishment. I would enjoy meeting them.'

Her face transfigured. 'Oh, thank you. Thank you!'

When her eyelashes lowered a second time, Jasim eyed her cautiously. He had a feeling the conversation was about to take a tricky turn. 'There's more, isn't there?'

He felt a light touch on his wrist.

'Jasim, I need another set of pigeons, ones trained to see Madinat Runda as home. Do you think that would be possible?'

He felt himself tense. 'Why do you need them?'

Her eyelashes lifted. 'To stay in touch with Sama.'

She lifted her shoulders in a nonchalant gesture, but Jasim wasn't fooled. He could sense the steel in her. The determination. She was desperate for his agreement.

He stared at her. He stared so long that if his mind hadn't been busy calculating what harm might come from her writing to her handmaid, he would have had time to count all the pretty green flecks in her eyes.

'Jasim? Do you know if there are homing pigeons in Madinat Runda? May I buy some?' Her fingers tightened on his wrist. 'Please?'

Jasim tore his gaze from hers and stared at a flower on the carpet. The idea of Zorahaida contacting her maid, or anyone else in the Alhambra for that matter, was deeply unsettling. 'I'd rather you didn't.'

She bristled. 'Sama is entirely trustworthy, I assure you.'

'I don't doubt it, my love, under normal circumstances.'

Dark eyes flashed. 'What might that mean?'

'Zorahaida, have you thought how the Sultan would respond if he intercepted your message?'

'He won't do that. My people—' She broke off, biting her lip.

'Zorahaida, I am sure you have many loyal, trustworthy servants in the Alhambra.' He softened his voice. 'I don't want to argue, but you yourself know that your father isn't above using violence to achieve his ends.'

'So, you forbid me to buy more pigeons?'

'For your own good, and that of Sama's, I believe I must.'

She gazed stonily at him. 'You said you weren't angry, yet it seems you are.'

He huffed out a breath. 'Don't be ridiculous.'

She tore her hand from his and pushed to her

feet. 'You don't trust me.' She began pacing up and down.

'Of course I trust you.'

She stopped mid-stride and shook her head. 'No, you don't. You feel threatened by the very idea of me writing to Sama.' Her voice softened. 'Jasim, there's no need to feel threatened.'

'I don't.' Rubbing his brow, wishing the conversation had taken a happier turn, Jasim stood. 'I simply would rather you left the palace and all it represents behind you.'

'I can't do that; it is part of me, and it always will be.' Biting her lip, she resumed her pacing. 'This is about asserting your authority, isn't it?'

He stared at her, aghast. 'What?'

'You are my husband, and you think that means I should bow to your every wish.'

He sighed. 'That is unfair. As I mentioned in the carriage on our way here, where matters are contentious, I would prefer we had open discussions and found common ground. I meant it. Zorahaida, I'd like our marriage to be a partnership.'

She glowered at him. 'Whatever you say, you are resentful and angry. You can't forget that I drugged you, even though it was in your best interest. You want blind obedience. I have to say,

I don't much like it.' Her voice cracked. 'Especially when all I want is to write to Sama.' She turned away.

Jasim stared bleakly at her rigid back. He had no desire to come across as domineering, but he didn't want her to come to harm. His chest ached, he could feel her distress and it was tearing him in two. If he wasn't careful, this marriage was going to be a disaster. Already, he felt as though he had failed her.

Without doubt, a better man would know how to handle her. He had no idea. He was the son of an insignificant second wife who had died in childbirth, and she was a Nasrid princess.

Had he overreached himself, asking for her hand? Did she think he was beneath her? Was that what this was truly about?

He had sought her out with the best of intentions, and despite every effort they were arguing.

Jasim didn't understand women. He never had. Except…

The face of his cousin, Fatima, jumped into his mind. Fatima liked him, she always had. As children they'd been inseparable. They would chase around the water gardens; they would creep into the kitchen to steal almond biscuits cooling on the table. To be sure, the bond between him and his cousin had weakened when he had begun his training as a knight, but he and Fatima remained close.

'Fatima,' he murmured. He understood Fatima.

She swung round, glowering. 'I beg your pardon?'

Ignoring her scowl, Jasim took her hand, pressed a kiss into her palm and folded her fingers over it, hoping she would understand what he was unable to put into words.

Know that you are precious to me, precious above all things.

'Zorahaida, I shall consider your request to write to Sama. In the meantime, I would ask you to wait. Now, if you would excuse me, my love, I need to speak to Fatima.'

Zorahaida stared frowningly at the door after her husband had gone. It took a few moments more for her to realise that the prickling behind her eyes meant that tears weren't far away.

Irritated that a brief exchange of words with Jasim was able to upset her so, and uncomfortably aware that in accusing him of wanting to assert his authority over her, she was doing him a disservice, she tutted under her breath and went to kneel before the travelling chest Maura had placed along one wall. Where was her writing box?

As she tossed silks and satins aside in the search for the box, she wondered if Jasim would learn to forgive her for giving him that poppy juice. He must. She truly hated being at odds with him.

She told herself she ought to know better. Over the years, she'd been at odds with her father the Sultan many times. She'd been angry with him. She'd disobeyed him. Lightly she touched her cheek, remembering how humiliated she'd felt when her father had struck her.

She leaned back on her heels and wrapped her arms about her middle. Her stomach was churning. This was much, much worse.

How was it that a relatively minor disagreement with Jasim made her feel utterly bereft? There'd been times when she'd hated her father. Loathed him. And not once had he made her feel as though the world was falling apart.

A mere frown from Jasim, on the other hand...

This is ridiculous, she thought, diving back into her travelling chest. Jasim was just a man. She'd made the mistake of assuming that their sensual compatibility meant their minds would align in other, more important, ways. It was entirely possible that she and Jasim would spend the rest of their lives arguing.

No, she had to be wrong about that. Jasim would never hit her. He was honourable and chivalrous and very protective. He was the soul of generosity. He'd insisted on buying Spirit at the horse fair, and unlike her father, Zorahaida was confident he would never use the mare as a means of bending her to his will.

She and Jasim hadn't been together for long. They would learn to get on, eventually. They must.

Where on earth was that writing box? Ah, there it was, hiding beneath an embroidered shawl.

Reverently, she drew it out. The box was in-laid with mother of pearl in orderly, geometric patterns. Leonor had given it to her years ago, at a time when Zorahaida had no need to write letters. The precision and neatness of the design had always appealed. Zorahaida gave an ironic smile as she lifted it from the travelling chest and took it to a side table. Leonor could have had no idea how indispensable the writing box would become. These days, it was in constant use, and that seemed likely to continue.

Drawing up a stool, Zorahaida lifted the lid.

Parchment rustled as she took it out. She trimmed a quill, uncorked the ink, and hunched over the parchment only to discover that it wasn't as easy to order her mind as it ought to be. Being at odds with Jasim was truly unsettling. She stared at a circle on the side of the writing box. Was she wrong about Jasim? Might he prove to be as intransigent as her father?

With a groan, she pushed Jasim from her mind and forced herself to concentrate.

Leonor must be told what had happened. She needed to know that Zorahaida had married and was living in Governor Ibrahim's house in Madinat Runda. Zorahaida would also tell her that Jasim had agreed that he and Zorahaida could visit Leonor and Alba in Castile.

At last the three of us can meet again!

Thoughtfully, she chewed the end of her quill. All was not lost as far as Jasim was concerned, he had been extremely amenable regarding her sisters.

Dipping her quill into the ink, she started to write.

The letter was half-written when the door opened and Hunter scampered in, swiftly followed by Fatima. Hunter clambered on to her lap, forcing Zorahaida to put the quill down and cork the ink. Hunter had a bad record as far as ink was concerned and she had no wish for ink to spill on the beautiful carpet.

'Excuse the interruption, Princess,' Fatima said. 'I was wondering if you would care to accompany me to the infirmary.'

Zorahaida lifted an eyebrow. 'You've been speaking to Jasim.'

'Aye, he mentioned that you were in the habit of visiting the hospital in Granada. Our hospital will undoubtedly be smaller than the one you are familiar with, but Jasim knows I occasionally help there. He thought you would like to see it.'

Zorahaida guided Hunter to her shoulder and rose. What else had Jasim told his cousin? Was Fatima meant to keep her occupied so that she would forget about wanting to write to Sama? Was this an attempt to divert her?

'I would love to see your hospital,' she said, smiling. 'Do we ride or go on foot?'

'It is only around the corner, so we will walk.' Fatima grimaced. 'Even so, Jasim insists we take an escort.'

'Very well.'

Fatima waited by the door whilst Zorahaida found her veil and cloak. Zorahaida was pretty certain that whatever Jasim had said to Fatima, he wouldn't have mentioned her wish to buy another set of pigeons. The only way to find out was to ask.

'Fatima, did Jasim say anything about homing pigeons?'

'Homing pigeons? No, he didn't.' She paused. 'You brought some with you, I know. Why do you need more?'

Zorahaida made her voice light. Casual. 'I need birds trained here so they will return to Madinat Runda. Then, if I can find a means of getting them to Granada, my friends there will be able to write to me. Is there a pigeon loft in town? I should like to visit it after we've been to the hospital.'

'Very well.' Fatima glanced toward the curl of parchment lying next to the writing box. 'And your correspondence?'

'That can wait.'

The infirmary proved to be close to the tavern favoured by Jasim's brother and several men were grouped around the tables in the square.

As Zorahaida and Fatima strolled by, Zorahaida peered round their guards, looking for Usayd. She couldn't see him, not that she was certain she would recognise him. Besides, a cursory glance was enough to tell her that today's customers were a rough-looking, edgy group. To a man they were scowling. Their beards were unkempt, and they were wearing stained leather jerkins with a distinctly military look to them. Zorahaida had never knowingly seen a mercenary, but these men were surely soldiers for hire. There wasn't a weapon in sight. None the less, instinct told her they were armed and dangerous.

Anxious to avoid drawing their gaze, Zorahaida tugged her veil closely about her and looked elsewhere. She would have felt happier with Jasim at the head of their escort, not that that would serve today. She wanted to buy those pigeons, just in case her husband wasn't as amenable as she hoped.

The tour of the infirmary passed without incident and Zorahaida and Fatima retraced their steps past the inn, still amid their escort.

It was a relief to see that the rough-looking men had gone. Breathing more easily, Zorahaida turned to Fatima.

'The pigeon loft?' she asked.

'This way.' Fatima spoke to Captain Bashaar

and they left the square and turned down a quiet side street.

Zorahaida could see that the street had once been lined with shops, but the shutters were up and there was little sign of life. A lone water carrier, a pot on his head, was calling for custom.

'It is sad to see so many of the shops are closed,' Zorahaida murmured.

'Aye, this was the street of the carpet sellers. It used to be a hive of industry. Usayd dreams of reviving it.' Fatima pointed down the street. 'The pigeon loft is on the corner at the end.'

If the pigeon trainer was surprised to see two veiled ladies and an armed escort on his doorstep, his face didn't betray it. With a flourish he indicated a rickety flight of stairs.

'This way, if you please,' he said, whistling slightly as he spoke thanks to the gaps in his teeth.

Zorahaida glanced at Captain Bashaar. 'We shouldn't be long. Please guard the door.'

The stairs creaked as they climbed and at one point Zorahaida even felt them shift. She turned to the pigeon seller. 'These stairs are safe, aren't they?'

'Been here for years, Mistress. I reckon they'll see me out.'

Fatima gasped as the door to the loft was opened and a pungent smell reached them. 'Ugh, that smell.'

Behind her veil, Zorahaida smiled. 'It's one of the perils of bird-keeping, I'm afraid. It will be even stronger inside. If you can't bear it, you could wait here on the landing.'

'You're too kind,' Fatima said in a choked voice. 'I believe I will.'

Zorahaida ducked her head and entered the loft as behind her, the stairs groaned. The walls of the pigeon loft were so thin, sound carried well. Fatima, she thought with a grin, was going back downstairs.

The aviary was filled with plump-looking, contented pigeons. Zorahaida decided to buy a basket at once, in case Jasim proved to be intransigent about her writing to Sama. She was reaching for her purse when she heard a bang and a muffled cry.

'What on earth?'

Outside, a man screamed, and she heard the chilling clash of steel hitting steel. Their guards were under attack! The building shook in a succession of thunderous bangs and crashes. The pigeon seller whimpered.

'Fatima?' Wishing that Jasim was with her,

Zorahaida dashed for the door. Her heart was banging like a drum and her mouth was dry. '*Fatima!* Are you all right?'

The door flew open and a bear-like shape charged straight at her. A huge fist lifted and struck the side of her head. The last thing Zorahaida heard was the shriek of the pigeon keeper as a black cloud swallowed her whole.

Chapter Thirteen

Jasim climbed the stairs to the women's quarters. On reflection, he'd decided to agree to his wife's request to communicate with Sama and he wanted to tell her immediately. He gave a wry smile. Zorahaida would probably write to her handmaid anyway and he would gain nothing but rancour in trying to prevent her. He risked pushing her away and he didn't want that.

Almost by accident Jasim had found the woman of his heart. The odds against them meeting, let alone marrying, had been steep from the start. A chance in a million had led him to offering for her. And yet another chance in a million had forced Sultan Tariq into agreeing.

Jasim wasn't sure he believed in destiny, but he was beginning to think that their marriage was written in the stars. He'd never imagined he would feel so passionately about any woman. It was most unexpected. And not entirely pleasant. What if he lost her?

It was a chilling thought. As was the realisation that he was largely responsible for her happiness. A happy wife would ensure a harmonious marriage.

All of which meant that he couldn't afford to let her brood about writing to Sama. If fortune was with him, he would catch her before she left for the hospital with Fatima.

He pushed open the bedchamber door. 'Zorahaida?'

The songbirds were singing but the chamber was empty. Fatima had obviously got there first.

Lying on a side table was a fabulous writing box. Wandering over, Jasim ran his fingers admiringly over the mother-of-pearl inlay. The workmanship was second to none. Seeing a small roll of parchment next to the box, he idly picked it up. She was writing to her sisters.

Not wishing to invade her privacy, he dropped the parchment back on to the table.

'Jasim? Jasim! Where the devil are you?'

Recognising Usayd's voice, Jasim strode from the bedchamber and on to the gallery overlooking the courtyard. He leaned over the railing.

'Get down here, Jasim. This is important. I've been looking for you everywhere.'

At the foot of the stairs, Usayd gave him the briefest of arm-clasps. 'Sorry to be abrupt, it is good to see you, Brother.'

'And you. Usayd, I've been meaning to ask you—'

Usayd shook his head. 'Later. I have pressing news concerning your wife. Come with me. Farid is saddling Blade as we speak.'

Jasim gripped his brother's arm. 'My wife is in the infirmary with Fatima. She is fine.'

Usayd shook his head. 'For your sake, Jasim, I hope that's true. For pity's sake, listen. I fear we have little time. I was at the tavern earlier, and before you say anything, I was not drinking. I was listening. The past few days have been interesting, to say the least.'

By the time they reached the stables, Jasim understood the need for urgency. If what Usayd suspected was true, the Sultan had sent a band of mercenaries to Madinat Runda to wait for Zorahaida's arrival. The mercenaries, not having a grand procession to slow them down, had been able to travel at speed. They'd overtaken Jasim and Zorahaida and had been using the tavern as a base for some days.

'Those men are close as clams,' Usayd said, whilst Jasim dragged on his riding boots. 'I am not certain what they're planning but they seem desperate enough to murder their mothers for a silver dirham. Be that as it may, I heard enough to raise my suspicions. Is it possible they are the Sultan's men?'

Jasim thought about the slow and stately wedding procession through the Emirate, and grimaced. 'It's entirely possible,' he murmured, pushing to his feet. 'I'll explain fully shortly, but in brief, the Sultan was reluctant for us to leave, and my wife decided we would be safer if we left the palace quietly. However, once free of Granada she made a grand show of our progress. It was like a circus—baggage carts, servants, outriders. We travelled at a snail's pace. A band of mercenaries could easily have overtaken us.'

Usayd nodded. 'So I thought.'

Cold sweat broke out on Jasim's brow. He had wondered if they might be followed but it had never occurred to him that they might be overtaken. If his beautiful wife hadn't drugged him out of his mind, it might have done.

'You think they have orders to kidnap her?'

Usayd grimaced. 'Possibly.' His eyes said something else. His eyes said that kidnapping was merely one of the fates that the Sultan had in store for his daughter.

Blade was waiting by the stable door, Jasim snatched the reins from Farid, vaulted into the saddle and dug in his heels.

Usayd's voice chased him into the street. 'Where are you going?'

'The hospital.'

'I'll follow with Farid. You might need help.'

A flock of pigeons had taken over the square outside the hospital, the air was full of feathers and whirring wings. Jasim urged Blade past the birds on the ground and rode directly to the infirmary door. He pounded on it until a porter slid back the grille.

'Can I help, Master?'

'I'm looking for my cousin, I believe she visited earlier with a friend.'

'You missed them, Master,' the porter said. 'The ladies were here earlier, they left about an hour ago.'

Jasim frowned. 'An hour ago?'

The infirmary wasn't far from the palace, they should have returned long since.

'Did you notice if they brought an escort?'

'Indeed, Master. I noticed it most particularly

as I've never seen your cousin with more than a couple of servants before.'

Ignoring the icy feeling in his guts, Jasim nodded his thanks and wheeled Blade about. Several pigeons rose from the ground, wings beating.

Usayd and Farid trotted into the square and as they joined him, more pigeons took to the air.

'No luck?' Usayd asked.

'They left an hour ago.'

'Where could they be?'

Jasim found himself watching the pigeons and something clicked into place. Zorahaida wouldn't be trying to buy pigeons, would she? Not when he'd told her that he was still considering whether she might write to Sama.

'She is a Nasrid princess,' he muttered. 'Of course she would.'

His brother looked at him. 'Eh?'

'Usayd, Farid, come with me.'

The street of the carpet sellers resembled the aftermath of a battlefield. Heart in his throat, Jasim's gaze skimmed over a guard whose eyes were gazing sightlessly to heaven. He had known the fellow since boyhood. Regret sliced through him. Another of his uncle's men was bent over a comrade, efficiently using the cloth from his

turban as a tourniquet to stem the flow of blood.
A couple of other bodies in filthy clothing he
didn't recognise lay nearby. Doubtless they were
the mercenaries Usayd had warned him about.

There was no sign of Zorahaida or Fatima.

Jasim dived from the saddle. He was through
the door of the pigeon-keeper's house so quickly
he almost tripped over Fatima, who was lying at
the bottom of the stairs, groaning.

'Fatima, what happened?' He helped her into
a sitting position and whipped off her veil. She
looked utterly dazed. 'Is Zorahaida in the loft?'

His cousin seemed to be having difficulty
focusing, but she managed a slow headshake.
'She's gone.'

Jasim's stomach fell away. 'Gone?'

'Strangers stormed in. Vicious men. They
shoved me down the stairs and they must have
hit Zorahaida, because when they dragged her
out of here, she was insensible.'

Rage descended on him, like a red mist. 'And
then?'

Fatima gave him a blank look. 'One of them
struck me. I must have fainted. I'm sorry, Jasim,
I saw nothing else.'

Leaving Fatima in the care of his brother, Jasim

galloped to the southern gate next to the garrison. Fortunately, the sergeant recognised him.

'Welcome home, Jasim ibn Ismail.'

'My thanks, Sergeant. I'm afraid the niceties will have to wait. I need help.'

The sergeant straightened. 'I am honoured to be of service.'

Unfortunately, the sergeant had grim news, for upon enquiry, he confirmed Jasim's fears. A band of about eight men had left Madinat Runda an hour since. They looked, the sergeant told him, like traders down on their luck, for their cart held a single, moth-ravaged carpet. 'It would take more than a miracle for someone to buy that carpet,' the sergeant said. 'It was filthy.'

Jasim ground his teeth. It sounded as though the Sultan's men, for he was in no doubt as to who was behind this, had bundled an unconscious Zorahaida into a carpet. Still, all was not lost, Blade would have no trouble catching up with a cart.

'Thank you, Sergeant.' Jasim wheeled Blade round to face the road. 'I need you to drum up a *conroi* of knights from the garrison.'

The sergeant's eyes widened. 'How many knights?'

'As many as you can muster. Tell them to

follow me, I shall be tailing that cart. Oh, my brother Usayd and my squire may well come after me. Be so good as to tell them what I'm doing.'

The sergeant saluted. 'Yes, Master.'

Jasim found the cart abandoned a few miles down the road. A rumpled heap of carpet lay in the dust next to it. A vivid vision of Zorahaida lying lifeless beneath it catapulted him from the saddle.

Pulse banging in his ears, he flicked back the carpet. Nothing. Warily, he leaned in and sniffed, hoping to catch the scent of roses, anything that might indicate he was on the right track. Again, nothing. Just the musty smell of ancient carpet.

He was examining tracks left by the mercenaries when the thud of hoofs alerted him to the contingent of knights from the garrison. And not just the knights, his brother Usayd and Farid were with them.

Usayd looked enquiringly at him. 'Your wife?'

'Gone,' Jasim said, clearing his throat.

'She's alive?' Usayd asked, bluntly.

'I can see no other reason why they would take her.' Mastering his emotions with difficulty, for to believe otherwise would unman him, Jasim remounted and pointed in the direction the mercenaries had taken. 'Judging by the hoofprints, one of their horses is bearing extra weight.'

'She's sharing a horse with a mercenary.'

'Aye. It's odd though, they appear to be headed south. It makes more sense for them to be taking the westerly road.'

Thoughtfully, Usayd stroked his beard. 'I disagree. They're heading for the coast.'

Jasim blinked. 'They're putting her on a ship?'

'I believe so. Merchants use them all the time. Given a fair wind, a ship can travel a hundred miles a day. Maybe more.' He gave a crooked smile. 'Even with several changes of horse, we'll struggle to match that. If the mercenaries are taking your wife back to the Alhambra, my guess is they'll board a ship bound for Salobreña.'

'That makes sense,' Jasim said. He remembered Zorahaida mentioning that she and her sisters had lived in the Salobreña fort when they'd been children. 'Sultan Tariq has strong links with Salobreña. We'll head for the coast. There's a chance we'll catch them before they board.'

Usayd was frowning at the bedraggled heap of carpet. 'Those men will be hard pressed to pass as merchants with a woman as prisoner.'

His mouth twisted. 'They might be slavers, I suppose.'

Jasim lifted an eyebrow. 'Usayd, do you truly believe mercenaries in the pay of Sultan Tariq will care what people will think?'

Jasim gave Blade his head and the rest of their party thundered after him. Anxiety churned in his belly. He felt vulnerable and nauseous. He was afraid. Which was fine. Fear had its uses— in battle it kept you alive. Fear had to be controlled though, you couldn't permit it to swamp you.

As one of the most celebrated knights in Al-Andalus, Jasim was renowned for his cool head. For his calm. Yet now he felt as though he was riding into battle without his armour.

He needed to regain focus. His glanced at his squire. In practice sessions, Farid often needed reminding to concentrate on his goals and to put everything else out of his mind. Jasim must follow his own advice.

They would catch the mercenaries before they boarded ship. He would rescue Zorahaida.

Despite Jasim's efforts, focus remained elusive. As they pounded towards the coast, he couldn't stop worrying. Saving his wife was his goal, so that was fine. It was allowed. The problem was that his imagination didn't stop there. It kept throwing up images of Zorahaida hurt. Of her being beaten into submission and tied up. Of her being taken back to her father and locked up in that isolated tower for all time.

Losing her like this made his earlier dream for a harmonious marriage appear laughable. A harmonious marriage? Worthless. He wanted her back on any terms.

She could tempt him every day, she could argue all she wished and lead him a merry dance. That was what he wanted. He lived to see her again.

If he could only get her back in one piece, all would be well.

Some days later

When Zorahaida woke, she could scarcely move. Her head felt as though it was four times its usual size, and her throat was so dry she couldn't swallow. When she tried to speak, nothing emerged but a horrible croak.

Disorientated, she had one thought. Water. She was desperate for a drink.

Hand to her head, she rolled on to her side. It was then that she saw raw marks on her wrist. It throbbed. Rope burns? Her other wrist was equally sore. Had she been tied up? She couldn't remember.

Frowning, she thought back, vaguely wondering why it was so hard to think. If she weren't so thirsty, she'd go back to sleep. This was surely a nightmare.

Images, fragments of memory, it was hard to say what they were, passed through her mind. She had been looking at pigeons. A bear of a man had hit her. He must have tied her up. She remembered lying, half out of her senses, across a horse's withers. The horse had been badly groomed, and it stank. When she'd woken, she'd complained of thirst. Rough hands had forced something down her throat, and she'd slept again.

This had happened again and again. She'd heard men talking, though none of them had addressed her directly. As far as they'd been concerned, she didn't exist. She'd been a ghost. There'd been much jolting and banging and then, after a particularly long sleep, a rocking motion. The only good thing she could remember was the smell of the sea.

Had she been on a ship? She must have been, the smell of the sea was most distinctive, she remembered it from when she'd lived at Castle Salobreña.

Her head thudded. Why couldn't she tell reality from fantasy? Everything was such a jumble. Everything except...

Jasim! Where was Jasim?

Thirst temporarily forgotten, she sat up so fast, her head swam.

'Maura?'

The chamber in which she was lying came slowly into focus and goosebumps formed on her skin. The ceiling above her, with its froth of delicate plasterwork, was chillingly familiar. She must still be dreaming. There was no Maura, not here. Maura was in Madinat Runda, whilst she...

She was in her tower bedchamber in the Alhambra Palace.

Jasim was miles away in the west.

A carafe and glass of juice sat by the bedside. Hand trembling, for Zorahaida didn't think she'd drunk fruit juice in an age, she reached for the glass. It was orange juice and it tasted like heaven. Shakily, she poured another glass, drank it and fell back against the pillows, exhausted. She was as weak as a kitten.

Her father had brought her back to the Alhambra. He'd had her drugged.

Tears prickled at the back of her eyes. Was

this how Jasim had felt after she'd given him the poppy juice? Utterly wretched?

No wonder he'd been so angry.

The questions went round and round, blurring in her mind like a fleece of wool before it had been spun into yarn. Where was Jasim? Had he tried to follow her?

God let him come after me. Please.

But, no, that wouldn't do. Even in her bruised and wounded state, Zorahaida was hopeful her father wouldn't kill her. But Jasim? Jasim was another matter. If he had the temerity to appear in the palace, his life would end. Pain pierced her. Jasim mustn't die! It would be far better if he remained in the west and forgot she ever existed.

Zorahaida pushed the sheet away. She must see her father. It was imperative she knew his state of mind, his plans... Stifling a groan, she rolled out of bed. Her head thumped and waves of blackness swam across her vision. She could barely see.

She picked up the silver handbell. Who would come? Sama? Or had her father, in his fury, dispensed with Sama? She rang the bell.

Merciful heaven, let Sama answer this summons.

It was a while before anyone came. While she

waited, she forced herself to stumble about the chamber. Her legs had lost all strength, it was as though she hadn't used them in days. And that, she realised, was most likely the truth. Had her abductors drugged her the entire time?

She reached the spot where the gilded birdcage had once stood. Cleared of her belongings, the chamber looked empty and impersonal. There was no lute, no Hunter peering out from beneath the bed. No colourful shawls draped across the window ledge, nothing to show that the room had once been hers.

At length a footstep sounded on the stairs. A key grated—she had been locked in!—and the door opened.

'You rang, Princess?' a veiled maidservant asked.

The maidservant was tall and strongly built. Zorahaida didn't recognise her voice. She took a slow, steadying breath. 'I should like to speak to Sama.'

'Sama is not here,' the maidservant said.

'Where is she?'

'Princess, I have no idea. Your handmaid has disappeared.'

The maidservant stepped towards her and a bunch of keys at her waist chinked. This was no maidservant, Zorahaida realised. This was her jailer. She kept her head high and her voice steady.

'To whom am I speaking?'

'I am Amira.'

'Amira, I should like to see my father the Sultan.'

'Very well. If you are ready, I have instructions to take you to the bathhouse. After that you may see the Sultan.' Amira turned briefly towards the door and lowered her voice. 'I should warn you, Princess, you must brace yourself. Your father is very ill.'

That turn to the door suggested that Amira was wary of being overheard. Was she or wasn't she her jailer? Confused and still struggling to order her thoughts, Zorahaida decided to withhold judgement. If Amira felt like talking, she might prove useful.

'My father didn't wish to lose me,' Zorahaida murmured. 'It is possible he is feigning his illness to get attention.'

'Princess, I haven't been in service here long, but I understand Sultan Tariq is genuinely ill. He asks for you every day. Sometimes, he seems to have forgotten you are married. There have been many days when he appears to believe you never left this tower.'

'And on other days?'

'On other days he appears relatively well. Overall, I have no doubt he is pining for you.'

Clad once more in the finest Granada silk, Zorahaida passed line after line of guards and was bowed into one of the smaller throne rooms.

The Sultan was alone, seated on a cushioned couch. In the weeks since Zorahaida had seen him, he was much changed. He looked gaunt and grey. Shrunken. His white robes swamped him. The enormous ruby glinted in his turban, but today its size served only to belittle him. Sultan Tariq looked lonely and sad and very, very old.

Holding back a gasp of shock, Zorahaida prostrated herself on the cool tiles.

'My dove, at last.' Her father's voice, thinner and higher than she would have thought possible, floated over her head. 'Where have you been? Please, come and sit beside me.'

Concern warred with shock. The word 'please' wasn't usually in her father's vocabulary.

Rising, unable to take her gaze from her father's face, she went towards him. Amira hadn't lied. Her father was seriously ill.

Was he dying?

Tossing back her veil, the better to see him, Zorahaida approached the couch.

Her father's mouth turned down as he, in turn, studied her. 'You are too thin, my dove,' he said. 'Have you not been eating?'

'No, Father, I don't believe I have.'

'That won't do.' Smiling weakly, he gestured at a golden dish on a stand. It was filled with sugared almonds. 'Your favourite sweetmeats are waiting for you. Please, help yourself.'

Again, that 'please' was disturbing. Zorahaida's head throbbed as she stood before him, struggling to work out what was wrong.

'Father, those men you paid to abduct me—'

His head jerked. 'You were abducted?'

His expression was one of shock and innocence and it looked convincing. Whatever was wrong with her father, Zorahaida would swear that at this moment he truly had no memory of what he had done.

'Father, you must remember. Your men drugged me. They dragged me hither and yon for days without food. I believe I was bundled on to a ship, but whatever they gave me was so powerful that I cannot be sure. When I came back to myself, I found myself in my tower apartment.'

She received a look of utter bemusement. 'Weren't you here, all long, my dove?'

'No. I am married. Father, you must remember. I went to live with my husband.'

Her father gave her a helpless look and it came to her that Sultan Tariq had become a bear without claws. He was sitting alone in his den, waiting to die.

'No sweetmeats, my dove?'

'No, thank you, I need something a little more sustaining. Father, I shall return to my apartment.'

I need to think.

A wrinkled hand reached out. It shook pitifully. 'You will visit tomorrow?'

'I shall try.' Perhaps by then she would feel a little stronger. There was so much to absorb and in her weakened state, she was overwhelmed. Grief. Anger. No, not anger, frustration. Fury. Her father had coldly set about separating her from Jasim, yet it felt wrong to challenge him on it when he was so ill. That would be beyond cruel.

'You will eat?' he said, plaintively. 'I can't have you fading away.'

'Be assured I shall eat.' Torn, Zorahaida drew in a breath. Her father might be ill, but he must surely have some memory, and although she was faint with hunger, she couldn't leave without mentioning Jasim. 'Father, do you remember Jasim?'

'Jasim?' Slowly the Sultan shook his head. 'I don't believe so.'

'Jasim ibn Ismail, he is a knight, a champion and he—'

'Ismail?' Her father's eyes turned to slits. 'I remember Ismail ibn Osman. Damned renegade.'

'Jasim is his son. I married him; do you remember?'

The Sultan stiffened and his dark eyes flashed with a hint of the old fire. 'Madinat Runda. You deserted me and went to Madinat Runda.' The fire faded as quickly as it had appeared, and he gave a sickly smile. 'Still, you are back where you belong and that pleases me, very much. My dove, are you sure you won't have a sugared almond?'

Zorahaida drew down her veil and turned away. Her father's voice came after her, weaker than it had been when he was in his prime, but audible, none the less.

'Daughter, you will be pleased to know what you will not be returning to Madinat Runda. Ever. You will forget Jasim ibn Ismail. If you as much as mention his name in my presence, an assassin will be dispatched to the west with orders to kill him. And, champion or no, Jasim ibn Ismail will die.'

Chapter Fourteen

Jasim tipped his head back and frowned at the dark shape that was the Princess's tower. A stiff breeze had been blowing through Granada all day and a mass of cloud obscured the moon and most of the stars. Autumn was on its way.

Tonight, the change in season was a blessing. Light glimmered faintly in the top window and his spirits lifted. Jasim had got a message to and from Captain Yusuf ibn Safwan, so he knew that Zorahaida was back in her tower. That light was a beacon of hope. She was up there.

It was time his luck turned. When Jasim and his party of knights had reached the coast, autumn had been working against them. Frustratingly, they had missed the mercenaries by the narrowest of margins and when they'd tried to board the next ship to Salobreña, a sudden squall had prevented their ship from casting off. Even more frustrating, a quick succession of storms had followed, further delaying their departure. Jasim and his knights had been forced to spend several days in port.

In short, the mercenaries—and Zorahaida—had escaped them. However, as Jasim's brother Usayd had pointed out, since they knew Zorahaida was being taken to the Alhambra, her destination was scarcely a secret.

Jasim had no wish to encounter Sultan Tariq. He'd given the man enough chances, but over and over he had shown himself to be a tyrant and a bully. The Sultan had no sense of honour and not a shred of decency.

Zorahaida's abduction proved without doubt that negotiating with the Sultan was impossible. Her father was governed by self-interest and whim—dealing with him was like walking on shifting sands. What the Sultan agreed to one day was likely to be overturned the next.

Which was why Jasim was, once again, standing in the dark at the foot of the Princess's tower, listening to the grasses rustle in the dusk. He put his hand on the rope, preparing to climb.

Usayd's doubtful whisper reached him through the gloom. 'Jasim, this is madness.'

'Have faith, Brother. I've done it before and survived.'

Usayd sighed. 'That's a mercy, but are you sure there's no other way?'

'Her apartments are in this tower.'

'Well, I am thankful you have found someone to love,' Usayd responded in his matter-of-fact voice. 'Although I'd rather there was another way of getting her back.'

'If there were, I wouldn't be doing this.' Jasim paused. The word 'love' was ringing in his mind like an alarm bell. 'Usayd, how are you so sure I love her?'

Usayd snorted. 'I've been watching you since we left Madinat Runda. You've been your usual single-minded self, but I've never seen you gnashing your teeth quite so much. Frankly, you're a wreck. You adore that woman. You wouldn't be going to this trouble if you didn't love her.'

Jasim's mind raced. Did he love Zorahaida? For days he'd been conscious of an urgent and terrible need to see her again. To hold her. To make her safe for all time. The feeling was relentless, it had him in its grip and he was coming to see it would never let him go.

'She is my world,' he said slowly.

'That's it. That is love. It is exactly how I feel

about Aixa.' Usayd gripped his shoulder. 'Have you told her?'

'We're usually too busy arguing,' Jasim admitted ruefully. Could what he felt for his wife truly be love?

'You're an idiot, Jasim, a stubborn idiot.'

'Most likely.'

Jasim tested the rope. It held firm. Captain Yusuf ibn Safwan was proving to be a staunch and efficient ally; he had sent word that the rope would be in place, and so it was. Training his gaze on the top of the curtain wall, Jasim marked the places where lights were showing. If his memory served, each light signified a guard post.

'Usayd, swear to me that if you hear an alarm, you'll take to your heels.'

By way of response, his brother indicated a small basket sat at his feet. He'd brought it from Madinat Runda, Jasim had noticed it tied to his brother's horse before this, though he'd been too eaten up with worry to concern himself about the contents.

'Jasim, I need to warn you, I'd like to—'

Jasim made his voice firm. 'Whatever you're about to suggest, no. No heroics, and no delays.

Aixa would have my head if you came to harm. The first sign of trouble, get out of here.'

Clapping his brother on his shoulder, Jasim started to climb. He took it slowly and steadily even though he felt as jumpy as a cat. His nerves were torn to shreds. The last time he'd done this he'd been obsessed with trade agreements and full of noble ideas. He'd been gambling on the possibility that winning the Princess would bring hope to his district and free the Princess from her tyrant of a father. Fired up after winning the Sultan's tournament, he'd been playing the hero.

This time, far more was at stake. He was fighting for the woman he loved.

Usayd was far too perceptive.

I love Zorahaida.

The realisation was so disconcerting Jasim almost lost his grip. He paused for a moment and hung at the midpoint with the rope shifting from side to side and his knee bumping against the wall.

I love Zorahaida.

Jasim had always assumed love wasn't for him. Having lost his mother as a babe, he couldn't claim to understand it. Long ago, he'd concluded that such feelings were an indulgence. An indulgence? Zorahaida was far more than a mere indulgence. Having her at his side was a necessity.

I love her.

He smiled.

'Jasim, all is well?' Usayd hissed from the base of the tower where a small light glowed. His perceptive fool of a brother had opened the lantern.

'Never better. For pity's sake, shut off that light.'

A creaking noise caught Zorahaida's attention. It was vaguely familiar. Her heart leaped and she stared in disbelief at the window facing the mountain range and the wilderness beyond the palace wall.

The shutters were ajar. Her gaze fixed on a sturdy-looking rope fastened around the central pillar. Heart in her mouth, she nudged a cushion to the window and dropped to her knees. The rope was rough to the touch and pulled so taut someone must be climbing it.

Jasim! Holding her breath, she pushed the shutters open the rest of the way and leaned out over the window ledge.

A light flickered briefly below. Zorahaida glimpsed a rope trailing down and a man climbing up. Another man was standing in the gully, lantern in hand. Then the light went out and all she could see was the top of the rope, secured to her window. The creaking resumed. The wilderness beyond the palace wall was dark. Apart from the groan of the rope it was unusually quiet.

Jasim, it must be Jasim.

A laugh bubbled up inside her. Joy. He had come for her. He had found her.

A hand appeared and gripped the central column. She backed away to give him space and watched his red-gold hair appear. Wide shoulders squeezed through the gap. She was smiling so much her face felt strange.

He stepped into the chamber and bent over, hands on his thighs, catching his breath. Amber eyes devoured her.

She swallowed. 'You've lost another turban.'

'So I have.' Straightening, he opened his arms. 'Are you ready to come home?'

With a sob, Zorahaida flew towards him. His arms closed about her and everything was right with the world. Jasim was nuzzling her hair and kissing her neck. Being in his arms was like being given a taste of paradise—a paradise that had been stolen from her and unexpectedly restored. Frantic with need, acting on instinct, she kissed every bit of him she could reach. They exchanged mindless, blissful kisses that were more potent than any drug.

She kissed him to let him know how he filled her mind. Somehow, Jasim had become part of her. She kissed his chin and the pulse at his neck, again and again. She couldn't stop. When she nibbled the muscle at the top of his shoulder, she was rewarded by a deep groan she felt in her toes. He smelt delicious, strong and male and incredibly reassuring. Jasim.

'Zorahaida.'

He nipped her ear. His hands were busy, sending sparks of delight all over her body. He explored her waist, he caressed her buttocks, he cupped her breasts. Abruptly, he lifted his head and frowned.

'My life, did those dogs forget to feed you? I can feel your ribs. You are far too thin.'

'I'm not sure. I don't remember much after going into the pigeon loft.' She touched her head. 'Something hit me. After that most of the journey is a blur.'

The frown deepened; careful fingers explored her scalp and he turned his head to see for himself.

'It's all right, Jasim. It's healed.' She pressed closer.

Kiss me again. Please.

'You've eaten tonight?'

'Yes.'

'We can't have you fading away.' He placed his palm again her cheek, eyes filled with tenderness. His thumb brushed lightly against her lip. 'Zorahaida.'

With a sigh he wrapped his arms about her waist and pulled her flush against him. Gold-fringed eyes searched hers.

'The journey lasted days and it was a blur? Those fiends must have drugged you.'

'I am sure of it. They drugged me every day. I have no memory of eating, but they forced me to drink.'

A muscle ticked in his jaw. 'Do you know what they gave you?'

She shook her head. 'All I can tell you is that it tasted utterly vile.' Hoping to lighten his mood, for she wanted nothing to spoil this reunion, she lifted an eyebrow and smiled. 'It tasted far worse than the poppy juice I gave you.'

He gave her a considering look. 'You tested that out personally, did you?'

'I only tasted it. We consulted one of the palace herbalists, she assured us it wouldn't harm you.'

It was hard not to look at his mouth, it was so

tempting. He hadn't kissed her properly yet and he was handling her far too gently. Either he remained angry or he thought her too fragile. Neither possibility was acceptable.

She slid her fingers into his hair. 'Jasim, have you forgiven me?'

Turning his head, he kissed her palm. 'My life, all anger burned away when you were abducted. Have you forgiven me?'

She stared. 'For what?'

'For failing to protect you.' Hauling her closer, he touched his mouth to hers. 'Forgive me, my life.'

His kiss was careful, light and gently searching. It wasn't enough. Against her belly, she could feel that he was fully aroused, but he was holding back. Zorahaida pressed herself against him and was pleased to hear a smothered moan. She didn't want him to hold back. Jasim continued to stroke her hair, and he ran his hand down her spine. He was being far too decorous. It was as though he feared she might break.

Zorahaida wanted more, she needed him to renew his claim on her, as thoroughly as he had done after their marriage. Equally important, she needed to renew her claim on him. They had been strangers when they'd married and making love had been exquisite. What would it be like now, when they had grown to like and respect each other?

I love you, Jasim.

She kept the words locked tight in her heart and there they would have to remain, though they burned in her brain. She would never use them. She felt ridiculously shy.

Love was the most unsettling of emotions. Even now, Zorahaida wasn't confident she understood it. Her father claimed to have loved her mother the Queen, yet he'd refused to allow her to return to Spain.

Her father's behaviour was beyond disturbing. He'd dragged her back from Madinat Runda, he called her his 'little dove' and offered her sweetmeats, yet he seemed perfectly happy to confine her in the tower, just as he'd once confined her mother.

Love was dangerous. Besides, Jasim wouldn't want to hear. A warrior like him, a successful champion, would have no time for such a messy, confusing emotion.

She could, however, spend the rest of her days showing him how much she appreciated his determination to keep her. She would enjoy showing him that he had become the centre of her world. She gave him a crooked smile and threw caution to the wind. Shyness was of no use here. That Jasim, a great warrior, had asked her for forgiveness was more than she ever expected.

'Jasim, you did nothing wrong. What happened was my fault, not yours. If I hadn't disobeyed you by going to the pigeon loft, they would never have caught me.'

She looked up at him through her eyelashes and slowly, determinedly, slid her hand down. Down over that beautifully sculpted chest, down to his waist. She eased back and went further. Through the fine linen, she folded him in her hand. He was fully aroused.

'Jasim, I need you. It's been too long.'

A pained expression crossed his face and he bent to rest his forehead against hers. 'Believe me, Zorahaida, I need you equally badly. But you are not thinking clearly. This is neither the time, nor the place, we have to get out of here.'

Setting her at arm's length, he pressed a kiss to her forehead and released her. His smile held regret.

'Be patient, my love. God willing, we shall soon be home. We will have all our lives to give each other pleasure.' He cleared his throat and his voice became brisk. 'In the meantime, you haven't seen a sling lying about?'

'A sling?'

'To use with the rope. Unless, of course you can climb a rope.'

'I can't climb a rope!'

He grinned. 'Well, you are so resourceful, I couldn't be sure. Relax, Zorahaida, you don't have to do any climbing. Your man, Captain Yusuf ibn Safwan has been most helpful. When I explained I intended to help you escape, he arranged for the rope to be put in place.' He bent to peer under the bed and his voice became muffled. 'Devil take it, he promised to leave a sling. Where can he have put it?'

Straightening, Jasim shoved his hand through his hair. 'It must be somewhere; I'd take my oath the Captain remains your man.'

A faint chink caught his attention. When he heard it a second time, the hairs rose on the back of his neck.

He and Zorahaida exchanged glances and went to the window overlooking the palace gardens. She slipped her hand into his.

The gardens were ablaze with torches and the grounds were bright as noontide. The path to the tower bristled with palace guards. The guards stood in silence, if it weren't for the occasional clink, they would never have been heard. Helmets gleamed; light bounced off the points of dozens of spears. The quiet was ominous. Eerie.

Zorahaida's eyes were hunted. 'God help us, we're surrounded.'

'The Sultan's men must have caught your Captain Yusuf with the sling. Your father knows I'm here.'

'Yusuf wouldn't betray us!'

It was a point Jasim wasn't prepared to argue. As he backed away from the window, pulling Zorahaida with him, logic told him there was little they could do. Notwithstanding, his mind sprang into action.

There must be a way out, there must be. Regrettably, the sling had been crucial, without it, there was no way to get Zorahaida out of the tower before the Palace Guard broke in. And Jasim wasn't going to leave without her. They were trapped.

'How many servants do you have here?'

'Only a handful.'

'I assume Sama is one of them?'

Zorahaida took a shaky breath. 'Apparently Sama has vanished. The new maidservant told me no one has seen her for a while.'

With that, Zorahaida manoeuvred Jasim across the chamber to the window facing the ravine. She gestured at the rope hanging over the ledge. 'Jasim, you must go. Please.' Her voice cracked. 'I won't have your blood on my hands.'

'No.' Firmly, he laced his fingers with hers. 'We stay together.'

'Jasim, I don't think my father will hurt me, but you…?' She shuddered. 'Go, I implore you.'

'I won't lose you again.' He cupped her face with his palm. 'Come what may, we face this together.'

A door banged. Loud voices floated up the stairs. Someone barked a sharp order.

Jasim gripped Zorahaida's hand. He was watching her face as the door opened, praying that this wouldn't be the last time they would be together.

Zorahaida let out a gasp and her face transfigured. The change from grim defiance to delight was extraordinary.

Sama stood under the arch, beaming from ear to ear and she hadn't come alone. Prince Ghalib was with her, a wry smile on his face. As Jasim's eyes met those of the Prince, Prince Ghalib inclined his head.

'I wish you good evening, Jasim ibn Ismail. May I enter?'

Zorahaida darted across and flung her arms about her uncle. 'Come in, Uncle, please.' She turned to Sama and, after embracing her too, drew her to one side. The women began talking, nineteen to the dozen.

Jasim returned Prince Ghalib's bow, mind working furiously. The Prince's appearance could only mean one thing. There had been a palace coup. 'The men outside—I assume they owe allegiance to you rather than the Sultan?'

'They do indeed.' Triumph gleamed in the Prince's eyes. 'And before you ask, my brother the Sultan has no idea you are here.'

'God is good,' Jasim said as Zorahaida came over. She tucked her hand in his and rested her head against him.

The Prince glanced fondly at her. 'I don't know how much my niece has told you, but your father by marriage is extremely unwell.'

Jasim raised an eyebrow. 'I'm afraid we haven't discussed Sultan Tariq's health.'

The Prince's eyes danced. 'You have other matters on your mind, I am sure.'

Jasim ran his hand around the back of his neck and the Prince gave a bark of laughter.

'I see how it is, and I am happy for my niece.' Prince Ghalib's eyes lit on a carafe on a side table. He snapped his fingers and another maid-servant materialised as if by magic. 'Wine, if you please.'

By the time Jasim and the Prince had finished their wine, Jasim had learned much.

The Prince was refreshingly candid. He had long been concerned about the balance of Sultan Tariq's mind and apparently matters had grown worse after Zorahaida and Jasim had married.

Bouts of ungovernable rage had been followed by periods of appalling melancholy and self-pity. The Prince admitted that the Sultan's nature had always tended that way, and after Zorahaida left for Madinat Runda, he deteriorated fast. The Sultan had lost his appetite. Daily, the Prince had watched his brother become more irascible and more unreasonable. The Sultan was now so sick, the Prince informed Jasim, that he had taken refuge in a handful of chambers.

'He rarely leaves them, he has become a recluse,' the Prince concluded.

Jasim looked thoughtfully at the Prince. 'So you are, in effect, ruler of Al-Andalus.'

'That is so. All of which means you and my niece are free to return to the west.' The Prince met Zorahaida's gaze and his face creased into a smile. 'You won't be needing that sling, Niece. You may leave in style through the main gate.'

'If you know about the sling, great Prince, Captain Yusuf ibn Safwan must answer to you.'

He was met with a quiet, clever smile and a slow nod. 'Captain Yusuf ibn Safwan and I came to terms shortly after my niece left the palace.'

Jasim felt a flash of irritation. 'Then why the devil didn't he permit me to enter by the main gate? It would have been a lot easier.'

The Prince smiled easily. 'The Captain wasn't confident that everyone in the palace answers to me. I set him right just before coming here.'

Jasim replaced his cup on the table and found himself remembering the gossip about palace intrigues and secret networks. He nodded in Sama's direction. 'Tell me, did you take my wife's handmaid into your household too?'

'Aye, she appealed for help when the Sultan took against her. She feared for her life. I decided it was best to keep her out of the way until my brother forgot about her.'

Jasim nodded. Prince Ghalib was, it seemed, a far better man than his brother the Sultan. With him in power, the entire kingdom would be a happier, safer place.

Movement in the window caught Jasim's attention. Incredibly, the basket Usayd had shown him earlier slid on to the ledge. A hand followed and then his brother was staring at him, eyes wide and desperate.

'Jasim, for pity's sake, help. I can't hold on.'

In a heartbeat, Jasim was at the window, elbowing the basket aside. He gripped his brother's arm. 'I have you.'

Usayd's belly was large and it was a struggle getting him through the narrow gap, but Jasim hauled for all he was worth and at length they managed it.

'My thanks, Brother.' Usayd's brow was dotted with sweat. He sucked in a lungful of air and gave a self-deprecating grin. 'How you made it look so easy, I've no idea. I'm spent.'

Jasim shook his head. 'You shouldn't have done it, I warned you to stay put.'

'Had to,' Usayd said simply. He smiled at Zorahaida. 'You must be my brother's princess; I am delighted to meet you.'

Jasim glowered at Usayd. 'You could have been killed.'

'Brother, I will never make a knight, but I thought you might need help.' He paused. 'Besides, you're not the only one with a mission.'

Jasim blinked. 'Oh?'

With a cough, Prince Ghalib stepped forward. 'Allow me to introduce myself. I am the Princess's uncle.'

Usayd bowed deeply. 'Please forgive my rudeness. I am Usayd ibn Ismail. Blessings be upon you, Prince Ghalib.'

Prince Ghalib inclined his head. 'And on you, Usayd ibn Ismail.'

'Great prince, I am at your service.' Hand on his heart, Usayd gave another bow. 'It is most fortunate that you are here, for you are the very person I wanted to see.'

The Prince looked enquiringly at him.

'Great Prince, I came to discover if you are willing to discuss reopening the trade routes to the west.'

Prince Ghalib's mouth twitched. 'You have chosen an unusual approach, Usayd ibn Ismail.'

Jasim swallowed down a sigh. If Usayd was going to start talking about trade, none of them would get any sleep. He slipped his arm about Zorahaida's waist. Happily, the Prince noticed.

'Usayd ibn Ismail, my niece and her husband are clearly exhausted. We should pursue our discussions elsewhere.' The Prince sent Jasim a knowing smile. 'For now, I and my people will leave you in peace. You are my most honoured guests. Rest assured, you will be free to leave whenever you wish.'

'Thank you, Uncle, thank you,' Zorahaida murmured.

The Prince headed to the door. Usayd took up the basket and followed him.

Jasim frowned thoughtfully. 'Usayd, what the devil have you got in that basket?'

Usayd let out a bark of laughter. 'I thought you'd never ask.' He grinned at Zorahaida. 'I've had it with me since we left Madinat Runda and my brother was fretting about you so much he barely noticed it. I got the idea from you, so I'll warrant you'll know what's inside.'

Zorahaida gave the basket no more than a glance. Her lips curved. 'Pigeons, you brought Madinat Runda pigeons to Granada.'

Usayd returned her smile. 'I have a feeling they will come in handy.' He moved to stand with the Prince by the door. 'When the trade routes are open again, we will need an efficient means of communication between the districts.'

With a laugh, the Prince beckoned Sama over. 'Come, Sama, your mistress and her husband wish to rest. Please find my friend Usayd accommodation and see he has everything he needs.'

Chapter Fifteen

Zorahaida and Jasim were alone.

'At last, I have you to myself,' he said, kissing the back of her hand and pulling her firmly into his arms.

Zorahaida swallowed. Despite her determination to set her nervousness to one side, her mouth was dry. One would have thought she had never done this before. They were together again, there was no need for fear.

Yet she felt hopelessly at sea. Why?

In the early days of their marriage, she'd hidden behind excitement. What she felt this evening was altogether different. They could take this slowly. Calmly. Was that the problem? Taking it slowly was challenging. It meant revealing more of herself and her emotions than she was comfortable with.

He might see too much.

His amber gaze caught hers. She thought she

glimpsed a heady mix of desire and hope. 'Zorahaida?'

She moistened her lips. 'I feel…'

'You are exhausted. I will make no claim on you until you are fully rested. We are together again, that is all that matters.'

She was directed carefully to the bed and encouraged to lie down.

Candlelight played over Jasim's red-gold hair. The lamp behind him silhouetted his champion's body as he kicked off his boots and unbuckled his belt.

Greedily, Zorahaida drank in the sight of him as he tossed his clothes aside. Jasim's body was magnificent, she was blessed to have him as her husband. His wide shoulders and strong arms were nothing less than perfection. Yet that wasn't the sum of him, there was more than strength built into those muscled limbs. They answered to a mind which understood more than brute force. When Zorahaida admired Jasim's body, she was looking at far more than power. She was looking at a man who would protect her with his life. Jasim would never use his body to force himself or his will on her. It was true they sometimes quarrelled, but with them both being so headstrong, perhaps that was inevitable. He was amazingly protective of her needs and wishes. It was an astonishingly attractive quality.

He must care about her. Did he love her? She ached to know. Jasim hadn't mentioned love and likely he never would, but his actions in coming back to Granada, in getting a message through to Captain Yusuf and climbing up to her bed-chamber all spoke of a man who would guard her with his life.

Already Jasim treasured her in ways her father would never understand. Her father might claim to think only of her well-being, but all he truly wanted was for her to remain at his beck and call for ever. That had been the case when Zorahaida and her sisters had first been brought to the Alhambra. Nothing had changed.

Sultan Tariq was worn down with age and his mind was weakening, yet his need to dominate remained unquenched. Life had taught her father nothing. He wanted her on hand to pander to his whims. As far as the Sultan was concerned, Zorahaida was a toy. Try as she might, she would never get him to understand that she was far more than that.

She had a will of her own. A life to lead. God willing, she would spend it with Jasim.

Jasim joined her in bed and she went eagerly into his arms.

He kissed her forehead. 'Sleep, my sweet.'

She nuzzled his chest. She was still clothed, although she could feel him well enough. She loved the careful way his body cradled hers. Her head lay on his chest, his arms held her tightly against him and their legs were entwined. Jasim wanted to make love with her, she could feel him hard and hot, pressing against her belly. Yet he made no move because he thought her exhausted. He was willing to put his desires to one side, for her. Jasim would never treat her as a toy.

'Jasim?' She drew a circle on his chest with her forefinger and felt the shiver that went through him. Desire. 'I won't be able to sleep until you have answered some questions.'

'Aye?' His voice was husky, it was the voice of need, barely held in check.

She hid a smile. She burned for him too, but her questions were important.

'What happened to Fatima at the pigeon loft? Is she all right?'

A large hand ruffled her hair. 'She is well, I thank you.'

'That's a mercy. I saw nothing of what happened after I was hit. I've been worrying about her.'

'Fatima will be fine. She was worried about you too.'

'I like her, very much.'

'I'm glad.'

'Jasim, what happened to the men who made up our escort? Did the mercenaries attack your uncle's guards? Was there a fight?'

He hesitated. 'I'm afraid so.'

At her urging, Jasim launched into a description of the aftermath of the fight. No detail was spared. He told her about the pigeons fluttering loose in the square outside the hospital, and he mentioned that some of his uncle's guard had been killed. It was clear he grieved for them. He explained that the Sultan's mercenaries led him and his party first to the coast and then, when the storms had blown themselves out, to Salobreña.

Zorahaida heard it all with a sinking heart. 'Jasim, I am truly ashamed that my father's orders mean your uncle has lost faithful soldiers.'

'You are not to blame for your father's sins.'

'You are generous.'

A pensive silence fell. Zorahaida drew away and stared at the lacy plasterwork ceiling. The flickering lamplight cast ugly shadows. Men had died because of her. She took a deep, pained breath. 'When we get home, perhaps I may be allowed to make amends.'

'Truly, there is no need.'

She turned her head to look at him. 'I disagree. Jasim, Fatima told me about her work at the hospital in Madinat Runda. Will I be permitted to support her? As you know, I visited the infirmary in Granada. I like to help, and I have experience.'

'If that is your wish, of course you may.'

Zorahaida let out a small sigh. 'Thank you. I didn't doubt you for a moment, but it is good to know my dreams have at last come true.'

She felt a gentle tug on her hair. 'Your dreams?'

'I have married a chivalrous knight.'

He kissed her lightly on the lips and an eyebrow lifted. 'I believe you once set your heart on a Spanish knight.'

Jasim's tone was casual but something in his eyes warned her that her answer mattered to him.

'Enrique de Murcia?' With an airy wave, Zorahaida consigned Enrique de Murcia to the past. 'He is nothing. I never knew him; I saw what I wanted to see. Much later, I discovered him to be both dishonourable and cruel. A liar.' Leaning forward, she kissed Jasim's shoulder. 'The best I can say of him is that he taught me to hope that somewhere in the world, there was a chivalrous man and that he would find me.' Angling his head to hers, she inched slowly and carefully up his body until her mouth was inches from his. 'God be praised, you did.'

With a groan, he caught her up and their mouths met.

The kiss intensified. Fire raced along every vein. Their tongues met and played, and the air filled with sighs of pleasure. Relief made her desperate. Want made her greedy. She wanted this to last for ever. Perhaps it would. They were both kissing each other as though their lives depended on it.

Inevitably, she found herself on her back with Jasim leaning over her. His tender expression warred with a bemused frown.

'My life, we should not be doing this,' he said, shaking his head. 'You have been half-starved, and you are exhausted.'

With slow deliberation, Zorahaida circled her hips, relishing in the feel of the hard ridge pressing into her belly. When his eyes glazed, she smiled. 'Jasim, it's plain you desire me. You do realise I feel the same?'

His eyes darkened. 'Zorahaida, you spent too long in the harem. Those women are trained to give pleasure. To give it. They have little choice but to simulate enjoyment. It is a trick designed to enhance their partner's pleasure.' He shrugged. 'Every man likes to believe he is a marvel in bed.'

Puzzled, Zorahaida pushed her fingers into his hair. The feel of those bright, silky strands was tempting her beyond endurance. What was he saying? It came to her that despite the consideration Jasim had shown her in bed, despite the delicacy he had shown her after their marriage, he never truly believed she desired him.

On reflection, his questions about the Spanish knight Enrique de Murcia revealed more than she'd first realised. Jasim didn't understand she'd been content to marry him from the first.

Did he think women were incapable of desire? Would he be shocked if she admitted that she desired him?

She sifted her fingers through the hair at the nape of his neck. 'Jasim, I need to tell you something. It might shock you. I hope not, but I have to tell you.'

His body tensed.

'Go on.'

'Jasim, I am fortunate to have you as my husband. I confess that when we married our goals may not have aligned, but you need to know that I do not regret it. I couldn't.'

His mouth twisted. 'You like being my wife?'

'Very much. Being with you makes me happy. I enjoy talking to you.'

An eyebrow shot up. 'Talking? Zorahaida, we spend much of our time arguing.'

'Exactly. I am free to say what I wish to you and whilst we often disagree, I know you will never force me into submission. When we married, I wasn't sure what to expect. Why, I've learned more since I met you than I would in years of study in the palace library.' Cheeks heating, she looked sideways at him through her eyelashes. 'I enjoy looking at your body and I enjoy touching it.' Matching actions to words, she kissed his chest, over his heart.

Careful fingers brought her head up. 'Zorahaida, I confess to being a little confused. Are you saying that you enjoy making love with me?'

She nodded. Her throat was so tight she had to force the words out. 'I love it.' More words, revealing words like *I love you* threatened to tumble out too, but she held them in. 'Jasim, your body gives me pleasure and that is no pretence. It is real. I confess that when we first married, you intrigued me. I'd never expected my father to allow me to marry and I was curious about what making love felt like. Jasim, I adored it.'

He grinned and shifted closer to nuzzle her cheek. His breath warmed her neck and his teeth closed lightly on her earlobe. 'You weren't alone in that,' he breathed.

'I am happy to hear it. A moment, Jasim, let me finish. I was ignorant then.'

A huff of amusement stirred the hair at her temple. 'Now that is a lie. Believe me, wife, you were far from ignorant.'

She nudged his shoulder with her nose. He was lying very still, and she knew she had his full attention. 'You're wrong, I was very ignorant. So much so that it took me days to realise that the way our bodies responded to each other was extraordinarily rare. I've thought about it since, believe me. I could only respond so freely with someone I trusted and liked. And I trusted and liked you from the first, more than any man I'd met. Jasim, I could only have given myself to you. Only to you.'

Those telling words were back, hovering on the tip of her tongue. *I love you.* It was becoming harder and harder to hold them in.

'Jasim, I hold you in the highest esteem.'

'Esteem,' he muttered.

She frowned. He sounded almost…disappointed. She sighed. The women in the harem had warned her that misunderstandings between husbands and wives were commonplace. Men didn't like talking about feelings, she was probably boring him.

Experimentally, she wriggled against him and her smile returned. He was pressed against her belly, hot and firm as ever. Bored or no, he still desired her. Well, she could help with that.

She draped her leg over his hip and loosed a series of kisses on his chest, his shoulder, his chin.

Hooded eyes met hers. 'You are weak and tired, my temptress.'

She laughed. 'Jasim, I need you. I won't sleep, otherwise.'

A slow smile dawned. 'You're certain?'

'Never more so.'

He touched his mouth to hers and a languorous kiss consumed them. She sucked his lower lip and he sucked hers. She edged closer and her breathing quickened. Jasim stroked her back, her bottom, her thighs…

Abruptly, he lifted his mouth from hers, frowning as he unwound her shawl from about her waist. He threw it to the floor and pulled impatiently at her clothes. 'Why are you still clothed?'

Fingers collided in a decadent scrabble to undress her. Silk whispered as it followed the shawl to the floor. Linen rustled.

The sun was slanting in through a crack in the shutters when Zorahaida woke. Judging by the lozenge of light splashed across the floor, the day was well advanced. She was alone. Slightly concerned, she pushed up.

'Jasim?'

Silence. Telling herself he must have gone downstairs to break his fast hours ago, Zorahaida scrambled out of bed and into a robe.

He was on the floor down below, sitting cross-legged on a cushion, next to a bowl of bread and figs.

'At last you are awake,' he said, rising and coming across to take her hand.

He smiled down at her and memories of their bodies coming together the previous night, of their mutual pleasure, flooded into her mind. Just so had he looked at her before their bodies renewed their knowledge of each other. The soft touch of his lips had led to a gradual increase in tempo. They'd ended with a wild, unrestrained celebration of their marriage. They were together again and thank God, he seemed to be as pleased about it as she was.

He stroked her arm tenderly and something inside her shifted. Jasim invariably treated her with respect. From the very beginning, he'd told her that he hoped there would be affection between them. She'd understood him to be telling her what he thought she wanted to hear. Well, she would settle for that, even though she wished with all her heart for more than affection.

Life with Jasim wasn't going to be easy with her craving his love. Still, it was better than life without him. He was intelligent. Kinder than most, he would be mortified if he believed she was unsatisfied with their marriage. He must never learn that she yearned for his love above all else.

'I am thankful you slept so soundly,' he said.

Smiling, she shrugged. 'I felt safe for the first time in days.'

With a nod, he drew her towards the cushion by the bread and figs. 'You must be hungry.'

As Zorahaida settled on to the cushion, Jasim rang the handbell before taking his seat beside her.

When Sama appeared, her face was bare. She had discarded her veil as she had done immediately after their wedding, when Jasim had moved into the tower.

'Princess.' Sama bowed. 'Would you care for more to eat? Prince Ghalib has asked me to remind you the kitchens are entirely at your disposal.'

'Thank you. For now, bread and fruit are enough, although I will admit to a craving for meatballs with rice and almonds.'

'The spicy ones?'

'That would be marvellous. I haven't had meat in an age.'

'Very well.' Sama hesitated. 'Princess, may I speak freely?'

'Always.'

Sama drew closer. 'Princess, I am aware you have seen your father, so you know how ill he is. You might like to know that since you left, the Alhambra has changed beyond recognition. Sultan Tariq has lost all power. The Prince commands loyalty throughout the palace. Your father's guards, the army, his servants and stewards have transferred their allegiance to your uncle.'

Zorahaida felt Jasim's hand on her arm, warm and reassuring.

'Thank you, Sama. After last night that was plain. Tell me, is Captain Yusuf truly safe?'

'Aye. The Captain and his troop—with all the men who guarded you so bravely—are sworn to the Prince.'

Jasim cleared his throat. 'You believe the Prince is a just man?'

'Indeed, Master. The atmosphere in the palace is utterly changed.'

Jasim nodded. 'That is all to the good.' He smiled at Zorahaida. 'My brother will be thankful to be dealing with a rational man.'

Sama moved to the door. 'Princess, I shall let the kitchen know about your wish for meatballs and rice.'

'Thank you.'

When Sama had gone, Zorahaida looked ruefully at Jasim. 'Do you think my departure prompted all these changes?'

'It's possible.'

Pensively, she picked up some bread and tore off a small piece. 'Perhaps I should have run away with my sisters. If Father had lost all his children, he might not have become so controlling.'

Jasim made an impatient sound. 'That's absurd. Your father's cruel reputation preceded your sisters' flight to Spain. If you'd gone with them, we would never have met.' Strong fingers encircled her wrist. 'I, for one, cannot regret our marriage.'

There was a look on his face she was unable to interpret. She thought she saw a hint of uncertainty. Oddly, it gave her heart. She covered his hand with hers. 'Jasim, I would never regret our marriage. And I am certainly pleased for everyone in the palace if my uncle is truly in power.'

'If?' Jasim's eyebrows lifted. 'After last night's show of force, how can you doubt it?'

She stared at the bread. 'I know my father, and his state of mind troubles me. He has always been the most manipulative of men. He tricks people. He woos them to his will and then, like the toss of a coin, he changes direction.' She sighed. 'Father deteriorated suddenly, what's to say he might not recover equally suddenly? Jasim, I'd like to go home as quickly as possible.'

Amber eyes searched hers. 'You fear he might stage a swift recovery. My heart, after last night's show of strength by your uncle I am convinced your fears are groundless. Prince Ghalib is firmly in power.'

'Nevertheless, I would prefer to go home.' She shrugged. 'I don't mean to be difficult, Jasim, but—'

'Say no more. You wish to leave today?'

'If you please.'

'Very well.' Lithely, Jasim got to his feet. 'Home it is. I shall find Usayd and warn him that if he wants to travel with us, he will have to conclude his negotiations swiftly.'

The plan was to be clear of the palace by late afternoon. Prince Ghalib lent fresh horses to the men who had accompanied Jasim from Madinat Runda and their party now comprised the knights Jasim had commandeered from the Madinat Runda garrison, as well as a detachment of the Prince's guards and a small retinue of servants.

'Zorahaida, you saved my beloved Yamina,' the Prince said, eyes twinkling as she surveyed her attendants. 'It is my pleasure to ensure your comfort on the journey.'

'You are very generous, Uncle, thank you.'

The Prince's expression became sombre. 'We shall miss you. My main regret—apart from losing you, of course—is that I didn't move sooner to curb your father's power.'

'Father would have had you executed. The time was not ripe.'

'It's possible.' His face lightened. 'Be that as it may, your swift action in saving Yamina and the bravery with which you confronted your father afterwards were an inspiration. Zorahaida, I salute you. Not only did you teach me that inaction might serve to keep me alive, but you also showed me that if I waited too long to assert myself, I risked losing my soul.'

'You are too kind,' she murmured.

'Kind? No, I merely speak the truth as I see it. I learned much from you and from those who quietly gave you their loyalty. Loyalty that was well deserved. I beg you to remember that you will always be welcome here. Please, put those pigeons of yours to good use, write whenever you wish.'

'I will write often.'

The Prince glanced at Usayd. 'Thanks to your husband's brother, I also now have the means of writing to you.'

Zorahaida ran her gaze over their party. It was smaller and leaner than her wedding procession and that, she knew, was down to Jasim who had explained their wish to travel more swiftly. Thankfully, no one had suggested she bid her father farewell. Everyone understood she had no wish to see him again.

As she was helped into the saddle and their

party trotted out through the palace gates, she breathed a sigh of relief.

With several changes of horse, they should reach Madinat Runda in about a week.

Chapter Sixteen

Mondragón Palace, Madinat Runda

Zorahaida felt as though she had barely drawn breath after reaching Mondragón Palace, though in truth Governor Ibrahim gave her and his nephews half an hour's grace to refresh themselves before asking them to join him in the pavilion overlooking the water garden. Recalling several instances when her father had summoned her to his presence, Zorahaida felt a shiver run down her spine.

'What's this meeting about?' she asked, as she and Jasim left her apartment and made their way downstairs.

Jasim shrugged. 'It will be a family conference. My brother's wife Aixa is also attending. Doubtless, my uncle wishes everyone to know what happened in Granada.' He looped Zorahaida's hand through his arm and led her down the path towards the pavilion.

'Is it not strange that your uncle has included Aixa and me in this conference?'

'Strange?' Jasim laughed. 'Not in this household. Fatima will be coming too; she usually has much to say.'

Zorahaida fell silent as they entered the first courtyard, marvelling at the world of difference between the Governor's household and her father's. She knew she didn't have to say a word for Jasim to understand that she was stunned at being included in a family discussion. Did Governor Ibrahim truly treat the women in his family as valued members of his household? Her father would never have done such a thing. In truth, the Sultan didn't value anyone. He feared that if he did so, his authority would be undermined.

Her father was weak. He had always been weak and for decades had hidden his weak character behind bluff and bluster. It was staggering to think that the Sultan ruled by fear because he himself was afraid.

Governor Ibrahim appeared to be cut from a different cloth. Well, she would soon see for herself. Nerves were still fluttering in her belly, but she was no longer fearful.

She looked sideways at Jasim. 'What is Aixa like?'

'You haven't met her?'

She gave a slight headshake and bit her lip. 'I have a feeling she's been avoiding me.'

Jasim stared. 'Why on earth should she do that?'

She gave a small shrug and said softly. 'Perhaps she has taken against me because my mother was Spanish.'

He halted mid-stride. 'Zorahaida, that is certainly *not* the case.' He gestured at himself. 'Look at my eyes. My hair. I know very little about my mother, but I do know she was of mixed ancestry. Like you, I have the blood of more than one race flowing in my veins.' He grinned. 'Likely more than two races, if the truth be known. Aixa hasn't taken against me. No more will she take against you.'

Zorahaida nodded and smiled and prayed he was right. 'Very well. I am glad to hear it.'

A footfall behind them made them turn, Fatima was hurrying towards them, Hunter on her shoulder. When she got within two feet of them, Hunter made his joyful chattering sound and flew to Zorahaida.

Whilst Zorahaida juggled with Hunter, Fatima gave Jasim a brief hug. 'It is marvellous to see you back in one piece. I did worry.' She glanced at Hunter, rubbing his head against Zorahaida's neck. 'That animal is the most outrageous flirt.'

'That he is.'

Fatima squeezed Zorahaida's hand. 'Thank God you are safe. What did your father say when you saw him? How did you get away?'

Jasim shook his head. 'Later, Fatima. First, we must answer your father's summons.'

'Of course.' Fatima linked arms with Zorahaida and the three of them continued down the path to the pavilion with Fatima talking non-stop.

'Jasim, Father knows that you and Usayd are fully reconciled,' she said. 'When I explained that you had both rushed to Zorahaida's rescue, he looked happier than I've seen him in some while. The only person who wasn't happy to learn where you'd gone was Aixa.'

'That's understandable,' Jasim said. 'I knew she'd be frantic with worry, but Usayd insisted on coming.'

'Aye, he's been obsessed with renewing the

trade agreements with Granada for an age. Was he successful?'

They entered the water garden and Jasim smiled. 'Patience, Fatima, and all will be revealed.'

The pool that took up most of the water garden was rectangular and with the sunlight shining on the surface it gleamed like a bright pathway, pointing straight to a pavilion at the other end. Myrtle bushes glowed like green fire and a pair of pomegranate trees were bowed down with ripe fruit. Jasim led his wife and cousin down the left-hand path, ducked under the central horseshoe arch and entered the pavilion.

Governor Ibrahim was sitting cross-legged before a low table, with Usayd and a woman who had to be Usayd's wife, Aixa.

'Welcome home, Princess, Jasim. Please, be seated.' The Governor clapped his hands and a manservant appeared.

'Master?'

'Hisham, my nephews and the Princess have been travelling for days. We'll take those refreshments now, if you please.'

Zorahaida blinked as, for the second time since returning to Madinat Runda, the ground shifted beneath her feet. The women were to eat with the men? Her father would never countenance such a thing. She'd only ever known him share a meal with a handful of favoured concubines.

The manservant didn't appear at all startled, he nodded easily, as if this was a normal, everyday occurrence.

'Very good, Master.'

Zorahaida watched, fascinated, as Hisham gestured and more servants appeared with jugs and glasses. Hunter left her shoulder and crouched near the table, beadily observing everything.

'Master, the wine has been chilled in the icehouse, as you directed,' Hisham said.

'Very good.'

While the servants bustled about with wine and jugs of sweetened lemon juice, Jasim squeezed Zorahaida's hand.

'My heart, this is my brother's wife, Aixa,' he said.

The two women smiled at each other and Zorahaida found nothing in Aixa's posture or manner to suggest ill will. She felt herself relax.

'It is a pleasure to meet you.'

'Princess, the pleasure is all mine.'

Pottery dishes were set within arm's reach. They were piled with stuffed vine leaves, honey pastries flecked with pistachio nuts and tiny balls of cheese rolled on to sticks. Aixa picked up a colourful bowl of vine leaves and held them out.

'Princess, these are worth trying. They are made to my mother's recipe.'

'Thank you.' Zorahaida took one and sampled it. The leaves were tender, and the delicate blend of herbs and spices made her mouth water for more. Eagerly, she reached for another. 'They are delicious.'

Aixa passed the bowl on. 'If you are interested, I will share the recipe.'

'You cook?' Zorahaida asked, startled. Much as she loved food, she had never been allowed anywhere near the kitchens. She looked to Jasim. If she was to given access to the kitchen, her life would be altered beyond belief. 'I might learn to cook?'

'If that is your wish.'

'It would interest me very much.'

Governor Ibrahim reached for a jug of wine. 'We will share supper later, of course,' he said, easily. 'This should tide you over until then.'

'Thank you, Uncle,' Jasim said.

Hunter chose that moment to lunge at a bowl of dates. Snatching up a handful, he raced away, chattering.

'Hunter, no!' Zorahaida flushed. 'I am so sorry; I fear he is badly trained.'

Fatima laughed, the Governor smiled and Zorahaida saw Jasim exchange rueful looks with his brother.

A strange feeling welled up inside and to Zorahaida's shame, tears stung at the back of her eyes. Whatever this feeling was, she was at a loss to identify it.

Too choked to speak, she looked around the pavilion, determined to puzzle it out. Most of the servants had slipped away, only Hisham remained. Usayd and Jasim were smiling at Hunter's antics. The women in the family were openly laughing. The family...

That was it, for the first time in her life she felt as though she was part of a real family. She belonged here. The feeling was new and strange and altogether wonderful.

Jasim covered her hand with his. 'You are well, my life?' he murmured.

She smiled through her tears and nodded. 'Aye, very well.' She met the Governor's gaze and inclined her head. 'I wish to thank your uncle for welcoming me into his family. Indeed, I'd like to thank all of you.' Her voice thickened. 'Until today I have never known what it is to be part of a proper family. I thank you all.'

Fatima reached out to squeeze her hand. 'We are delighted Jasim chose you for his wife.'

The Governor cleared his throat. 'Aye, Princess, you are indeed welcome.' He gestured at the manservant hovering near the arch. 'Thank you, Hisham, we shall call you if we need you.'

As Hisham effaced himself and walked away across the water garden, Governor Ibrahim reached into his tunic and withdrew a small scroll.

'Princess, you need to know that two days ago a carrier pigeon arrived from Granada.'

Zorahaida felt the blood drain from her face. 'It's from the Sultan?'

'No, my dear, it is from your uncle. It's addressed to me, although the contents concern you. It is of a personal nature. Do you care to read it?'

Mind whirling, Zorahaida took the scroll. Had her father died? She'd been so upset and angry about his high-handed treatment that she'd never gone to bid him farewell. Had he discovered that she'd gone and flung himself into a rage? Had he given himself an apoplexy?

Fingers trembling, she smoothed out the scroll,

vaguely aware of Fatima turning to Aixa and of Jasim muttering softly to his brother. Bless them, they were giving her space to read her uncle's letter in peace.

To the most respected Governor of Madinat Runda, Ibrahim ibn Osman, from Ghalib ibn Mustapha, heir designate to Sultan Tariq of Al-Andalus.

Greetings,

Forgive the hasty nature of this missive. Once again circumstances in the Alhambra have changed, and I thought it best that you received my account before the rumours reached you.

Firstly, it was a rare honour to welcome your nephews, Usayd and Jasim ibn Ismail to the palace, although I deeply regret the reason for their visit. Princess Zorahaida is dear to my heart and, whilst I understand the esteem in which the Sultan holds her, I cannot condone the cruel and high-handed manner in which he brought her back. For a man, particularly a sultan, to stoop so low is completely abhorrent. I fear that my brother has little respect for anything save his own wants and desires.

My brother's actions bring shame upon

the Nasrid family. I make no excuses, but you need to know that the Sultan is ailing. I fear that his mind is unhinged and that it has been for some while. He is reluctant to accept treatment, if treatment for a malady like his should truly exist.

When the Sultan learned that the Princess had left Granada for a second time, what little sense he had left deserted him completely.

In brief, Sultan Tariq has proclaimed his daughter's death. He mourns her. He wanders the palace courtyards like a shadow. He rends his clothes and appears to believe his fabrication is truth.

No one is permitted to mention her name.

I am sure my niece will be desolate when she learns of this. However, all is not as dark as it seems. When her sisters fled to Spain the Sultan banished them, on pain of death. That, at least, will not be Zorahaida's fate.

Ibrahim ibn Osman, you need to know that the reins of power are in my hands and that the Sultan is little more than a puppet. I do not recommend that Zorahaida returns to Granada quite yet, but should she choose to do so in future she will be welcome.

Further, if her sisters care to return to the land of their birth they too will be welcome.

Zorahaida blinked as the loops and curlicues of her uncle's handwriting started to blur and waver. Her father had announced her death. She stared blindly at the scroll, trying to analyse what she felt. Nothing. She felt numb. What should she do? What did this mean? Clearly, such tidings would not be absorbed in a day.

Blinking rapidly, she forced herself to finish the rest of the letter.

Governor Ibrahim, the best that can be said of Zorahaida's abduction is that it brought not only Jasim ibn Ismail to the Alhambra, but also Usayd. It gladdens my heart to see brothers capable of working together instead of treating each other as rivals.

Your oldest nephew, Usayd, is brimming with ideas to rebuild traditional trade alliances. Improved trade will benefit citizens throughout Al-Andalus. It was a privilege to talk to him and I look forward to furthering a prosperous association between our districts.

In the meantime, I would be grateful if you

could convey my warmest greetings to my niece. A place in my heart is reserved for her.

May peace be with you,
Sincerely yours,
Ghalib ibn Mustapha, Prince and Heir Designate of the Emirate of Granada

Conscious everyone had fallen silent, Zorahaida looked up to find all eyes were trained on her.

She touched Jasim's hand and swallowed hard before she could speak. 'My father has declared me dead.'

Jasim went pale. After a moment's appalled silence, he slid his arm about her and pulled her against him, visibly struggling for words.

'Zorahaida, I am so sorry.' He gestured around the pavilion. 'All I can say is that I hope you are able to accept our comfort. You belong with us. We will love and cherish you, as you deserve.'

Stunned, Zorahaida stared into steady amber eyes. Love. It was the one word that could heal any amount of hurt and betrayal. Love.

Jasim had said, 'We will love and cherish you'. *We.*

That meant him, did it not?

Praying no one could hear the wild pounding

of her hopeful heart, she gathered her dignity about her like a cloak and eased away from him. Had he meant it? Had he even noticed?

The words *We will love and cherish you* became a refrain in her head. She needed to think. Away from Jasim, away from his family.

She rose and when Jasim attempted to do the same, she held him in place with a hand on his shoulder. Smiling, she shook her head and took refuge in subterfuge. 'I'd like quiet to think about my father's announcement.' She turned to Jasim's uncle. 'Governor Ibrahim, I thank you for including me in this family gathering, it means a great deal. However, considering Prince Ghalib's letter, you will understand, I hope, my need for reflection.'

Bowing her head, she left the pavilion and went upstairs.

The silence in her apartment was absolute and the bedchamber empty. No one was about and the songbirds were dozing on their perch.

She closed the door. The chamber was a mess, Maura hadn't been in to tidy up. Her travelling clothes were strewn across the bed, tangled with Jasim's. Scooping the lot into a bundle, Zorahaida was putting it out of the way on a coffer when something caught her eye.

The unfinished letter to her sisters sat where she had left it on the side table. Goodness, it was the same letter she had begun an age ago to inform them of her marriage. The one she'd started writing before going to the infirmary with Fatima.

Sitting by the side table, she picked it up. What with her abduction and Prince Ghalib's news, it was hopelessly out of date. She would have to start afresh.

She leaned her hand on her chin. Her sisters must still be told about her marriage to Jasim. They would be glad to hear that he had shown an interest in meeting them.

She stared into space. How best to tell her sisters of their father's state of health? It wasn't easy to think because almost at once her mind wandered back to what Jasim had said in the pavilion.

We will love and cherish you.

It could simply have been a turn of phrase, a courtly expression to let her know that she was welcome in his family. She hoped it meant more than that. She longed to believe that Jasim had mentioned loving and cherishing her as a declaration of his feelings for her.

Could it be possible? Aching to believe it, she

wrapped her arms about her and held in a moan. If only this pain would leave her. No, no, that was a terrible lie. This pain was the sweet agony of loving Jasim, and though the idea that he might not love her tore her to shreds, she wouldn't wish it away for all the gold in her father's treasury.

And the reason for that was obvious. She loved him. She always would.

Was this what Leonor and Alba felt for their husbands? Had they gone through similar torments?

She'd not been in the bedchamber long before swift footsteps pulled her from her thoughts and the door opened.

Jasim. Her love. She sat at the side table and looked at him, he was after all a joy to behold. Tall, strong and true, and so very handsome. Her husband, the champion.

He lifted an eyebrow. 'My life, are you ready for company?'

With a smile, she held out her hand. 'If that company is you, always.'

He pulled her to her feet and drew her against him. 'Zorahaida, to my mind, your father has declared you dead because he knows it will wound you. You can't allow him to succeed.'

She rested her head against his chest and put

her hand against his heart. 'He hasn't wounded me. Rather, I've lost hope he will ever change.' She curled her fingers into his tunic. 'As you know, Father banished my sisters from the Emirate. He could do the same to me and he hasn't. It occurs to me that he didn't do so because he knows my place is here in Madinat Runda. Perhaps he—'

Long fingers tipped up her chin and amber eyes searched hers. 'What are you saying?'

'By declaring me dead Father might, in his way, be giving me permission to remain in the Emirate. He is allowing me to remain with you.'

Jasim huffed out a breath. 'There is no way that man is considering your interests. You might want to think so, but it is impossible.'

'Is it?' she said, sadly. 'I find myself wanting to believe that he loves me, at least a little.'

'Zorahaida, that man doesn't deserve you. He has a dark soul and he has treated you abominably.' He frowned. 'Your sisters lost patience with him and walked away. You did your best to redeem him, to no avail. Zorahaida, you mustn't look back.'

'I won't, it's just, well, he is my father. And as far as he is concerned, hope has become a habit.'

'Hope's wasted on Sultan Tariq.'

Zorahaida looped her arms about Jasim's neck and kissed his chin. 'I won't look back, I promise.' She gave him a coy look. 'After what you said in the pavilion, I have more important matters to think about.'

He stilled and faint colour tinged his cheeks. 'Go on.'

She cupped his jaw and looked deep into his eyes. She yearned for his love and she rather thought she had it. But she also remembered Jasim telling her that he had no memory of his mother. A man who had grown up without a mother's love might need a lesson in expressing his emotions. He wouldn't find it easy to tell her how he felt.

Her cheeks stung with heat; she would have to show him the way.

'Jasim, when we married, you spoke only of the affection that might exist between us.' Trembling inside, she held his gaze. 'We haven't been married long, and already I feel more than affection, much more. Jasim, you have brought happiness and hope into my life. You've taught me the meaning of love.' She paused. 'I love you.'

His breath stopped. Hers did too, for his eyes were shining and his smile—it simply dazzled.

'Zorahaida, my life.' He kissed her eyelids.

'You mean everything to me. I love you. I thought you understood.'

She drew her head back. 'You never told me.'

'That's not true, I've been telling you for some while. You are my life. My life.'

She fell silent. *You are my life*. It was an expression she had never heard until Jasim used it. 'You first called me that after my abduction, when you climbed into the tower bedchamber for the second time.'

He grunted and kissed her temple. It was a hot kiss. It was loving and affectionate and it stirred her blood.

'Zorahaida, I started to accept what you meant to me when I found you gone. The idea of life without you was unendurable. Miserable. Empty and worthless.'

She gave a quiet laugh. 'My life,' she said slowly. 'I am your life and you are mine. I like it. Jasim, it expresses what I feel for you very well.'

They loved each other. Relief weakened her knees and perhaps it weakened Jasim's knees too, because before she knew it, they had tumbled on to the bed and were kissing and caressing as though they'd been separated for a thousand years instead of for a brief half-hour.

* * *

As the afternoon melted into evening, Zorahaida learned much. Jasim touched her reverently, innocently and there was wonder in that. He stroked the robes from her body, and his lightest touch told her how much he loved her. In response, her body softened as it prepared to receive him.

Loving a man was, she realised, not the same as knowing how to make love to a man. Knowledge certainly helped, though it wasn't everything.

She frowned at his turban and began to unwind it, eventually pushing it from him so it fell to the carpet with a soft thump.

'I love your hair,' she murmured, winding a bright strand around her fingers. 'I never dreamed that touching a man's hair could bring such pleasure.'

Jasim lowered his head and gently bit her neck. 'Hmmm?'

He was licking his way from one breast to the other, as intent on her as she was on him. With love between them, his touch felt different. Warmer. More real. New feelings flowed from him to her with every caress. Feelings of joy and contentment.

Her blood was heating under Jasim's hands. She bit back a moan and when he looked up, she framed his head with her hands and guided his mouth to hers. It was her turn to give him pleasure. She ran her tongue over his lips to tempt and to taste, and when he opened her mouth, her tongue swept in. 'Jasim.'

He groaned. As Jasim moved over her and they became one, her last conscious thought was, mysteriously, that loving him had restored her innocence.

Shortly after cockcrow, came a knock on the bedchamber door.

Jasim rolled away from Zorahaida and opened an eye. Sama was setting a tray on a side table whilst Zorahaida slept on.

'Your breakfast,' Sama said cheerfully.

Jasim grunted. 'We need sleep more than we need breakfast.'

Sama shrugged. 'My apologies, Master. The Governor has asked that you and my mistress meet him in the pavilion in the water garden as soon as you have broken your fast.'

Jasim rubbed his face and turned back to Zorahaida.

* * *

Shortly afterwards, he and his wife were walking arm in arm through sun-splashed courtyards, past the glassy pool, the myrtle bushes and the pomegranate trees. Save for the Governor, the pavilion was empty. The distinctive fragrance of mint was coming from a pot on the low table.

Jasim could only see three cups. He came to an abrupt halt and raised his eyebrows.

'I thought this was to be a continuation of yesterday's meeting, where is everyone?'

Indicating they should sit, his uncle smiled. 'There are matters you and I must settle before I take things further.'

Puzzled, Jasim took Zorahaida to a cushion and sat beside her. 'Very well. I am guessing you are concerned about Zorahaida's so-called death.'

To his surprise, his uncle laughed. 'Not in the least, your wife looks extremely healthy for a dead woman. However, in part this does concern her. Jasim, you will recall that when you set out for Granada to enter the tournament, I had mixed feelings about your ambitions. Put bluntly, I feared you might prove to be as impulsive as your father. I feared more conflict between the districts, and I feared for your life. Yet you handled the Sultan with great subtlety.' The Governor gave Zorahaida a gracious smile. 'You won his daughter and despite the Sultan's machinations, you and Usayd joined forces to mend fences with Prince Ghalib. In short, you have proved yourself equal to almost anything. Jasim, I've long suspected you had diplomatic potential and since you and your brother are reconciled, I am even more convinced of it. You and Usayd have become a team. The newfound co-operation between the two of you has given me hope for the future. With your consent, I should like to name you the head of the family after my death. You will be the next governor.'

'Uncle?' Jasim's mind raced. His uncle was going to nominate him as a candidate for the governorship?

The Governor had no son, and in such circumstances, it wasn't unusual for the head of a family to designate another male relative as his successor. Nor was this Spain where the eldest male heir tended to take precedence. In Al-Andalus, positions of great office were awarded according to merit.

Still, Usayd was the older nephew...

'Uncle, Usayd is the firstborn.'

His uncle stroked his beard and made a negative gesture. 'Usayd's destiny lies on a different path, he has the heart of a merchant. There's no shame in that, it takes rare talent to make agreements that satisfy more than one party. Jasim, your brother doesn't have the makings of a governor. He will be relieved if you accept, he has no head for politics. Consider this, if our district is to avoid a repeat of what happened when your father fell foul of authorities in Granada, its Governor would also need a firm grasp of military matters. Not only do you command the loyalty of the Madinat Runda fort but your marriage to the Princess will be invaluable.'

Jasim nodded. 'Aye, Zorahaida and the Prince are close.'

His uncle took a deep breath. 'Jasim, relations between east and west have been sour for too long. It is my earnest wish that you will at least think about my proposal.' He directed a warm smile at Zorahaida. 'You might like to know that my daughter's testimony helped me reach this decision. Fatima thinks as well of you, Zorahaida, as she does of your husband.'

'Thank you,' Zorahaida murmured. Under cover of the table, she slid her hand into Jasim's.

'Well, Nephew, do you agree?'

Jasim felt a swift tug and glanced at Zorahaida. Her eyes were bright, they were shining with pride and confidence. He could see that she wanted him to agree and his heart warmed to see her faith in him.

'Uncle, I am honoured, but—'

'But?'

'I've no wish to see you dead. God willing, you will be Governor for many more years.'

His uncle smiled. 'It is never too soon to prepare for the future.'

Zorahaida leaned forward and caught Jasim's eye. 'I am sure the position of Governor is a weighty responsibility; however, it strikes me you must consider it.'

'And so I shall.' Jasim bowed his head. 'Thank you, Uncle, I shall give you my decision tomorrow.'

Chapter Seventeen

Dawn was lighting the bedchamber when Zorahaida awoke and the first thing she saw was Jasim, asleep at her side. As the chamber brightened, his hair took on the colour of fire. Not wishing to disturb him, she lay on her side watching him and counting her blessings.

Jasim had come after her. He had braved her father's wrath to bring her home and, best of all, he had confessed that he loved her.

Jasim loves me.

During the night the sheet had slipped, allowing her gaze to wander freely over his well-muscled chest. Her warrior husband. As she studied his rare colouring, she smiled. He was magnificent, she loved everything about him.

Thank God, Jasim and Usayd had set aside their differences. It was odd to think that all they'd had to do was to come to terms with themselves. After that, accepting each other had followed as naturally as day follows night.

A lock of red-gold hair fell across his eyes. Zorahaida leaned a little closer and carefully brushed it back. It was impossible not to press a light kiss to his shoulder and breathe in his scent.

He loves me. And I love him.

As the light strengthened, she was too comfortable to do anything other than lie there. This was happiness.

Someone tapped lightly on the door. After a pause it opened and Sama peeped in, her eyes bright with excitement. Zorahaida looked pointedly at Jasim and put her finger to her lips.

Sama beckoned. 'Quickly,' she whispered. 'You must get up.'

Intrigued, Zorahaida slipped out of bed and headed for the washbowl. Her handmaid was next to her before she had done more than splash her face.

'No time for that,' Sama murmured.

Her handmaid appeared to be in a great rush. Without bothering to ask permission, she slipped a heavy silk robe over Zorahaida's head. A heartbeat later, she had a girdle fastened about Zorahaida's waist. Eyes shining, and filled with something Zorahaida couldn't read—joy, perhaps?—Sama snatched up an embroidered shawl and shoved it at her.

The comb was next. Before Zorahaida had time to blink, Sama was dragging it through her hair, working so briskly she brought tears to her eyes.

'Ow!'

'Hurry, Princess.'

Zorahaida wound the shawl about her shoulders, put on her house slippers and allowed herself to be drawn out of the bedchamber and into the adjoining room.

Carefully, Sama shut the bedchamber door.

'You need to go down to the central courtyard, my lady. Now.'

'But my hair isn't properly dressed.'

The strangest of smiles flitted briefly across Sama's face. 'That won't matter. *Hurry.*'

Borne along by curiosity and her handmaid's excitement, Zorahaida flew down the stairs. Hunter was in the courtyard before her, chattering in such a high pitch Zorahaida knew he too was excited. Shawl tight about her shoulders, she paused under one of the arches.

Two foreign knights were standing in the courtyard with two heavily veiled women. They were speaking quietly in Spanish. It had been years since Zorahaida had seen the knights, but she recognised them instantly. One was Rodrigo Álvarez, Count of Córdoba and the other was Inigo Sánchez, Count of Seville.

They were married to her sisters.

Heart in her throat, she stared at the women. Hunter was riding on the shoulder of one of them, tugging insistently at her all-enveloping veil. Zorahaida didn't need that veil to be lifted to know who she was looking at.

'Alba!' she cried, voice cracking. With greedy happiness, she turned to the other woman. 'Leonor!'

As one, the sisters flew into each other's arms.

'Let me see you,' Zorahaida said, choking with emotion.

Leonor and Alba dragged off their veils and the three of them kissed and hugged.

Zorahaida's sisters were clad in Moorish costume, undoubtedly to avoid attracting unwanted attention on their journey. Tears of joy gleamed in their eyes as Hunter screeched and danced from one to the other like the little devil he was. For a time, conversation took second place to hugs and kisses. Then, as the sisters calmed, words started to flow.

Zorahaida was the first to recover. She shook her head in amazement and, since all three sisters spoke Spanish fluently and it was important that her sisters' husbands understood what was being said, she chose to speak in Spanish. Using their mother's native tongue had been the Princesses' way of hanging on to their heritage. The Queen their mother had died when they were too young to remember much about her, and the Sultan had refused to talk about her. The language had been their way of honouring their lost mother.

'I was writing to you both, but I never finished and the letter wasn't sent,' Zorahaida said. 'How on earth did you know where to find me?'

Leonor linked arms with her. 'Dearest, news of your marriage reached Castile. We heard about a ridiculously extravagant marriage procession that wound through the Emirate until it reached Madinat Runda.'

With a coy look, Alba took her other arm. 'We also heard about a Moorish knight, a chivalrous warrior who won the Sultan's daughter at a tournament and bore her off.'

Count Rodrigo stepped forward with a smile and a deep bow. 'Princess, once Leonor got wind of your marriage there was no stopping her. She was determined to come and find you, to see that you were happy.' His smile dimmed. 'I am sorry to say Leonor was blind to the dangers of returning to the Emirate with a sentence of banishment hanging over her head. She refused to listen to reason.'

With a wry laugh, Count Inigo joined them. 'Reason? Rodrigo, your wife is a Nasrid princess. You've been married to Leonor for almost three years and you still expect reason?'

Alba tutted, though her eyes smiled. 'Inigo, please, you might try for some courtesy.'

'I am always courteous, my love.' Count Inigo gave Zorahaida a charming bow. 'It was the same with Alba. Once your sisters knew of your marriage, Rodrigo and I had no peace until we had agreed to escort them here. Incognito, of course.'

Delighted though she was to see them, Zorahaida sobered. 'You ran a great risk, all of you. However, you need to be aware that there has been, shall we say, a change of the guard at the Alhambra. The risk was not as great as it might have been.'

'A change of the guard?' Leonor blinked. 'We heard curious rumours about Father, you will have to explain.'

'Certainly. However, since you appear to have travelled through the night, I assume you are hungry and thirsty?'

'Breakfast would be most welcome,' Count Rodrigo said.

Catching sight of Sama hovering behind a pillar, Zorahaida caught her attention. 'Sama, we shall break our fasts in the pavilion, if you please.' She turned back to her sisters and their husbands. 'Please come this way. I shall explain all as we eat.'

Zorahaida led her most welcome guests to the pavilion and when her sisters were sipping mint tea and their husbands were holding cups of ale, she summarised the goings on in the Alhambra in recent years. Not wishing to cast too much of a cloud over their reunion, Zorahaida didn't tell them everything. She left out many of their father's cruelties, although she did mention that, rather than mellowing with the years, he had gradually become more cruel and more tyrannical. If they wished for chapter and verse, that could come later.

She mentioned Prince Ghalib, and Leonor and Alba smiled when she spoke about the slowly growing bond that had developed between her and her uncle.

'I am glad to hear the Prince is well,' Alba murmured. 'I always liked him.'

'I felt sorry for him,' Leonor added. 'Father caged him for many years, just as he caged us.'

'There is no need for sorrow today,' Zorahaida said. 'The Prince is no longer caged; he has come into his own. You should know that Father is very ill.'

Lord Inigo shifted. 'I heard he's quite frail.'

Zorahaida grimaced. 'My lord, the Sultan is certainly ailing, but he is not simply frail. His mind is more disordered than ever. He has become a kind of hermit.'

'A hermit?' Leonor looked sceptically at her. 'That doesn't sound like Father.'

'No,' Zorahaida said, soberly. 'Father is a changed man. He is a sad figure and he keeps to a handful of rooms. In summary, Prince Ghalib has taken over the running of the palace. The Guard, the palace officials, the servants—they have all transferred their loyalty to Prince Ghalib.'

'Sultan Tariq has become a puppet?' Lord Rodrigo asked.

'Aye.'

Lord Rodrigo looked meaningfully at Lord Inigo. 'If Prince Ghalib proves more tolerant than his brother, this could be excellent news for Spain,' he murmured.

'Indeed.' Lord Inigo cleared his throat. 'We need to discover whether Prince Ghalib would welcome the idea of friendship between our countries. Princess Zorahaida—?'

Alba set her mint tea on the table with a clack. 'Inigo, I don't think Zorahaida will toss us into the streets for a day or so. You'll have plenty of time to talk politics. First, I'd like to know about her marriage. Zorahaida, I have no need to ask if you are happy, I can see from your face that you are.'

Zorahaida felt herself blush. 'I've never been so content.'

Alba reached across and squeezed her hand. 'It is wonderful to see. Now you must tell us how you came to marry your champion.'

'Very well.'

Zorahaida launched into an account of their father's decision to hold a tournament, and of his rash and very public promise to present the champion of the day with the finest gem in his collection.

'As you have heard, Jasim won the tournament,' she finished slowly. 'He turned down a casket of gold then, instead, he asked to take me as his bride!'

'I'm surprised Father let him have his way,' Leonor said.

Zorahaida shrugged. 'He felt he had to. Once he had sworn before witnesses that the champion could choose between the casket of gold and the most prized jewel in his collection, he couldn't back down.'

'He was afraid of losing face,' Leonor muttered.

'That's it exactly.'

'It sounds very romantic,' Leonor said, reaching for a sliver of almond cake. 'Except that Jasim was a stranger and you've always been rather shy. Were you happy to marry a stranger?'

Zorahaida laughed. 'Jasim is very enterprising. By the time we married, we were no longer strangers. He contrived to speak to me once or twice before the tournament, and he understood the difficulties I'd been having with Father. Furthermore, after he'd won Father's agreement to the marriage, he climbed up into our tower and came to see me. That was before the ceremony.'

Leonor looked at her, open-mouthed. 'Jasim did what?' she asked faintly. 'Why?'

'He wanted to make sure I was content to marry him.'

Alba's eyebrows shot up. 'And how, pray, did he persuade you?'

Zorahaida felt herself flush. 'That, my dear sister, is private.'

A shadow fell over them.

Jasim was standing beneath the arch, quietly observing them. Sama must have told him that Zorahaida's sisters had arrived with their husbands, for he was wearing his wedding finery, the dazzlingly white turban and his princely cloth of gold tunic. His jewelled belt gleamed as he stepped towards them, smiling.

'Exactly what is private, my heart?'

Zorahaida's flush deepened and everyone laughed.

Jasim had honoured their guests by speaking Spanish. Despite this, Zorahaida found herself holding her breath. Her sister's husbands were Castilian noblemen, and thanks to the Sultan there had been years of bloody fighting in petty border disputes between the Emirate and the Kingdom of Castile. Count Rodrigo had lost a much-loved younger brother. At best, this could be an uncomfortable moment.

Amid the laughter, Count Rodrigo and Count Inigo got to their feet. Zorahaida and her sisters remained seated. There were different traditions between the Kingdom of Spain and the Emirate, but there were also similarities. In a meeting like this, it was traditional for the men to introduce each other before presenting their wives. Zorahaida and her sisters might be princesses, but it was a man's world.

The three knights, though hailing from different cultures, had much in common. They were extremely protective. And being protected by a loving husband, Zorahaida had learned, was not the same as being controlled by a tyrannical, power-hungry father.

'You must be Jasim ibn Ismail,' Count Rodrigo said.

His smile was so easy, so sincere, that Zorahaida felt her tension ebb away.

The Count gripped Jasim's arm, in the way of men. 'Your reputation for chivalry has reached Córdoba. I wish you good fortune in your marriage.'

Count Inigo nodded and then he too clasped Jasim's arm. 'You have my thanks for rescuing Constanza.'

'Constanza?' Jasim asked.

'Constanza is my Spanish name,' Zorahaida explained. She smiled at Lord Inigo. 'I rarely use my Spanish name. Here, I am Zorahaida.'

Lord Inigo nodded. 'I understand.'

Jasim bowed towards her sisters. 'I hope your journey was an easy one.'

Leonor pulled a face. 'Far from it. We didn't know that Father is no longer in power and Rodrigo was so concerned about what might happen if we were caught, that he made Alba and I travel in a coach. We weren't permitted to ride, not even for a mile, and we had to wear veils for the entire journey.' She sighed. 'I'd quite forgotten how restricting they can be. And the coach was fearfully uncomfortable. I'm bruised all over.'

'I know all about uncomfortable journeys,' Zorahaida said, with a shudder. She brightened. 'However, next time you come, you may travel in style. Prince Ghalib says you will not be penalised for visiting the Emirate.'

Alba gave her an arch look. 'Next time we meet, which I hope will be soon, you will have to visit us in Seville.'

'Oh?'

Alba put her hand to her belly in the age-old gesture of a woman who was with child.

'You're going to have a baby!' Zorahaida said. 'Oh, Alba, I know how you long for children. That is wonderful news.'

'Thank you.' Alba looked pointedly at Leonor. 'Your turn.'

Zorahaida's eyes widened. 'You too?'

Leonor laughed. 'I already have a baby. Diego is almost a year old.' She smiled across at her husband. 'We named him after Rodrigo's brother. So you see, Zorahaida, you and Jasim will have to come to Castile, so you can meet our growing family.'

'Thank you,' Jasim said. 'We would so enjoy that. I have long wished to see Castile.' He took Zorahaida's hand and slanted her a meaningful look. 'What say you to making a show of it, as we did with our marriage procession?'

Zorahaida caught her breath as she worked out what he was telling her. 'You're going to accept your uncle's offer?'

Jasim smiled quietly and nodded.

Leonor was watching them, eyes puzzled. 'What are you talking about?'

Zorahaida looked at everyone in turn. 'What Jasim is saying is that his uncle the Governor wishes to nominate him as his successor. God willing, you are looking at the future Governor of Madinat Runda.'

Count Inigo and Count Rodrigo exchanged glances.

'I told you good could come of this visit,' Inigo said. 'With the Sultan ineffective and our wives' sister married to the successor of the Governor of Madinat Runda, peace might finally be within reach.' He shrugged. 'And once peace is achieved, trade will surely follow.'

'*Madre mía*, Inigo,' Alba said, expression pained. 'Save the politics for later.'

Jasim arched an eyebrow at the three sisters. 'It seems to me that our ladies would like to continue exchanging their news.'

'If you please,' Zorahaida said. She had no wish to turn this reunion into a trade discussion.

'Very well.' Jasim gestured the Spanish knights towards the door arch. 'I should like to further my acquaintance with our Spanish guests, and I am sure my uncle the Governor would be pleased to meet you.'

'Lead on,' Count Inigo said.

'After that,' Jasim continued, 'if you and Count Rodrigo are interested, I can give you a tour of the palace and you can meet the rest of my family. My brother Usayd will assuredly want an introduction.'

As her sisters' husbands proceeded through the arch, Jasim looked back at the three Princesses and bowed. 'Ladies, for now, *adiós*. We shall see you later.'

Briefly, he held Zorahaida's gaze and his expression softened into a loving smile. Unable to speak her heart was so full, Zorahaida watched him guide her sisters' husbands past the pomegranate trees.

When the men had gone, she saw that Leonor and Alba were watching her, wreathed in smiles.

Alba took her hand and sighed dreamily. 'The way that man looks at you.'

Leonor lifted an eyebrow. 'Not to mention the way Zorahaida looks at him. It's positively scandalous!'

'No, it isn't,' Zorahaida said, laughing. She had escaped her father, she had the best of husbands, and the freedom to visit her sisters whenever she wished. 'It's—*wonderful*.'

* * * * *